A PERILOUS JOURNEY OF DANGER & MAYHEM

BOOK 3:
'THE FINAL GAMBIT'

A
PERILOUS JOURNEY
OF
DANGER&MAYHEM

BOOK 3:
'THE FINAL GAMBIT'

Christopher Healy

WALDEN POND PRESS
An Imprint of HarperCollins*Publishers*

Walden Pond Press is an imprint of HarperCollins Publishers.

A Perilous Journey of Danger & Mayhem: The Final Gambit
Copyright © 2020 by Christopher Healy

Library of Congress Control Number: 2020942252
ISBN 978-0-06-234203-4

Typography by Joel Tippie
20 21 22 23 24 PC/LSCH 10 9 8 7 6 5 4 3 2 1
❖
First Edition

To Stephanie Rivera, the teacher who somehow made my daughter love history more than she already had.

And to all the teachers.

PROLOGUE

Hidden
Buford's Bend, Ohio, October 17, 1884

MOLLY PEPPER HELD her breath and tried to ignore the spider crawling down the bridge of her nose. *It's just a spider,* she told herself. *I don't care about spiders.* This wasn't technically true. Under normal circumstances, Molly *loved* spiders. She once tried to keep an unusually fuzzy one as a pet, an experiment that sadly ended when the creature found its way down the back of her mother's dress. Ignoring this particular spider on her face, however, was proving more difficult by the second. The tickle of tiny legs skittering across her cheek was almost unbearable, but she dared not shake, scratch, or sneeze, because the slightest movement would disturb the sticks and branches piled on top of her and give away her hiding place. The people looking for her would find her. And then it would all be over.

She could hear dry grass crunching beneath the feet of her pursuers just outside the firewood bin, where she lay curled beneath the kindling. But the spider had reached her top lip. Carefully as she could, Molly thrust her lower jaw forward and attempted to blow the spider off. But if there's one thing spiders are good at, it's sticking in place.

"Where is she?" a frustrated voice griped nearby. "We've looked everywhere!"

"Don't worry, she's not getting away this time," came the reply. "Let's check the well!"

As the footsteps outside the bin began to recede, the spider decided to explore Molly's nostril. The sensation was more than she could bear. Twigs scattered and clattered as she leapt from the woodbin, wiping her face and blowing vigorous puffs of air from her nose.

"Drat!" she grumbled, expecting to see her pursuers rushing back to her along the side of the barn where she'd just emerged from the woodpile. But they were nowhere to be seen. She craned her neck to peer down the hill to the circle of stones surrounding the family well. No one. Where had they gone? There was no way they'd gotten far enough away that they wouldn't have heard the commotion she'd just made. It was a trap. Had to be.

She pressed herself against the barn's bright blue wood-plank wall and tiptoed to its rear. Peeking around the corner, she saw nothing but rain barrels. And a clear shot to the house—her cute little yellow house, with its cute little porch and cute little rocking chairs. If she could make it to the house, she'd be safe.

She took another glance behind her. They must have gone inside the barn. That was the only possibility. Her mother was in there. And Emmett. And while Molly didn't like using them as a distraction, she knew it might keep her pursuers busy long enough for her to make a run for the porch. She took a deep breath, rose onto the balls of her feet, and took off at a full sprint.

"Gotcha!"

A figure leapt out from behind the rain barrels, tackling her. Molly yelped as she and her attacker both hit the ground and rolled down the hill in a tangle of arms and legs. They came to a rest by the well and Molly lay in the grass, catching her breath for a few seconds before realizing she was on top of the other girl. "You okay under there, Orla?" Molly asked, unable to stifle a giggle.

"I win!" A small arm poked out from beneath her, raising a fist in victory. "Sometimes it hurts to win."

Laughing, Molly slid aside and freed her friend. Orla wiped her grass-stained hands on her gingham dress as another girl, much taller with a pointy nose and unruly hair, came running down the hill, laughing. "I tagged her, Luddie!" Orla crowed.

Luddie snorted. "You know that 'tagging' is usually done just with the hands, right?"

"Since when do I do things *usual*?" the petite girl said proudly.

"We should hire you out to a rodeo show in need of a

bull," Molly said, helping her up.

Luddie gave Molly a playful shove. "You're it this time," she said.

"Okay," said Molly. "But I would advise against hiding in the woodbin unless you don't mind spiders in your . . ." She trailed off as she noticed a wagon coming up the road. "Captain Lee's back from town!" Molly said, running off. "He's gonna have the mail."

"Wait!" Luddie shouted. "Spiders in your *what*? You gotta finish that sentence!"

"Yeah, and I wanna know about that rodeo bull thing," Orla added. "Is that a real job? 'Cause I could see myself doing that."

Molly ran up and around the front of the barn, passing the open front doors and giving a cheerful wave to her mother and her best friend, who were hard at work inside. Cassandra Pepper, the unsung genius inventor, was back to doing what she did best: creating astonishingly imaginative and useful machines. And Molly's more-brother-than-friend, Emmett Lee, was working as Cassandra's apprentice—and looking more confident than Molly had ever seen him. Together, the two were putting the finishing touches on her mother's Daedalus Chariot, a new flying machine to replace the one that had been stolen by their archenemy, the diabolical madman Ambrose Rector.

Cassandra, soldering wires in grease-smeared

coveralls, looked up, waved, and proudly flashed the medallion that she wore on a chain around her neck. It wasn't really a medallion—it was the lid to a pickle jar—but Molly had etched the words "World's Greatest Inventor" into it as a gift for her. Emmett, balanced on a stepladder to oil the chariot's spinning overhead propeller, flashed Molly a smile as well. Seeing those two so happy, realizing their mutual dreams of being inventors, gave her warm tingles. (The good kind of tingles, not the kind caused by a spider up your nose.)

The horse neighed as Captain Lee's wagon pulled up to the hitching post by the little yellow house. Molly bounded onto the porch and threw herself into one of the comfy rocking chairs that Cassandra had designed to sway in smooth, silent, fluid motion. She glanced around—at the vibrant paint that she still couldn't believe they'd talked Captain Lee into letting them use, at the adorable hummingbirds hovering around the feeder that Emmett had installed, at the window to her very own bedroom. Molly had never thought she'd be able to live this way. Coming here was something she did for the others, she told herself—an act of self-sacrifice. But she could no longer deny that it was pretty darn nice. Even if part of her wished it wasn't.

Captain Wendell Lee hopped down from the wagon with a wave and a smile. Molly wondered if it was still weird for Emmett to no longer be an orphan, after believing he was for so many years. But ever since they'd rescued his father from that cavern in Antarctica the prior year, Emmett was now just a half-orphan, like Molly. Bonding over their missing parents had been one of the things that initially brought Molly and Emmett together as friends. But Molly always felt worse for Emmett, because she at least had fond memories of her father, who'd been such a big part of her life for her first nine years, but Emmett's mother had died giving birth to him back in China; he'd never known her at all.

Captain Lee unloaded two burlap sacks from the wagon, one filled with flour, the other with iron bolts. "Guess which of these your mother requested?" he said with a grin.

"Did you get the mail?" Molly asked.

Captain Lee furrowed his brow. "A hello would be nice."

"Hello, did you get the mail?" Molly asked.

The captain sighed and carried his bundles inside. "It's on the seat."

Molly ran to the cart, gave the old gray horse a friendly pat on the nose, and grabbed the two envelopes and a newspaper that sat on the driver's bench. Back on the porch, she tossed the envelopes onto a small wooden table—she didn't care about those—and began flipping through the paper, scanning, as she always did, for the name of their long-lost friend, investigative journalist

Nellie Bly. Months earlier, on their mission to find Captain Lee, Nellie disappeared on the island of Barbados. She had gone to seek aid from a man named Grimsby, whom they later learned was an employee of Ambrose Rector. No one had heard from Nellie since.

And this newspaper didn't seem like it was going to change that situation. Molly sighed as she folded back the last page. There, she saw a name that made her breath catch in her throat. And it wasn't Nellie Bly's. It was the name of someone who was supposed to be dead. Someone she knew was dead. And yet, there this person was in the newspaper, talking to reporters.

"C'mon, Molly! We're waiting on you for the next round!" Luddie called from the lawn. "Get educated on your own time!"

"Yeah," added Orla. "Unless you are already playing and you're trying to hide behind that newspaper. In which case . . . we found you."

Molly barely heard them. She couldn't tear her eyes from the article.

"Come on, Molly! You're it!"

"I know," Molly muttered as she reread the sentence for the third time.

There was only one explanation for what she was seeing: Ambrose Rector was back.

PART I

1

Deception on the High Seas
Somewhere off the Florida coast,
January 17, 1884

MOLLY AND EMMETT stood at the rail by the bow of the *AquaZephyr*, an experimental high-velocity ship designed by the world-famous Alexander Graham Bell—and their home since the previous September. It was on this vessel that they, along with Cassandra and their friend Nellie Bly, sought refuge after their own boat sank in the Caribbean Sea. It was also on the *AquaZephyr* that they and Bell were held captive by Ambrose Rector, the madman whom they'd prevented from killing thousands at the World's Fair that spring. This was the same ship in which Rector and his henchmen dragged them all the way to Antarctica on his quest for more Ambrosium, the mysterious alien ore that he used to power his doomsday weapons. But once they were in Antarctica,

Emmett and the Peppers had sought to achieve more than just thwarting Rector: they'd also hoped to uncover evidence as to the fate of Emmett's father, who'd been marooned by Rector on those icy Antarctic shores four years earlier. What they *hadn't* expected was to find the man himself, alive and well. So it was on the decks of the *AquaZephyr* that Emmett and Wendell Lee began the long but joyful process of getting to know each other again.

Now they were all heading home. Well, most of them. Nellie had vanished in Barbados, Rector's henchman Icepick and the backstabbing federal agent Archibald Forrest had both met gruesome ends during the hunt for Ambrosium, and Rector himself had been, in an ironic twist, left stranded in Antarctica. Molly was not naive enough to count him out, though. There was no logical reason to believe anyone would survive alone in the frigid Antarctic wastes, especially after a cave-in destroyed the oasis of warmth, food, and shelter that had been keeping Captain Lee alive. But this was Ambrose Rector, the man who had already found his way back from Antarctica once before, the man who'd held thousands hostage at the World's Fair with his Mind-Melter threatening to liquefy their brains, who'd used his uncanny talent for impersonation and disguise to fool them far too many times in the past. The man who had tried to kill the Peppers a dozen times over, the man who still haunted Molly's dreams every night. They might have left him helpless in the icy wastes, but Molly would be forever awaiting the moment when Ambrose Rector would worm his way back into their lives.

Molly tried not to think about him, though. Or the others who were gone. She was just grateful they hadn't lost Robot, her aluminum friend who unfortunately owed his life to Ambrosium. Robot may have started out as a clockwork automaton, created by Alexander Graham Bell to sing at the World's Fair, but after a chunk of Ambrosium granted him a life and mind of his own, he became another full-fledged member of Molly's patchwork family. Molly had believed she'd lost Robot along with Nellie in Barbados, but it turned out he'd flown all the way to Antarctica to find her again. Robot was a very devoted robot, and Molly was a very devoted sister to him. The only problem was that the shard of Ambrosium in his chest, which also gifted him with powers of flight and magnetism, shrank a bit every time Robot used those powers. Once that glowing orange rock in his torso was gone, so was Robot.

But that wasn't the only threat to her mechanical friend. There was also Alexander Graham Bell, their supposed ally, who, despite repeated promises never to do so, couldn't seem to keep himself from constantly mentioning how much he'd like to dissect Robot and tear his heart out. He may never have used those specific words, but Molly knew that's what Bell meant every time he suggested "experimenting" on her friend. Molly had stopped trusting Alexander Graham Bell the moment he broke his promise about changing the rules of the all-male Inventors' Guild so that they could start admitting women (namely, Molly's mother).

"Gorgeous night, isn't it?" Bell strolled up and took a spot at the rail between Molly and Emmett. The children exchanged knowing glances. Bell had taken to doing this every night for the past few weeks as they sailed back toward the United States. The inventor stroked his thick black beard and stared out at a star-filled sky over dark, swirling waters. "Believe it or not, I think that, once we're home, I might miss being at sea." He had a slight Scottish lilt to his speech, a remnant of his European childhood.

"I don't know, Mr. Bell," said Emmett. "I'm looking forward to my stomach staying in just one part of my body again."

"You still get seasick after all these months, Emmett?" Molly asked.

"The steady diet of barnacles probably hasn't helped," Emmett replied.

"Don't worry," said Bell. "In a few days' time, you'll be back on solid ground."

Molly snorted. "You've ridden a wagon down those New York streets, right? They don't feel very solid to me.

My eyeglasses bounce right off my face."

Bell harrumphed. He had never quite taken to Molly's sense of humor. Or humor in general. He stared out at the horizon. "Children, do you see? It might be difficult to make out in the dark, but that bit of land rising up in the distance—that's Florida. Well, the Florida Keys most likely, but still American soil. We may be back in New York sooner than expected."

"Speaking of which," Molly said, "have you given any more thought to your plan for us when we get to Manhattan?"

"You know, with the government having warrants out for our arrest?" added Emmett.

Bell patted the boy's head. "I've told you before: all will be taken care of. Once I explain to the authorities that you helped me stop Ambrose Rector—"

"But we broke federal secrecy agreements," Emmett said. "No one was supposed to know about what happened at the World's Fair; no one was supposed to know that Ambrose Rector even existed. But we told. And we told a journalist, of all people."

"Well, *I* did," Molly said. "You and Mother just got roped in by being connected to me. Still feel bad about that."

"It doesn't matter anymore," Emmett said. "It happened. And somehow I don't think the Feds are just going to forgive and forget. Especially when we don't know where Nellie is; they'll probably think she's hiding out there, waiting for the right moment to blow open the whole Rector story, including the cover-up."

"Children, children," Bell said. "Don't forget that I'm the co-president of the Inventors' Guild. I have influence. I can make things happen."

Like getting my mother into the Guild? Molly thought. *You told us you'd make that happen too.* But what she said was, "That's right, Mr. B. I keep forgetting how lucky we are." Behind Bell's back, Emmett squeezed her hand. He was so good at knowing when Molly needed a little "I know how you feel" hand squeeze.

Bell's eyes went back to the stars. "Ah, as much as I enjoy the thrill of seafaring, I do look forward to getting back to the Guild, back to my lab, back to inventing," he said wistfully. "Without the specter of Ambrose Rector hovering over me, I can finally focus on my work. There's so much I long to do."

Here it comes, Molly thought.

"It would be fascinating, for instance," Bell continued, "if I could finally get a more in-depth look at our friend Robot."

Emmett squeezed tighter.

"It's really for the best that I haven't examined him here on the ship," Bell said. "The instruments in my workshop at the Guild Hall will allow for a much more thorough investigation—thorough, but not harmful, of course. I gave my word that Robot would never be in any danger and I meant it. In fact, now that I think about it, if anything should go wrong and you folks do end up temporarily in police custody, you can count on me to care for Robot in your absence."

Molly pulled her hand from Emmett's and thrust her finger in Bell's face. "That's—"

"Venus!" Emmett redirected Molly's arm so she was pointing up over Bell's head. "Yes, Molly, that's Venus up there. Good astronomy lesson. Well, look at the time. We should really be heading to bed."

"Look at the time?" Bell echoed. "There's no clock out here."

"I can tell time by the stars," Emmett said. "Can't you?"

Bell straightened his tie. "Naturally. And, uh, bedtime it is. I should wake up early to start packing my bags anyway." He began ambling down the starboard deck to his cabin.

"Good night, Mr. Bell." Emmett nudged Molly.

"Yeah, good night," Molly grumbled. As soon as Bell was out of earshot, she added a quiet, "Sorry." She was annoyed at herself. Of all nights to almost start an argument with Bell. She could've blown their whole plan.

"It's okay," Emmett said. "Honestly, I wanted to do more than just stick a finger in his face. But—"

"I know, now is not the time," Molly finished. "Do you

feel guilty at all about what we're about to do? You were pretty close to Bell before you met us."

Emmett took in a deep breath of salty air. "Well, he basically got me off the streets after my father disappeared," he said. "I'll always be grateful for that. I don't think he's a bad person. But he and the Guild are too closely tied to the same government folks who want to see us behind bars. Besides, it's kind of our only choice. I have a hard time imagining us stepping off Alexander Graham Bell's super-ship in New York without a circle of federal agents waiting for us."

Molly nodded. "Well, you certainly made us hash over the plan long enough."

"That's because your original 'plan' involved hopping on the back of a passing dolphin."

"Which still sounds funner, but, yes, this new plan is better. See, I'm not afraid to admit when I'm wrong." Molly flashed him a cheesy grin. "By this time tomorrow, we'll be kicking our feet up on a train back to New York."

"Or keeping our *heads down* on a train to New York. Because, you know, those arrest warrants?"

"Either way, we'll be returning to New York on our terms. We're going to have to reckon with the charges against us eventually, but we might as well do it when we're good and ready, rather than the moment we hit the docks."

"I know. I helped make this plan, remember?" Emmett said. "Sneaking back on our own will give us time to figure out how we're going to get the Mothers of Invention out of jail, for one thing. Those women risked everything to keep us safe. Helping them is our top priority."

"Absolutely," said Molly. "And once we've freed them, they can rub their spectacular brains together and help us clear our names. And get Pepper's Pickles back. And fix Robot."

"If anybody can do those things, it's the MOI."

Molly got horrible pangs of guilt every time she thought about the way the brave, ingenious women of the MOI had held off a squad of federal agents long enough for Molly, Emmett, and Cassandra to escape on the boat they'd built for them. Those courageous and talented women, who'd previously put their lives and futures on the line to help defeat Rector at the World's Fair, had ended up in handcuffs solely for the crime of aiding the Peppers yet again. But as Cassandra always reminded Molly, the MOI knew what they were doing; they'd sacrificed themselves because they knew the danger presented by Ambrose Rector and they wanted to make sure the Peppers had the chance to stop him. Of course, they'd also hoped that the act of stopping Rector would bestow fame upon them and help them enact change in the inventing world, such as getting women allowed into the Inventors' Guild. But that part hadn't quite worked out yet. If they managed to pull off tonight's plan, though, there might still be a chance for Molly and her friends to achieve the kind of recognition and status they deserved.

"It's been long enough," Molly said. "Let's check on him." Molly and Emmett crept to Bell's cabin door and listened until they heard the sound they were waiting for: a wet, rumbling, eardrum-grating snore. They nodded to each other, and grabbed the two carpetbags packed with supplies and changes of clothing that they'd stashed inside a large coil of rope earlier that day. They slid their arms through the secret shoulder straps that Cassandra had sewn into the bottoms of the bags, and slung them onto their backs like mountaineers' packs before hurrying to the wheelhouse. "Bell's out. Time to move," Molly whispered to Captain Lee, who was at the helm. The captain nodded, silently adjusted a series of dials on the control panel, and joined the children on deck.

Molly didn't know if the captain's silence was him trying to be stealthy or just him being him. In the dozen or so weeks she'd known him, Molly, who considered herself to be an excellent judge of character, had not been able to get a good read on Wendell Lee. He was quick to waggle a finger at Emmett for slurping his soup too loudly, but then he'd let out an impressively resounding belch after the meal. He would frown disapprovingly whenever Cassandra burst out into a boisterous rendition of "Polly Wolly Doodle" or "Yankee Doodle Dandy" (or any of the "Doodles," really), but then he'd grab Emmett's hand out of the blue and start dancing a little jig with him. Molly didn't know which was the *real* Captain Lee: the stern and serious man, like the fathers in so many of the books she'd read, or the fun and goofy guy, like her own father had been before they'd lost him to tuberculosis.

Even more fascinating—Emmett didn't seem to know either. When Molly had asked him what his father used to be like, Emmett replied, "Strict. Never silly like he has been lately. I lived with a strong set of rules for so long. That's why it was difficult for me to adjust to life in the Pepper household. Remember how shocked I was the first time I saw you throwing pickles at your mother to wake her up?"

To which Molly responded, "We live in a pickle shop! What was I supposed to throw? Apricots?" But she understood Emmett's point. The captain's time in Antarctica had changed him. But was this new, more entertaining version just a mask, or was this the real Captain Lee finally coming out? Molly hoped for the latter, because "Silly Captain" seemed less likely to take his son away and break up Molly's family. "Serious Captain," though? Serious Captain had already made far too many comments about "getting our lives back to the way things were before." And by "our lives," Molly was pretty sure he meant just him and Emmett. The Peppers weren't part of "before." Aside from her mother, though, there was no one who meant more to Molly than Emmett, and if being back with his father was what Emmett wanted, Molly promised herself she would not be the one to get in his way.

The trio slunk along the portside deck to Cassandra's cabin and gave the secret knock. The door cracked open and Molly's mother poked her head out, grinning like a child at a birthday party. "Is it time?" she asked. Molly nodded and stepped aside to make space for her mother and Robot, who shuffled out together, carrying the engine that Cassandra had spent the last two weeks secretly building out of loose parts and stolen gear from the *AquaZephyr*.

"Good evening, friends. And a happy secret escape plot to you all," said Robot as moonlight glinted off his silvery cheeks. The tall metallic humanoid had blocky feet, a barrelish chest, and long pipelike arms. His metal mustache twitched as he tipped his hat—a dirty brown derby that had belonged to Bell until the inventor finally got tired of Robot asking to borrow it.

"Keep both hands on the motor, please, Robot," Cassandra said, referring to the heavy-looking block of pipes, gears, and pistons they were toting. She turned to the others. "Lady and gentlemen, may I introduce you to our way off this boat. No, wait—that's not correct. Our way off this boat will be stepping over the railing into the rowboat. Lady and gentlemen, may I introduce our way back to land. Well, technically the rowboat will be—"

"It's okay, Mother," Molly said. "We all remember the plan."

"Ah, good," said Cassandra. "I can't wait to try it!"

Emmett furrowed his brow. "Try what? The plan or the engine?"

"Both," Cassandra said with enthusiasm.

"I thought you already tested the motor," Emmett said, failing to disguise his concern.

"I did," Cassandra said. "In my cabin, for five minutes. But I'm reasonably certain that twelve hours on the ocean shouldn't cause it to explode or anything."

Captain Lee raised an eyebrow. "I can't tell if you're joking."

"Oh, when I'm joking, you'll know it," Cassandra said. "I assume. I have no way of knowing how my jokes sound to someone else. Am I funnier than I think I am?"

"Let's discuss this when we're safely on our way to Florida," Emmett suggested, retrieving a bag of tools from Cassandra's cabin. "Emphasis on the *safely*."

"Should Robot be lugging that thing?" Molly asked as they made their way toward the ship's stern. "We need to conserve his Ambrosium, right?"

"Do not be concerned, Molly," the metal man replied.

"Mrs. Pepper surmises that normal mechanical motions, such as walking or lifting, do not erode the meteorite, as I was capable of performing such actions before I received my Ambrosium."

"Yes, it's only the more magicky things that put a drain on his battery, as it were," Cassandra explained. "Magnet rays, defying gravity, mind reading . . . Wait, *can* you read minds? No, forget I said that! And don't try it, because if you can do it, it would be one of the things you shouldn't do. Anyway, flying is the worst of it, which is why all five of us are squeezing into one dinghy instead of having Robot just zoom off to Miami to wait for us."

Molly tried not to worry about it, but couldn't help wondering why the mecha-man was stooping, seemingly having a tougher time lugging the engine than her mother was. Back when she had first encountered Robot in a dark vault, she'd been terrified of him. But now she looked upon his clunky hands, goofy handlebar mustache, and big, round, perpetually shocked eyes with nothing but affection. And not just because Robot had saved their lives on multiple occasions. Even as dented and scuffed as he'd become over the course of their misadventures, he was still a thing of beauty in her eyes.

"Do not fear," Robot said. "I am not an easily broken thing, such as glass. Or an egg. Or a glass egg." Metaphors had never been Robot's strength.

They stopped along the port rail, by a shiny chrome

control panel with multiple levers and a crank wheel. Emmett flipped the switches to open a panel in the side of the *AquaZephyr*'s hull, from which emerged a steel platform bearing a four-person rowboat. Emmett hopped the rail with the tool bag, then helped Cassandra into the dinghy with the motor. They immediately began working to secure the engine to the rear of the small wooden craft. Molly looked up and down the deck. There was only one more person they needed for her plan to be complete.

"I am here, escaping friends! Right on time! I am very good at being prompt." Roald, the *AquaZephyr*'s ten-year-old Norwegian cabin boy, bounded around the corner and was greeted by sharp shushing from everyone. "Ah, yes, we whisper for secrecy. Have no fear, I can speak so silently none will hear it." He moved his lips noiselessly. "Did you hear that? If you say yes, you are not being truthful. Because I was faking. I said nothing."

"I'm going to miss you, Roald," Emmett said, helping his father over the rail into the rowboat.

"Are you sure you don't want to come?" Molly asked. "It's a pretty packed boat, but maybe you can sit on Robot's shoulders."

"I have wide shoulders," Robot said, climbing clumsily into the dinghy and offering his arms to the boy. "Like a buffalo. Think of me as an aluminum buffalo."

"Thank you, but no," Roald said. "I will be saddened

by your parting, but Uncle Lars is my responsibility. He is a true criminal, unlike you five. He is in the brig for now, but Mr. Bell and I will have to see he is properly dealt with when we make port. Besides, if I go with you, who will lower your getaway boat?"

Molly gave him a hug before climbing into the dinghy. "That's very mature of you, Roald."

"I am very mature," Roald replied proudly. Then his face turned suddenly serious. "Molly and Emmett, you have been good friends to me. Perhaps my first real friends. And Robot, you have been my . . . shiniest friend. Mrs. Pepper, you have been kind and welcoming to me. And Mr. Captain Lee, I do not know you as well. But I like your eyebrows. Thank you all for everything."

Molly was surprised to find herself misty-eyed. "You've been a true friend, Roald," she said. "I hope we meet again, someday."

"Come with us, Roald," Cassandra said. "I'm sure Bell can handle your uncle—"

The boy shook his head. "As long as we can still get this ship to New York, I will be all right."

"The navigation coordinates are preset," said Captain Lee. "And I've left detailed instructions in the wheelhouse."

"Then here is to the future!" Roald said, saluting them. "Oh! And do not forget this. For your train tickets." He fished a wad of American dollars out of his pocket and handed it to Cassandra.

"Are you sure about this, Roald?" Cassandra asked. "It still feels wrong to take your money."

"Pish posh," said the boy. "You need it more than I right now. And it is Uncle Lars's money anyway. He is locked up in the brig, so it was very easy to steal."

"That actually makes me *more* uncomfortable," said Captain Lee.

"But it was money paid to my uncle by Mr. Rector," said Roald. "So really it is Rector's money that will get you back home."

"Okay, *that* doesn't bother me at all," said Emmett.

They thanked Roald as he gripped the crank wheel and began to lower the dinghy to the water.

"Don't forget: you're still going to be the first person to set foot on the South Pole someday!" Molly called to him.

"I know!" he replied cheerily. "I am very good at—"

"What's all the commotionation?" a voice called from farther down the deck. "Someone mucking about with the rowing boat?" It was Pembroke, a former gangster and Rector henchman who switched sides when he realized Rector had planned to kill him too. But Pembroke wasn't part of their escape plot; he was still loyal to Bell.

Roald stopped cranking and the escapees in the rowboat froze, unsure of what to do.

That's when Robot rose and hovered over the rail, back to the deck. Molly gasped.

"You are very good at distracting people, are you not, Roald?" Robot said. To which Roald nodded vigorously.

"Go keep Mr. Pembroke busy and I will lower the row-boat."

"We're not leaving you behind, Robot!" Emmett said.

"I will fly down to the rowboat once it is on the water."

"You can't," Molly warned. "You need to preserve your Ambrosium! You'll—"

Cassandra put her hand on her daughter's shoulder. "One thirty-foot dip isn't going to wipe him out," she said. "This might be our only way to make sure Bell doesn't follow us. Thank you, Robot."

There was a click as Robot nodded his metallic head and began cranking the wheel.

"Who's down there?" Pembroke called, and Roald rushed to cut him off before he turned the corner around the mess hall and spotted them. The group in the dinghy listened as their vessel slowly dropped toward the waves below.

"Mr. Pembroke! Mr. Pembroke, it is me!"

"What are you doing sphinxing around out here at this o'clock, Roland?"

"Roald."

"Whuzzat?"

"My name is Roald."

"You mean to tell me I been on this vesicle with you for nine weeks and I been calling you by the wrong monocle?"

"Come with me, Mr. Pembroke. Mr. Bell has a book

in his library that I would like to show you. It is called a dictionary."

The dinghy touched down upon the water and Captain Lee unhooked the ropes that fastened it to the platform. They pushed off into the open sea, out from under the arcing, crablike legs of Bell's hydrofoil, as the platform rose back up, nestling once more into its compartment in the upper hull.

Molly looked up. "Where's—"

Before she could finish the question, Robot came floating down from the deck and landed gently in the bow of the rowboat. "Success," he said.

As Captain Lee paddled hard to break free of the much larger vessel's wake, Molly inched down her bench toward Robot. "Can we take a quick peek inside? Just to check."

After a pause, the metal man put a hand to his chest plate and clicked open the small panel at its center. Molly, Emmett, and Cassandra all leaned in to peer at the dimly glowing bit of orange stone cradled by a nest of wires and springs. Back at the World's Fair in March, when the Ambrosium was first placed inside Robot, it was bigger than a human fist; now it was roughly the size of a thumb.

"Thank you, Robot," Cassandra said soberly. "You can close up now."

"And no more flying," Molly said. "That was it, okay?"

"I can fly," Robot said, rather haughtily. "But I will not. I will be like a penguin."

"You know, penguins don't just stay on the ground because they like it," Emmett said. "They literally don't have the ability to fly."

"Then I will be like a penguin with a flying machine… that he does not use," Robot said.

Emmett shrugged. "I guess that works."

Molly bit her lip with concern. Robot's life expectancy was growing shorter by the day. And if trouble *was* waiting for them back in the States, who knew how long it would be before they could fix him? *If* they could fix him. Without getting their hands on more Ambrosium, the possibility felt frighteningly out of reach.

"We are far enough from the *AquaZephyr*," Captain Lee said, pulling in the oars. "Time to show us what that motor of yours can do, Mrs. Pepper."

Cassandra wiggled her fingers in anticipation. "Hold tight, everyone. I don't know how much of a kick our little friend here will have." Throughout the boat, fingers gripped seats and walls as Cassandra pulled a long cord and a rumbling purr arose. "Get ready. Things are about to get—"

The boat took off on its own, the engine propelling it forward at a reasonable speed.

"—smooth and comfortable, apparently. Well, this is a pleasant surprise. I honestly hadn't ruled out an explosion."

Molly and Emmett tried to stifle their amusement at Captain Lee's poor attempt to hide his discomfort. As the *AquaZephyr* disappeared behind them, Molly leaned back into Robot's cool metal arms and decided to enjoy the ride. Within a few hours, the green Florida coast came into clear view.

"Land ho!" Molly said. She knew that even once they were off the water, they still had a long journey ahead of them. She just hoped it would lead them to a cozy little pickle shop and not a cold, bleak prison cell.

2

An Audience with the Swamp King

As THE SUN'S first rays lit up the swells, the motorized rowboat puttered north through the Gulf of Mexico. Molly stared off to the right at a seemingly endless stretch of greenery that was tantalizingly close. "Okay, *that* has got to be the actual *Florida* Florida," she said. They had already passed what seemed like a dozen perfectly good little beaches, but every time Molly had yelled, "Land ho!," Captain Lee explained that they were just passing islands—the Florida Keys—and it was pointless to stop before they reached the mainland. It made sense, but when someone is as tired, hungry, and cranky as Molly was after eight hours of bouncing over waves in the cramped little dinghy, sense isn't always what they're looking for.

"Yes, that is the Florida peninsula," Captain Lee said,

but he didn't tilt the rudder to steer them any nearer to shore.

"Soooooo . . . land ho?" Molly tried. "Can we finally get out of this thing? I can't be the only one whose stomach is out-rumbling the engine."

"I have no stomach," said Robot. "But I can make a rumble noise with my elbows. Would you like to hear it?"

"It's all swamp over there. Who knows if that vegetation we're seeing is even on solid land?" Captain Lee said. "Getting lost in the marsh would do us no good."

"Wait, is it a swamp or a marsh?" asked Cassandra. "If you don't know, how can you be so sure it's not safe?"

"Maybe it's a fen," Molly added.

"It doesn't matter," said the captain. "My point is that if you can just be patient, then in three more hours north, maybe four, we should find a legitimate port."

"Hours?" Molly moaned. "I'll be a skeleton by then! And do you have any idea how annoying it is to have to wipe sea spray off your eyeglasses every five minutes?"

Emmett wobbled in his seat with every rise and dip of the boat, his green-tinged complexion indicating that his old seasickness had returned. He'd barely said a word the entire trip, but Molly wasn't sure whether that was because of his nausea or his father. She had begun noticing a tendency in Emmett to grow quiet in the captain's presence. She didn't like it.

What bothered her even more, though, was her mother's silence. Cassandra sat with her shoulders slumped, staring glassy-eyed into the gradually brightening distance. Molly nudged her.

"THAT'S RIGHT!" Cassandra burst out, shaking the whole boat. "I'm sorry—I mean, Molly is right. About us being hungry. And tired. So very tired. If there's possibly *anywhere* in that swamp or fen or marsh—"

"What about a bog?" said Robot. "Perhaps it is a bog."

"I think they're all the same thing," said Cassandra. "But that is a debate I'd much rather have after a snack and a nap. So, Captain, if there is even a slight chance of stopping someplace closer . . ."

Emmett lifted his head. "Papa, are we sure it wouldn't actually be, you know, *safer* to get off the water here? There are no people around, at least," he said. "I mean, it's past dawn. Do we really want to pull into a busy harbor full of fishermen and dockworkers when people might be on the lookout for us?"

"I seriously doubt the New York police are looking for you in the Gulf of Mexico," Captain Lee said.

"It's not just that, Papa," he said weakly. "The Exclusion Act. Remember we told you about that? While you were in Antarctica, President Arthur—"

"Banned Chinese immigrants, yes." Captain Lee's face darkened. "I suppose that's a bit of news I would have liked to have forgotten. Not that I can really say I was surprised by it."

"I know," Emmett said. "But you see my point, right? It doesn't matter that we entered the country legally before the ban. If we come in through a busy port now . . ."

His father gave a solemn nod.

"Enough debate," Molly said. "Emmett's obviously on our side. That's three votes for stopping, so let's stop. Democracy in action."

"Technically," Captain Lee said, "a ship is not a democracy. The captain makes all the decisions."

"It's a dinghy," Molly said flatly.

"And *technically*, none of us here has a legal right to vote, but that doesn't mean we shouldn't," Cassandra added bitterly. "The point is, we're all in this together and most of us are about to melt into sleepy little hunger puddles. So, pardon me, Captain, if—"

"It's okay, it's okay, I intended that as a joke," Captain Lee said quickly. "Sorry if it came out wrong. I guess I'm a little rusty. The penguins were a pretty easy audience. They'd laugh at anything."

Molly saw Emmett view his father with a squint that said, "Rusty? When were you ever smooth?" Or perhaps that squint had more to do with the idea of laughing penguins.

"I'd be happy to forgive you, Captain," said Cassandra. "If you start steering this boat shoreward."

The captain did just that. "If people are hungry and tired, then we must address those needs," he said. "I apologize for not doing so sooner. I once went a week living on nothing but melted snow and fish scales, so I sometimes forget that not everyone has the constitution for sea travel that we Lees have."

"Um, I'm in just as poor shape as the others," Emmett said.

"Worse, I'd say," added Molly.

Captain Lee half smiled. "You just haven't grown your sea legs yet, son. But now that I'm back, we'll have plenty of time to remedy that, eh? You were too young before, Emmett. I can't wait to show you all my favorite things—fishing, boats, fishing boats . . ."

Emmett bowed his head. Molly couldn't see his face, but she could *feel* his frustration. She wanted so badly to point out that Emmett had spent the last five months on a boat and *hated* it. If his father was trying to win him over, promises of more seafaring were not going to make the sale. But she'd vowed not to interfere in Emmett's relationship with his father. Especially when she wasn't a hundred percent sure if she should be rooting for or against patching it up.

"In any case," Captain Lee continued, "we five are, for the time being, a team. And so, yes, majority rules."

Time being? Molly didn't like the sound of that. But before she could ask for clarification, her mother bounced in her seat, pointing toward the marshy shore and shaking the boat a bit too much. "Look there!" Cassandra said. "Something flattened out the reeds in that spot. It had to be a boat. That little inlet is going to lead us to people. Or a boat that drives itself. And frankly, I'm keen to see either."

"Let's not be hasty," said the captain. "For all we know those reeds were flattened by a—"

"Who votes we go down that inlet?" Molly called out. All hands except the captain's went up.

Captain Lee slumped in resignation and tilted the rudder, steering their boat toward the break in the reeds.

"Can I get some sea legs?" Robot asked. "They sound very useful. The last time I went in the ocean, it was quite difficult to get out."

As the purring motor pushed their craft upstream, Molly felt as though she'd entered another world, one that was nearly as alien to her as the crystal cavern they'd discovered in Antarctica. Despite it being midwinter, the air was thick and steamy—and filled with a cacophony of buzzes, chirps, and gurgles. Turtles and frogs watched them pass from floating logs. Carrot-sized dragonflies skimmed the surface of the brackish water, from which rose strange, warped trees that stood on gnarled, tentacle-like roots, and had long, mossy vines dangling like curtains from their limbs. The tall grass that lined either side of the murky stream was so like the reeds dotting the waterway that it was difficult to tell where the land actually started.

"We're going to get lost in here, aren't we?" Emmett said. "This is what I get for letting a primal urge like hunger overrule my normal need to create a solid plan."

Captain Lee scoffed. "You need to learn to stand by your choices, boy."

"You're the one who was afraid we'd get lost! I'm agreeing with you now!"

"Yes, but I'd be more impressed to see you agree with yourself."

Emmett arched an eyebrow. "Is that another joke?"

The captain looked down. "Um . . ."

"Gentlemen," Cassandra interrupted. "I believe I see a house."

Molly let out a victory hoot.

A short distance farther down the waterway, on what passed for land in a swamp like this, a grimy canoe lay among the thick weeds. Just a few yards inland, a small shack stood on splintery, mold-dappled posts that held it up out of the muck. Moss coated the roof and walls of the tiny home, which was constructed from uneven timbers, many still covered in rough bark. Its little porch might have been quaint had it not seemed likely to collapse in a mild breeze.

"You think the other two little pigs' houses are around here too?" Molly asked.

Captain Lee shut down the engine and used the oars to pull their boat ashore alongside the old canoe that lay among the thick weeds. "We should knock," he said, climbing out.

"I'm not sure that door can withstand a knock," Emmett said.

Molly and Cassandra followed the captain, their feet splooshing into soft, gushy mud as they tramped over to the rickety porch. Molly was grateful they were still wearing the men's sailor clothing they'd borrowed from the crew of the *AquaZephyr*. This was not a trek she would have wanted to make in her long black dress. And if her mother had been wearing a corset? They'd have had to lay her flat across the dinghy's benches, because there's no way she'd have been able to bend enough to sit properly in that tiny boat. As Molly often said, women's garments were not designed for maritime escapades.

Back in the boat, Robot crouched as much as his mechanical joints would allow, and Emmett covered him with a blanket, just in case.

Captain Lee gingerly rapped his knuckles against the door. "Hello?"

"Sounds like no one's home," said Molly. "Let's go in and see if they have any food."

"Relax, Goldilocks," her mother warned. "Whoever lives here might be our only hope of help for miles."

"If it is bears, I would like to come out and see them," Robot said from beneath the blanket.

Emmett shushed him and joined the others on the porch. His eyes were immediately drawn to a long, rusty machete leaning against the wall. "That looks . . . murdery."

"I'm sure it's just a tool," Molly said, trying to convince herself. "For cutting vines and such. The owners of this place probably—"

"Get away from my house!" barked a gravelly voice from the side of the shack.

They all turned as a man stepped up onto the porch with them. He was gaunt, with deep-set eyes and leathery skin. The crown of his head was hairless, while the white beard on his chin was long enough to be tucked into his pants (which it was). The man snarled and raised his left hand, in which wriggled a hissing, three-foot-long, red-striped snake. "I don't take kindly to trespassers."

"We're sorry! We were just looking for help!" Emmett blurted. "Please don't throw your snake at us!"

The man looked at the serpent writhing in his hand. "Gah! Snake!" he shouted, tossing the animal into the water. "Whew! That was a close one. Those things are deadly. Thanks, friend. I owe you one."

The Peppers and Lees looked to one another and shrugged.

"Well, perhaps you can be of help," Captain Lee said. "We're not from around here, and—"

"No one's from around here," the man said with a rough-throated chuckle. "That's kinda the point in living here." He held out his hand and Captain Lee shook it. "I'm Spurgeon."

"Spurgeon," Emmett repeated, also shaking the man's hand, though far more reluctantly. "Is that a first name or a last name?"

"Oh, it is, kiddo. It is," said Spurgeon. The man's voice sounded like he was on his tenth straight year of laryngitis. He walked past them and opened the shack's door. "Come in, let me show you around. I don't get many visitors."

"That could be because you yell things about not taking kindly to trespassers," Cassandra said as they cautiously followed him inside.

"No," said Spurgeon. "It's because this place is impossible to find."

"Um," Emmett started. "We literally just—"

Molly elbowed him.

The inside of the shack was crammed with various furry dead things that Spurgeon had obviously stuffed to use as decor. Most looked like large rats or perhaps woodchucks, but Spurgeon was a terrible taxidermist, so it wasn't easy to tell. It was also quite dim on account of the windows being far too small to let in adequate light. The room smelled like mushrooms and feet.

"I might regret asking this, but do you have any food, Spurgeon?" Molly said.

"Oh, I've got something special for the trespassers who saved my life," Spurgeon said.

"Half of that description puts me at ease," Emmett said.

After rooting through a wooden chest, Spurgeon laid an array of charred meat strips on his table. "Have a seat," he said. There were no chairs.

"So, um," Emmett began. "What kind of animal—"

"Better not to ask," Molly said, grabbing a piece and biting into it. Cassandra and Captain Lee cautiously nibbled some as well, but Emmett seemed afraid to even touch the stuff.

"This kind man is sharing his homemade delicacies, Emmett," Captain Lee said. "It would be rude to refuse. I once ate a whole octopus to be polite."

"You like octopus," said Emmett.

"That's beside the point."

Spurgeon looked on eagerly as Emmett sniffed the blackened chunk before him. "Thanks, but I think I'm still a little seasick," said Emmett.

Molly, in the meantime, was already using her teeth to strip the thin bone she'd found at the center of her meat. "So, Spurge," she said. "Which way's the nearest town?"

"No towns anyone would call 'near' in these parts," the swamp dweller replied. He sat down on what might have been a large stuffed possum. "And that's a good thing. 'Cause if I had neighbors, they'd all want a piece of my land—a piece of the fountain. Old Ponce de León couldn't find it, but old Spurgeon did."

"Ponce de León?" Emmett asked. "Are you talking

about . . . the Fountain of Youth?"

"Yessiree!" Spurgeon flashed a yellow smile. "Built my house right over it! How do you think I look so young? I'm thirty-four years old!"

Molly had pegged him at a hundred and four, so she said nothing.

"Well, you can rest assured we will keep your secret, Mr. Spurgeon," said Captain Lee. "But back to our question: There may not be any towns nearby, but what town would be the near*est*?"

"Punta Rassa, I s'pose. But it's a pretty rough place. 'Specially for womenfolk."

"Is there a railroad depot there?" Cassandra asked.

Spurgeon nodded.

"Then we're going to Punta Rassa," Molly said matter-of-factly. She wiped her hands on what might have once been a squirrel and headed for the door.

"You'll never make it on foot," Spurgeon said. "Gators'll get you. If the snakes don't get you first. Unless the gators get the snakes first and then they're too full to eat you. But that's probably not a good scenario to count on."

"How do *you* get to Punta Rassa?" Cassandra asked.

"I take my donkey cart."

"You have a donkey cart?" Molly asked in surprise.

"It's out behind the house," said Spurgeon. "Crazy, right? I keep expecting something out here'll eat the donkey. But the swamp critters don't go near him. Probably 'cause he smells like the devil's outhouse."

"Can you take us to Punta Rassa in your cart?" Molly asked.

Emmett tapped her shoulder. "Did you miss his description of the donkey? It was quite evocative."

"Emmett," his father chided.

"*He's* the one who said the donkey stinks," Emmett said.

"No offense taken," Spurgeon interjected. "Swamp stink is the price you pay for living in the marsh."

"Aha! See?" Cassandra said. "He just used 'swamp' and 'marsh' interchangeably. They're the same thing, aren't they, Mr. Spurgeon?"

"Now is not the time, Mother."

"But he's a swamp man," Cassandra said. "He would know!"

"You folks want that ride or not?" Spurgeon asked.

"Absolutely! But we'll need to load some . . . equipment onto your cart too," Molly said, thinking of Robot.

"How much? Is it heavier than a bushel of mudbugs?" Spurgeon asked.

"Yes?" Molly guessed.

"Then it'll cost extra," Spurgeon said.

The Lees and Peppers huddled.

"How much are train tickets to New York from Florida?" Captain Lee asked.

"I don't know the exact fare from Punta Rassa,"

Cassandra said. "But it's forty-six dollars from Miami."

"Wow, that's a lot of money," said Emmett.

"Wait, Mother, how do you know that?" Molly asked, baffled but impressed.

"From wistfully reading the train schedules for years," Cassandra replied. "I used to dream of traveling someday. Guess I can check that one off, eh? But the point is, Roald gave us two hundred dollars—"

"Wow, that's a lot of money," said Emmett.

"But it may not be *enough*," Cassandra went on. "As it is, we'll have to find a way to sneak Robot aboard without a ticket. An added donkey ride would undoubtedly put us over budget."

"Well, I'm not going to be alligator chow," Emmett said. He pulled a ring from his pocket, silver with a small green stone. "Will this be payment enough?"

Spurgeon snatched the ring and began sniffing it.

"Emmett, you can't give that away," Molly objected. "It's important." Back when Emmett had first found that ring, he thought it was his father's. It turned out that Captain Lee had never lost his actual ring, but until they learned that, Emmett had cherished his ring, always touching it, staring at it, spinning it on his finger. For a time, he'd thought of it as his only connection to his father.

"But it's not actually important, Molly," Emmett said. "I thought I'd found something I'd lost, but it turned out to be a disappointing imitation."

Spurgeon raised an eyebrow. "The ring is fake?"

"No, the ring is real," Emmett said. "And it's yours if you take us to Punta Rassa."

"Grab your stuff from your boat," Spurgeon said, pocketing the ring. "I'll go see if the donkey is still alive."

Grateful that aluminum was a lightweight metal, Cassandra and Captain Lee carried Robot, draped in blankets, to the rear of the shack, where Spurgeon waited with a small covered cart and (thankfully) a living donkey. "What's under the sheet?" the swamp dweller asked.

"It's an . . . oven," Cassandra said. "A portable oven."

"Portable . . . ?"

"Hey, what's your donkey's name?" Molly asked, hoping to change the subject as she and Emmett ran up with their bags.

"Why would I bother naming something that's probably going to be gator chow any moment?" Spurgeon said, before turning back to Cassandra. "So, you travel with an oven, eh?"

"I am an inventor," Cassandra said, grunting as she and Captain Lee hoisted Robot into the cart. "And this oven is a top-secret new invention of mine. As is the motorized boat that we left by your house. If you promise never to mention us to anyone, you can keep the boat too."

"But we worked so hard on that motor," Emmett moaned.

"Do you want to get home or not?" Captain Lee asked him.

Spurgeon flashed a knowing grin. "You folks are on the run. I knew it soon as I saw you. Well, worry not. Old Spurgeon knows how to keep a secret. No one else alive knows I found the Fountain of Youth, do they?" He pulled himself up onto the cart's driver's seat.

"But you told *us*—"

"Emmett, *shh!*"

The Peppers and Lees crowded into the small cart with Robot, and Molly whispered a quick "Good job" into where she assumed his mechanical ear was located beneath the sheet.

Spurgeon cracked the reins and the donkey began clomping off at a pace that made Molly wonder if the trip might actually be faster on foot. "This is going to take forever," she grumbled.

"Just so's you know," Spurgeon called back to his passengers, "there ain't gonna be no road for the first bunch of miles. Just a lot of thick weeds and tangled branches, probably an old skeleton or two. But don't worry—I know where I'm going."

"Thanks, Spurge. Very reassuring."

The Wild East
Punta Rassa, Florida, January 18, 1884

MOLLY COUGHED AND waved her hand to clear the air as their cart rumbled onto the raw-dirt streets of Punta Rassa, kicking up clouds of brown dust in its wake. Were it not for the swaying palm trees rising up behind the general store and the saloon, she might have thought she'd somehow crossed the country and ended up in the Wild West.

"Why did no one tell me Florida has cowboys?" she muttered in awe. Nearly everyone she saw was on a horse. And all the Punta Rassans wore tall boots, vests, and wide-brimmed hats, with bandannas around their necks and whips coiled at their belts. The men, at least. There were no women that Molly could see. Perhaps they were all inside, enjoying the shade on a warm January day. In that saloon, maybe. Or that coffin maker's shop.

"I've never met a real cowboy before," said Cassandra. "Perhaps this little detour will be more fun than we thought."

"Sure," said Emmett. "What could be more fun than dirt clouds, manure piles, and rugged manliness?"

Captain Lee gave his son a slap on the back. "Hey, you just described my life in that cave!"

Emmett furrowed his brow. "Manure piles?"

"You remember the size of those crabs, don't you?" his father replied.

The cart came to a stop and Spurgeon called for everyone to get out. Molly, Cassandra, Emmett, and Captain Lee all climbed down and stretched their stiff limbs. Molly scanned the buildings along the roadside as she and the others strapped their bags over their shoulders. She saw a barbershop, a pawnbroker, a small hotel, and a second coffin maker. "Where is the train station?" Molly asked as all four of them walked around to the front of the wagon.

From the driver's seat, Spurgeon pointed down the road. "Other side of town," he said. "Don't worry, you won't get lost. Place is basically one long street."

"Is there a reason you can't take us the rest of the way?" Captain Lee asked. "We have a lot to carry. Including our oven."

"Oh, yeah, the portable oven," Spurgeon said. "Not really so portable, is it? But hey, an oven is an oven. And having one would mean I can finally stop setting my old hats on fire to cook dinner. So I'm gonna consider it part of my fee. Have fun in Punta Rassa!" He cracked the reins and took off.

"Hey! Stop!" Molly cried, but Spurgeon just drove the cart in a wide half circle and headed back the way he'd come. "He's stealing Robot!" Molly cried. She and Emmett ran after the fleeing cart, but the old man picked up speed and quickly put some distance between them.

"Since when is that donkey so fast?" Emmett groaned as they slowed down, realizing the pointlessness of a foot chase. "That donkey lied to us!"

Captain Lee waved his arms and called out to a group of cowboys chatting outside the barbershop. "Help! That man is stealing our things!"

Most of the cowboys ignored him and continued their conversation. One laughed.

"There is a crime occurring right here in your town!" Captain Lee cried in frustration. "If you won't help, at least find the police! You must have police!" He paused and scratched his head. "*Do* you have police? I see plenty of taverns and coffin manufacturers, but . . . no police stations."

"He's going to get away with Robot," Molly panted.

"Let me try something," Cassandra said. "I hate this, but . . ." She ran in circles, screaming and waving her hands frantically over her head. "Help! Help! Thief! Can any brave soul save my precious belongings from that despicable thief!"

42

A broad-shouldered, scruffy-chinned man trotted up on his horse and gave Cassandra a tip of his hat. "Trouble, ma'am?"

"Oh, thank goodness!" Cassandra fanned herself with her hands. "A big, brave cowboy's come to our rescue!"

"I'm a cow*man*, ma'am," said the rider. "Name's Burl."

"Of course it is," Molly said, rolling her eyes. "It's okay, Mother, you can stop now. Listen, Burl: See that cart with the ridiculously fast donkey way down the road? The driver stole our stuff. We need you to help us get it back."

"Is that Spurgeon?" the cowboy asked, squinting at the dust cloud in the distance. "You folks wouldn't be the first to fall prey to that old marsh predator. Well, have no fear, ma'am. I'll get your belongings back."

"No, I said you need to *help us* get them back," Molly corrected. She was sitting behind him, having climbed onto the horse while he was talking.

"What are you doing, girl? Get off my horse!"

"Hey, time's a-wasting!" Molly snapped. "Ride, Burl! Ride like the wind!"

Flustered, the cowboy spurred his horse into a full gallop as Captain Lee gaped and Emmett hid his face.

"You get hurt, it's your own fault, kid," Burl said as they sped after the thief.

"It generally is," Molly replied, gripping the back of the cowboy's leather vest. As many times as she'd been in horse-drawn vehicles, she'd never experienced a ride from atop one of the animals. She was not prepared for the skull-rattling, up-and-down jostling, nor the dizzying speed with which the ground was flying by below her. It was best, she decided, to keep her eyes up. "So, Spurgeon tricks a lot of people out of their stuff?"

"Nah, I just said that to make your ma feel better," Burl replied. "Spurgeon couldn't trick a worm into wigglin'. Don't worry, though, ain't like he's gonna put up a fight once we catch him. And we're almost there."

They were close enough now that Spurgeon could hear them. He craned his neck around and yelped. He cracked the reins repeatedly, pushing his donkey harder, but Burl and Molly continued to gain on him. The horse was within a few yards of Spurgeon when Molly gasped. She could see movement in the back of the covered cart, glints of metal flashing out through the rear opening. *No, Robot!* she cried in her head. *Stay put! Just a few more seconds!* But soon there was a distraught aluminum face peering out at them. Molly threw her hands over Burl's eyes.

"What are you thinking, girl?" the cowboy shouted, trying to wriggle his head free of her grip. "I can't see!"

"Yeah, sorry about that," Molly said, shaking her head vigorously at Robot. "You're a cowboy—just ride straight!"

"What do you think a cowboy is?" Burl cried. They veered off road, the horse stomping through tall grass and thick ferns.

"What the heck is going on back there?" Spurgeon

yelled. He twisted himself around to gawk at the sight of Molly's arms wrapped around the cowboy's head, and his cart slammed directly into a palm tree. Two wheels popped off and rolled away as the wagon tipped to one side and Spurgeon fell off into the grass. The collision also sent Robot tumbling back into the cart's dark interior.

"Whoa!" Molly cried, removing her hands from Burl's eyes. The cowboy shrieked and pulled back on his reins. His horse reared up onto its hind legs, stopping mere inches from the crashed cart. Molly slid off and thumped to the mossy ground, sore but uninjured.

Spurgeon looked around for his donkey and found that it had broken free of its harness. He jumped onto the animal's back and took off into the weeds. "Go, Tidbit! Run!"

"Tidbit?" Molly cried, sitting up. "You *did* name that donkey, you liar!"

Burl stared down at her as if she were possessed by a demon. "You're nuttier than Aunt Beulah's cashew brittle, girl."

"Oh, yeah?" Molly stood between him and the cart. "If that's the way you feel about it, get out of here! I don't need you anymore anyway. Just leave me and my . . . oven."

The cowboy shook his head, turned his horse around, and took off, leaving Molly on the desolate road with the broken cart.

"Robot," Molly called softly.

Her friend's metallic face popped back into the open. "Hello, Molly. Did I do a wrong thing?"

"No, it's my fault. We should have made a plan about what to do if we got separated. Well, actually, Emmett's the one who usually insists we make a plan, and he didn't, so I'm going to blame Emmett on this one."

"I was afraid you would lose me," said Robot.

"And I was afraid *you* would lose *me*," said Molly.

"Well, that was silly. We were afraid of the opposite things."

Molly climbed into the cart and sat with him. "Remember how after the World's Fair, I used to complain about how boring life had gotten?"

"I do," said Robot. "You mentioned it every morning and most afternoons for eighty-two consecutive days."

"Well, I could use some of that boring right about now." A few minutes later, she heard her mother calling for her. "In here, Mother!" When they were sure the coast was clear, Molly and Robot climbed out to greet Cassandra, Emmett, and Captain Lee.

"We passed that cowboy halfway down the road," Cassandra said. "He does not have a very positive opinion of you."

"We have a problem," Molly said.

"The problem is me," said Robot. "Traveling without anybody seeing me is proving too difficult. You should go to New York without me. I will fly there to meet you and hope for the best."

"No," Molly snapped. "I just told you, you are *not* doing that."

"I do what I want," said Robot.

"She's right, Robot; there's no way you have enough Ambrosium to fly up the entire East Coast of the United States," Emmett said. "We don't know if you have enough to fly to the Punta Rassa train station from here."

"Our problem is just that we need something to hide you in," Molly said. "Because that blanket is not a long-term solution."

"Can we fix this cart?" Captain Lee asked.

"And take it on the train with us? No, we just need a box," Cassandra said. "And luckily for us, finding a large person-shaped box shouldn't be a problem in this town."

"Brilliant, Mother," Molly said.

"You are referring to the multiple coffin shops," Captain Lee said with a nod. "Yes, they do add a certain . . . creepiness to this place."

"I am confused," said Robot. "Is one of us dead? Because if so, I have misunderstood the concept."

"We're going to put you in a coffin to keep you alive," Molly said.

"I see," said Robot. He ran his metal finger along the brim of the derby on his head. "Can I still wear my hat when I am dead? I like hats."

Molly assured him he could.

Captain Lee cleared his throat. "I hate to be the voice of negativity . . ."

No, you don't, Molly scoffed to herself.

"But can we afford a casket?" the captain continued.

"That's not going to be a problem!" Emmett called victoriously from where he was rooting around in the front of the wagon. "Looks like Spurgeon lost something in the crash." He held up the ring he had given to the swamp dweller earlier.

"Excellent," said Robot. "Now, let us kill me so we can go home."

4

America's Most Wanted

AFTER SIX GLORIOUS months of wearing boy's trousers, Molly hated the very thought of squeezing back into her long black dress with its circulation-cutting cuffs and neck-to-ankle buttons. But passing themselves off as grieving members of a funeral party would be easier if they weren't dressed like sailors. Changing in the back of the broken donkey cart was a challenge, but Molly and Cassandra helped each other with all the tugging, tying, and buttoning. The most challenging bit was her mother's corset, which had, by Molly's estimation, roughly ten billion laces. Molly thought briefly about the fact that she was twelve and a half already; it wouldn't be long until people expected her to start wearing one of those torture devices.

Fully dressed and uncomfortable once more, they

climbed back out to the road, where Cassandra dug two black suits from her bag for Emmett and Captain Lee.

"Where did these come from?" the captain asked.

"Roald lent me a suit," Emmett said. "It's a little small, but it'll work."

"And mine?"

"Um, that was in Alexander Graham Bell's closet," Emmett said, trying not to make eye contact.

"You stole it?" Captain Lee asked.

"I'm already a wanted criminal, Papa!"

"I'm just saying that we've got a lot riding on what Mr. Bell tells the authorities when he lands back in New York," said Captain Lee. "So, maybe burgling the man's wardrobe wasn't the best way to ensure he stays on our side."

"I still think you're putting too much faith in the guy," said Molly. "Bell is a lost cause."

"Even if you're right about that . . ." The captain sounded flummoxed. "Do we have to . . . I mean, must we . . ." He sighed. "Now that I have a second chance to do so, I just want to be a good role model for my son."

Cassandra gave the man a sympathetic pat on the back. "Rest easy, Wendell," she said. "The only other parental figure Emmett has for comparison is me. And I'm a horrendous role model. Now climb in that broken donkey cart and put on your stolen suit for our fake funeral."

An hour later, the quartet marched solemnly into the open-air pavilion of the Punta Rassa railroad station, towing a pinewood coffin on a small handcart. Their clothes were creased and wrinkled and Emmett's pants only went down to his shins, but none of the "cowmen" seemed to look at them with anything other than sympathy. Molly had wanted to buy a fancier casket for Robot ("Show us your finest Egyptian-style sarcophagus," she'd requested), but Emmett reminded her that tickets to New York were going to be pricey and they needed to conserve the cash they'd earned from trading his ring to the local pawnbroker.

"What's it like in there, Robot?" Molly whispered while pretending to cry over the coffin.

"It is too dark to see, so I am using my imagination," he replied from within the box.

"Oh," said Molly. "What are you imagining?"

"That it is dark."

They paused along the tracks, by one of the squared-off wooden pillars that held up the depot's triangular roof. Thankfully, the station was not crowded. Aside from a handful of waiting passengers, the only other person in the pavilion was a sleepy-looking ticket agent standing at the center of a circular counter.

"Wait here with our things," Cassandra said. "I'll go purchase tickets."

Molly checked the clock above the ticket desk against the handwritten timetable posted on the slate chalkboard below it. The 7:43 p.m. train should be arriving any minute. They would soon be on their way home.

Molly was surprised by how intensely she missed New York. It had been a thrill to see Antarctic mountains, Caribbean islands, and Floridian marshes, but she longed to be back dodging oblivious carriage drivers in the streets, squabbling with obnoxious newsboys, and sucking in the vinegary air of Pepper's Pickles, her one true home. Would it still feel like home, though, if Emmett wasn't there? It was becoming increasingly clear that Captain Lee intended to take Emmett away from the Peppers. She could understand why the man would want to—Emmett was his son, after all. But Emmett was also her brother. Not in any legal or biological sense, but in all the ways that mattered. And there was no way Emmett would choose his father over them. Would he? She walked over to her best friend, who stood by a wooden column, wringing his hands.

"No need to fret so much, Goosey," she said to him. "This plan is going to work."

"Oh, it's not the plan," he replied. "I mean, I *don't* have much confidence in this plan, but that's not what's got me antsy. I'm thinking about what happens *after* we get home."

"Aha! You *don't* want to live with your father!" Molly said. "I knew it! C'mon, let's go tell him—"

"No," Emmett said quickly. "I *do* want to stay with him. I wish he'd stop acting so weird, but, yes, of course I want to be with him. I missed him for so long. It's just that we can't *all* live in your pickle shop, you know? That place is already overcrowded as it is. Being realistic . . ." He let out a long slow breath, like a balloon deflating. "I'm a terrible person. I got my father back from the dead—I should be nothing but happy!"

"You don't want to lose *me*! That doesn't make you a terrible person—that just makes you smart," Molly said. "I don't want to lose you either. And, hey, there's a chance the pickle shop's not even still standing. We'll *all* need someplace new to live, so maybe we can find a place together."

Emmett looked doubtful. "My father's not the kind of man who'd feel comfortable sharing his living space with another family. Or who knows, maybe he is now. I never know what to expect from him these days."

"I didn't want to be the one to say it, but, yeah, the man's tough to pin down. One minute he's scowling at a hilarious fart noise, the next he's making some embarrassingly corny 'gas' pun. It's like he keeps catching himself being a stodgy old grump and then trying to make up for it with the eye-rolliest jokes he can think up."

"Honestly, I think he's trying to compete," said Emmett. "He doesn't really know me, but he knows I've been happy with your family, so he's trying to, um, out-fun your mother. Which is not really in his skill set.

53

Looking at it that way, it's actually kinda sweet."

"And looking at it a different way, he's trying to steal you from us."

"He's not stealing me, Molly! He's my *father*. He didn't even want to steal the suit . . ." Emmett's eyes drifted up to a poster pinned to the column behind Molly. "Whoa. Look at that." He brushed past her for a closer look.

"Most wanted?" Molly read aloud as she rushed to his side. "Are we on it?"

"No, thank goodness," Emmett said with evident relief. "But look—"

"I mean, it would have been at least a teensy bit exciting to see my face on a wanted poster," Molly said. "But that's not really the way I want to get my name in the history books."

"You should be grateful for that too, Emmett." Captain Lee strolled up behind them.

"I am, Papa," Emmett said. "But—"

"There's a reason why I always warned you to stay on the right side of the law," his father went on. "Chinese people have to deal with enough distrust in this country as it is. Not that I don't understand the allure of the criminal mystique. I've read Robin Hood. I've always thought I would look rather dashing in one of those jaunty feathered caps, but . . ."

"Papa," Emmett started.

"You've got nothing to worry about, Cap," Molly said. "Emmett is *the* most law-abiding person I know. Aside from breaking the secrecy contract, he's never even—Whoa, look who's number one on that most wanted list! Oogie MacDougal!"

"That's what I was trying to show you," Emmett said. "It says he broke out of prison and should be considered armed and dangerous."

"Who is this MacDougal character?" asked Captain Lee.

"He collapsed a building on top of us once," Molly said casually.

"He *what*?" Captain Lee gasped. "Not that I'm, um, shocked by that or anything."

"Oogie was a partner of Rector's," Emmett explained. "He and his gang, the Green Onion Boys, helped Rector take over the World's Fair."

"Ah, of course," the captain said. "The only reason you know this gangster is because of Rector."

"Absolutely," Molly said. "Even though he already had a grudge against Emmett from back when Emmett worked for him."

"Emmett *what*?" Captain Lee burst out. "I mean, I'm impressed that you found employment, but . . ."

"Papa, I swear I didn't know who he was at the time!" Emmett blurted. "Oogie has such a thick accent, I couldn't understand—"

"Emmett, you should know better than to blame something on a person's accent," Captain Lee scolded. "English is not my first language—do you think I want people holding that against me?"

"But English *is* Oogie's first language!" Molly said. "He's Scottish! Seriously, you haven't heard the guy talk, Cap. And, anyway, Oogie only hates Emmett because Emmett stole a bunch of guns and money from him."

"He *what*?"

"Please stop 'helping,' Molly," Emmett grumbled.

"Everything okay over there?" the ticket agent asked Cassandra as he handed her four one-way tickets to New York.

"Oh, they're just excited about the most wanted list," Cassandra replied. "The man at number one? They put him behind bars."

The agent looked at her askance. "Um, okay. Well, that feller seems to be at large again, so . . . keep your eyes open."

"An excellent way to avoid walking into things," Cassandra said, slipping the tickets into her bag.

A piercing whistle sounded as a hulking black locomotive rumbled up alongside the pavilion. The brakes screeched as the ten-car passenger train jolted to a stop and a conductor in a pinstriped suit leaned out from between two cars to yell, "All aboard!"

As the captain asked the conductor to open a baggage car for their casket, Molly realized her mother was still at the ticket counter. She ran back to see what was keeping her.

"That MacDougal feller might be dangerous, but seeing as you folks are grieving and especially vulnerable, I feel like I should let you know that the men on that poster over there ain't the only ones the law is looking for," the ticket agent was telling Cassandra. From under the counter, he produced a sheet of paper. "These are the *most*-most wanted," he said. "The ones they don't put on the posters 'cause they don't want them to know they're looking for 'em. But we station managers get to see 'em. We're important like that."

"Thank you for your concern," said Cassandra. "We'll be sure to . . ." Her words trailed off as she saw her own photograph on the page. Molly's breath caught as she appeared by her mother's side and laid eyes on the picture that had been taken when Cassandra was admitted to the asylum on Blackwell's Island. Thankfully, the agent was too busy trying to impress his customer to realize that she had the same face as the wild-haired, sooty-cheeked woman in the photo. But one good back-and-forth look and he could very easily make the connection. Or read the names of the fugitive's listed accomplices: Molly Pepper and Emmett Lee.

"Train's here, Mother. Gotta go." Molly grabbed Cassandra's elbow and pulled her away, but not before grabbing a stick from the ground and jamming it between the hinges of the counter's short, swinging gate.

The ticket agent waved goodbye, then glanced down

at his paper. "Hey, this one almost looks like ..." He lifted the sheet to his eyes and squinted. "What's this? 'Traveling with two ch—' Hey, stop! Don't get on that train!"

"Ugh! I can't believe I'm actually on a wanted poster and they didn't have my picture!" Molly grumbled as they ran to join the others.

With the coffin stowed safely aboard, Emmett and Captain Lee were stepping up into the train, past the conductor. "Hurry, ladies!" the man called.

"We're hurrying!" Cassandra shouted back. "Believe me, we're hurrying!"

"Don't—um . . . Stay, train! Stay!" the ticket seller shouted, struggling to open the jammed gate.

Cassandra vaulted up the steps, past the conductor, into the train car. Molly, right on her heels, pushed the conductor into the car with her and pulled the door shut behind them.

"Excuse me, young lady," the conductor said. "But you can't—"

"Oh, Mr. Conductor Man, I'm so sad," Molly cried, putting on her most mournful voice. "That was my great-uncle Raspberry in that coffin! Oh, Uncle Razz, we're going to miss you so much! Your warm, caring eyes and your ... funny sneeze!"

"Oh, I'm, um, I'm sorry, little girl," the flustered conductor replied. "That's—that's very—um, I just need to check the—"

"Nothing will ever cheer me up again!" Molly howled. "Except maybe a tour of a real railroad train! Uncle Razz always said he'd take me on one. But he never got the chance."

"Um, uh, I—I think I can make that happen," the conductor said. He took Molly's hand as the train whistle blew and the vehicle began chugging down the tracks. As she passed them, Molly winked to her mother, who was whispering to Emmett and his father, presumably telling them about the most-most wanted list. "Okay, um, I guess we'll start with the dining car," the conductor continued. "Would that be all right, young lady?"

Molly nodded. She sniffled, realizing for the first time that the tears she'd worked up to fool the conductor had become real. This was their life now, wasn't it? Always running, always looking over their shoulders. For months, she'd been trying to prepare herself for the possibility that they would be fugitives when they returned to the US, but there was always a part of her that hoped for a smoother, easier transition to normal life. What were the chances now that they could move peacefully back into Pepper's Pickles? "Thank you, Mr. Conductor Man," she said. "You're so nice."

"It's okay," the conductor replied. "My grandpa used to have a funny sneeze. I miss him too."

Fugitives!
New York City, February 2, 1884

CERTAIN THAT THE stationmaster at Punta Rassa would have telegraphed a warning to other depots down the line, the Peppers and Lees quietly slipped off their train at a refueling stop in southern Georgia (not a simple task while carrying a loaded coffin). From there, they changed modes of transportation—and disguises—as frequently as they could. Inching northward in fits and starts, they went from being tourists in a coach to chefs on a freight train to apple pickers on a hayride to acrobats in a circus wagon to anglers on a fishing boat to cowboys (and cows) in a cattle car. By the time they reached the ferry station in Hoboken, New Jersey, two weeks later, the fugitives were haggard, hungry, scruffy, hollow-eyed ghosts of themselves, clad in a mismatched mishmash of patched coats and cowboy hats over workmen's coveralls, cooks' aprons, and sparkly leotards. But they finagled their way onto a boat to Manhattan nonetheless. It helped that they had transferred Robot to a crate marked "DANGER: DISEASED ANIMAL." No one wanted to get close enough to take a good look at them after that.

"Oh, joy. Another boat," Emmett grumbled as they surrounded Robot's crate on the deck of the ferry. "Well, at least it's not—"

It began to snow.

Emmett raised his face to the heavens and let the fat flakes settle on his reddening cheeks. "This is because I complained about the boat, isn't it?"

"Bah! It's just snow," Captain Lee scoffed. "I miss the snow, actually. Back in Antarctica, I used to make snowmen to keep me company. I am not a skilled sculptor, though, so they were mostly just piles with eyeholes poked into them. And they were terrible conversationalists."

After trekking through blinding blizzards in Antarctica, Molly felt the current flurries were barely worth mentioning. "I just hope the shop is still standing," she said.

"Afraid Jasper has burned it to the ground by now?" Emmett said with a little laugh.

Molly didn't want to admit that that's exactly what she was afraid of. The previous September, when the

Peppers were in a rush to vacate the premises, they left their family business in the hands of their loyal friend and only repeat customer, Jasper Bloom. Molly adored Jasper—he was chatty, cheerful, amusing—but he was also . . . well, eccentric would be putting it mildly. The Peppers didn't choose Jasper for his management skills; technically speaking, they didn't *choose* him at all. They handed him the keys simply because he happened to be there at the time. Molly prepared herself for the very real possibility that they would find him ignoring the store counter in favor of reading through her abandoned book pile or lying on the floor holding his belly because he'd eaten their entire pickle stock himself.

"Well, I trust Jasper," Emmett said. "The only reason he lost his ashman job was because he was helping us run from Rector. At worst, he's probably just bored with the lack of customers. If it turns out that anything *has* happened to the shop, my guess is that Agent Clark and his men would be behind it. Or the Jägermen. Maybe the Green Onion Boys. Or the Guild. Wow, for twelve-year-olds, we have a *lot* of enemies."

"Speaking of enemies," Molly said with sudden trepidation. "Bell is almost certainly back in New York by now too. I wonder how much he's told the authorities about us."

"Alec is more of an obstacle than an enemy, though, right?" said Cassandra. "I'm sure he's miffed about us skipping out on him, but certainly not so upset that he'd get us into more trouble. Right?"

Molly and Emmett exchanged glances, but said nothing.

"I cannot see your faces," Robot said from within the crate, "but I assume the uncomfortable silence is due to the others thinking that Mrs. Pepper is not necessarily correct."

"How are you doing in there, Robot?" Molly whispered to the crate. "Dry?"

"Dry would describe it, yes," Robot responded from inside. "Molly, do you remember how I once asked you to explain the concept of boredom? I no longer have need to ask that question."

"Well, we're almost home again," Molly said to him. Manhattan's western shore was coming up fast. She breathed in the icy air, letting it numb her nostrils. New York air had a quality all its own, a zest that even the biting Antarctic winds never carried.

"Before we disembark," said Captain Lee, "let's go over the plan one more time."

Molly tried not to let him see her rolling eyes. *This* was the one piece of evidence that Emmett and his father were truly related. "First thing we need is a base of operations," she said with the evident fatigue of someone who has had to explain the same thing a thousand times over. "Hopefully that will be Pepper's Pickles—"

63

"Definitely my first choice," said Cassandra. "We have coffee there." She stared off wistfully at what Molly assumed was an imaginary, steaming mug floating in the sky.

"But we all agree this is unlikely, correct?" Captain Lee said. "Because your shop is almost certainly going to be under surveillance."

"That's where you come in, Papa," Emmett added. "Since you're the only one of us the police won't be looking for. We need you to scout out the shop for us and make sure it's safe."

"That's assuming nobody stops me and asks me to prove I'm in the country legally," the captain said. "Which I won't be able to. Even though I am." He sighed. "It's a risk I'm willing to take to keep you safe. But what happens when I verify that your shop is indeed unsafe?"

"*If* that's the case," Molly continued, "then we'll ask Jasper to put us up."

"Do you think Jasper has a Brew-Master 1900 coffee maker?" Cassandra asked. "Probably not, right? Because I invented it?"

"I'm sure Jasper's apartment is tiny," Molly said, "but we'd only need to hide out there until we free the Mothers of Invention. Once they're out of jail, we won't have to worry about a place to stay anymore—the ladies have secret workshops all over the city."

"And from that point, the MOI can help us with all the

other stuff we've got to take care of too," Emmett said. "Clearing our names, reclaiming the pickle shop for the Peppers, solving Robot's Ambrosium problem, tracking down Nellie Bly . . ."

"And if we're aiming big," Molly added, "maybe even figuring out how to finally get credit for saving the world from Rector."

Her mother shot her a squinty glance that told her they were *not* aiming that high.

The captain raised a tentative finger. "If I may? I am sure these women are very intelligent, but should we really be relying on them for everything? Including my son's freedom?"

"I trust them," Emmett said.

"Yes," said his father. "But you also apparently trusted a man with the obvious criminal name of *Oogie*."

"I didn't know who he was!"

"All I'm saying," said the captain, "is, well, have we definitely ruled out *my* plan?"

"You mean turning ourselves in and telling the police that Emmett wasn't involved?" Molly asked, incredulous. "You were serious about that?"

"Well, when you say it back to me like that, I admit it doesn't sound like a very charitable suggestion," said Captain Lee. "But you have to understand, I hold out no hopes of Emmett getting fair treatment if he's apprehended before proving his innocence. You ladies, however . . . If you ladies explain everything to the authorities and tell them how you stopped Rector, they will surely go easy on you, no?"

"No offense, Captain, but you missed a lot," Molly said. "Granted, you had a good excuse, but you haven't gotten to see how relentless these federal agents are."

"Especially Agent Clark," said Emmett. "He already put Mrs. Pepper in jail once."

"I am not fond of the man," said Cassandra.

"He arrested all the members of the MOI just for sheltering us," Emmett said.

"Yeah, I think it's Clark's goal in life to see us all behind bars," Molly said. "He's like our very own Javert."

"Our very own what?" asked Captain Lee.

"Inspector Javert," said Emmett. "He's a police officer in the book *Les Misérables* who's obsessed with hunting down the hero."

"Hmph. This Javert fellow sounds a bit like Captain Ahab in *Moby-Dick*," said Emmett's father. "Now, *there* is a good book! Ships, whales, sea captains . . ."

"Personally, I'd rather read about revolutions than fish," said Molly. "But I think we've lost track of this conversation."

"We lose track of *every* conversation! Sometimes I wonder how you people accomplish anything!" Frustration was growing in Captain Lee's voice. "I'm sorry, I guess I just don't understand how you're going to secure your friends' release from prison without ever speaking to the police, or the governor, or—I don't know—*somebody* in authority?"

"We're going to *break* the MOI out, silly," said Molly.

Captain Lee furrowed his brow. "She's joking, right?" he asked Cassandra.

"If so, it's not one of her best," Cassandra said. "Those tend to begin with 'knock-knock.'"

"There is no way Emmett is taking part in something as foolhardy and risky as a prison break," Captain Lee said seriously.

"But, Cap—" Molly started.

"Look," he continued, "I've already done so many inadvisable things that I would never have done under normal circumstances—stealing clothes, jumping onto moving trains, getting within sniffing distance of circus folk—all in the name of keeping my son *out* of jail. But staging a breakout? We've got to draw a line somewhere. You must agree, Emmett, don't you?"

Emmett looked startled, like a student who gets called upon in class when they didn't do the required reading. "Well, um, we certainly shouldn't do anything rash," Emmett said. "I mean, we don't even know what prison the MOI are in. We'll have to think everything through before we commit to any course of action."

Captain Lee looked on his son with admiration. "*There* is the Emmett I remember."

The fire in Molly's cheeks felt hot enough to melt the snow accumulating on her head. Emmett caught her eye, then turned back to his father.

"But thinking it through means thinking *everything* through," Emmett added. "We shouldn't take anything off the table without considering it fully. Even a jail-break. If there's one thing I've learned from my time with the Peppers, it's that the most unexpected move can sometimes turn out to be the right one."

And there's *the Emmett I remember*, Molly thought. His father was no longer smiling, but she didn't care. She didn't want there to be a war between the family Emmett wanted to belong to and the one he felt he had to belong to, but if it came to that, she knew which side she'd be on.

"Christopher Street Pier! All passengers disembark!" shouted the ferryman.

"At least the weather means fewer people are out and about," Emmett said as the quartet rolled their crate through the slush along Bleecker Street on a wheeled dolly.

Fewer people, Molly thought, *but not none*. She couldn't help feeling that every bundled-up pedestrian they passed was taking an extra-long look at them as they walked by. Of course, that could have had something to do with the occasionally visible sequins peeking out from under their coats or the big "diseased animal" crate they were pushing.

They passed a newsboy hawking papers on the corner of Sixth Avenue. While the newsie, shivering in a threadbare vest, served a customer wrapped in thick woolen scarves, Molly snuck up and swiped a copy of that day's *New York Sun* from the pile behind him. She hurried back to her group, leafing through the pages and scanning not only for mention of Nellie Bly but also for any news about the MOI and where they might have been imprisoned. She barely got to see a half dozen headlines before Captain Lee snatched the newspaper from her hands. He strode back to the corner, brushed snowflakes from the paper, and returned it to the pile with apologies to the befuddled newsboy.

"No more stealing," the captain said to Molly. "We can't afford to draw any more attention to ourselves than we already are."

"The kid didn't notice anything until *you* brought it back," Molly complained. "And we have to go check that paper again. I think I finally saw something by Nellie!"

"Really?" Emmett asked hopefully.

"There was a headline on the back page: 'Best Pickle Shop in New York,'" Molly said. "Nellie was going to write that exact article when we first met her, remember?"

"I'm sorry, but that article was not by your friend,"

Captain Lee said, with genuine sympathy. "I saw the byline as I took the paper from you. The author was someone named Sherwin St. Smithens."

"Oh," Molly said. She supposed it would have been too good to be true.

"Let's move along, Molls," said Cassandra, gently rubbing her daughter's back.

"I'm okay, Mother," Molly replied. "I'm a little concerned about you, though. Normally in weather like this you'd have made yourself a snow brooch by now."

Cassandra sighed. "I'm just tired, Molls. We've been running and fighting for the better part of a year now. That sort of living takes its toll on a person. I'll be fine once we get a break."

As they walked, Captain Lee gaped up at the snowflakes dancing in the soft glow of electric streetlamps. "New York has changed even more than I realized," he said in awe.

"Those are new for us too, actually," Emmett said of the lamps. "Thomas Edison has obviously been busy in the time we've been gone. He had installed electric lights along the paths in Central Park before we left, but now they seem to be all over the city."

"I wonder what else the Guild has been up to in the past few months," Molly said. "Part of me wouldn't be surprised if we find Nikola Tesla or George Westinghouse running Pepper's Pickles when we get there."

"There it is—good old Thompson Street," Cassandra said with the warmth of someone reuniting with a long-lost friend. "This is our block!" She was about to turn the corner when Captain Lee stopped her.

"I go first, remember?" he said.

Molly nodded grudgingly. That was part of her plan, after all. She'd just stopped feeling generous toward the captain since formulating it. "Don't leave us waiting long," she said.

Captain Lee trudged off through the accumulating snow, while the others waited on the corner, pretending to inspect their crate for what passersby must have assumed were openings through which a diseased animal could escape. After an endless seven minutes, the captain returned. "I do not see any suspicious figures across the street from your shop," he reported. "But with the crowd outside, I cannot be certain there aren't any federal agents hiding closer to the storefront."

"Crowd?" Cassandra asked.

Emmett shook his head. "Oh, Papa. You must have looked at the wrong building."

"The closest Pepper's Pickles has ever come to a crowd was when the cucumber man and the vinegar man made their deliveries at the same time," Molly said.

"It's got a sign, for Pete's sake!" the captain said. "With your name on it! Go look for yourself."

"Wait with Robot," Cassandra told him as she, Molly,

and Emmett rushed around the corner.

They saw the familiar green awning, right in the middle of the block—and below it, a queue of waiting customers that stretched nearly to the opposite corner. There had to be fifty people in line, many of whom were reading the latest issue of the *New York Sun*.

Pepper's Pickles, it seemed, was the best pickle shop in New York.

Pickles, But No Peppers

THE PEDESTRIAN TRAFFIC jam in the doorway of Pepper's Pickles made it impossible for Molly, Emmett, and Cassandra to get inside.

"Can you believe this?" Emmett said, gaping at the crowd.

"I've read Jules Verne novels more believable than this," Molly replied.

Cassandra tapped several shoulders, but no one made way for her.

Molly crouched so she could peer between the legs of the people standing in the entryway. At least a dozen more sets of feet were lined up at the counter inside. She couldn't see Jasper from her angle, but she could hear him.

"What can I get for you today, sir? And may I add that

that is a spectacular tie you are wearing. I once had a tie like that, and by 'like that' I mean 'completely different,' and by 'tie' I mean 'fancy piece of string,' and by 'had' I mean 'stole from a bird's nest.' But the point is: I know a fashionable fellow when I see one and I see one before me right now. Although, apparently, fashion sensibility has no correlation to the speed with which one answers questions, because I am still waiting to hear what kind of pickle you want."

Molly snickered. Jasper had not changed one bit. The customer at the counter stammered and asked for a Hungarian Half-Sour.

"Hungarian Half-Sour coming right up," Jasper said. "Balthazar Birdhouse used to tell people he was half Hungarian. He also used to tell people he was half Welsh and half Canadian. But that's too many halfs by half."

"Who's Balthazar Birdhouse?" a customer asked.

"If you don't know, consider yourself lucky," Jasper replied. "I'll tell you one thing Balthazar Birdhouse definitely is not: half Hungarian. Now, half-sour, that I'd believe. Although the man's probably more like full-sour. You know, the first time someone offered me one of these half-sour pickles, I thought they was literally gonna give me half a pickle. Half a pickle. That sounds like half a problem. As in, 'That time that Balthazar Birdhouse told me he'd borrowed my potato masher but I did not own a potato masher, I knew I was going to be in half a pickle.' Why haven't you taken your pickle yet, Mr. Fancy Tie? I got other customers waiting. Or do you not see all those people standing around you? Here, take your pickle. That'll be five cents. I really do like that tie, by the way."

The waiting customers laughed.

"I'm not sure what you all find so humorous," Jasper said. "But go ahead and laugh it up. Laughter is a beauteous sound. Unless it's coming from Balthazar Birdhouse. That man's laugh will send shivers down your spine and up your esophagus. Sounds like a sickly seagull choking on a mouthful of hornets."

The customers laughed again and Molly couldn't take it any longer. She tried to squeeze between people.

"Hey, the line starts back there," a man yelled, jerking his thumb over his shoulder.

Emmett and Cassandra both sighed and started the trek to the end of the queue. "What are you doing?" Molly said in disbelief. "This is *our* shop!" She huffed and shoved past the people in the doorway.

"—and *that* is why Balthazar Birdhouse gave me the nickname 'Vinegar Teeth,' which I found quite unfair, seeing as I only made that mistake the one time," Jasper was saying as Molly worked her way to the counter. "It was a rather interesting insult to come from a man with teeth like pinto beans. And by that, do I mean they look like pinto beans, smell like pinto beans, or taste like pinto beans? The answer is—" Jasper finally glanced up from the latest pickle order he was wrapping. "Is that Molly Pep—I mean, is that a young girl I have never seen before?"

Molly bounced with glee. She wanted so badly to hug him.

"Little girl," a customer scolded. "If you want to order, you're going to have to go wait like every—"

"Hush!" Jasper snapped at him. "You're not the Pickle Man. I'm the Pickle Man. And the Pickle Man is taking a break!" He rushed out from behind the counter, shooing everyone to the door. "Everyone out! Not you three. But everyone else out!" Customers grumbled as Jasper physically pushed them out onto the sidewalk. "Sorry, we're closed!" he called to the people lined up outside. "Temporarily! Do not leave! We will reopen in ten minutes!"

"But we've been waiting," complained a woman with a frilly blue parasol. "In the snow!"

"And if you want pickles, you will wait some more," Jasper replied. "What are you gonna do instead? Go two blocks east to Pickle Palace? Or one block south to Let's Make a Dill? Neither of which has been named Best Pickle Shop in New York by the *New York Sun*?"

The people quieted.

"I didn't think so," Jasper said. "Now you all just wait here and we will reopen in ten minutes. But don't nobody check no clocks or anything. Whenever I open them doors again, just believe that it's been ten minutes. Thank you for your patience." He stepped back inside and locked the door.

"Well, look at you three," he said with an ecstatic grin. "I am overjoyed, I tell you. Overjoyed! I didn't know if I'd ever see you folks again. But I wanted to make you all proud of me, just in case, so I've been doing what I must say is a crackerjack job of selling your pickles, Peppers. But it's not just me who says that. Just ask a certain Mr. Sherwin St. Smithens of the *New York Sun*. Or any of those people outside. Just don't ask Balthazar Birdhouse, because I can't guarantee—"

"We know about the article, Jasper," Emmett said. "How did you manage that?"

"Mr. St. Smithens came in here his very self, and he must have been pleased with his service, because he decided to tell the world about it."

"Incredible," said Cassandra. "I wonder what brought him in here."

"My guess is he saw the long lines every day and got curious," said Jasper.

"This crowd isn't just because of the article today?" Molly asked.

"I suppose people just like me and my pickles," Jasper said with pride. "I mean *your* pickles—I have not changed the recipe one smidgen. I was the best ashman in New York, so I knew I would be the best pickle seller. And by 'knew' I mean 'hoped.' And by 'hoped' I mean 'genuinely doubted my capabilities.' But I was happy to be wrong about that. Honestly, I don't know how I do it. The people just like my stories, I suppose. They'd listen, listen, listen, then they'd come back the next day and bring some friends, saying, 'You gotta hear this guy.' Which is good advice, by the way. Everybody should listen to me. Folks seem to 'specially like hearing about Balthazar Birdhouse. Though don't ask me why. Every time *I* hear about Balthazar Birdhouse, I wanna cork my ears up with melon rinds, which is, ironically, something Balthazar Birdhouse once did to me while I was napping."

Molly smiled. "So, basically, you succeeded by just being you."

"I suppose so."

The Peppers looked around with admiration at the sparklingly clean countertop, the full jars on the shelves, the red-cheeked faces pressed against the big front windows . . . "Wow, is that a cash register?" Emmett asked, running to inspect the black metal, button-covered machine at the end of the counter.

"All the finest businesses have them now," Jasper said.

"I am thoroughly impressed," Cassandra said. "You turned Pepper's Pickles into a roaring success."

"Yeah," Molly said, trying to sound as enthusiastic as her mother. "A much bigger success than we ever did. Or ever could have."

A bell dinged as Emmett hit a button to open the register's cash drawer. "Wow, that's a lot of money!"

"Really? How much?" Cassandra ran over to look and her eyes opened wider than Molly had ever seen them.

"Take what you need, since I imagine you folks are in short supply, you being fugitives from the law and all," Jasper said. "It's your money, anyway. I am but your humble employee. By the way, I love your sparkly fairy shirt, Molly. Not many people could pull off that look. Just you and Balthazar Birdhouse."

"Thanks, I stole it from a circus."

"Speaking of the law," Emmett said, "how is it that this store isn't being watched?"

"Oh, it is," said Jasper. "Come look, but be very quiet." Holding his finger to his lips, he motioned for them to join him by the dividing screen that separated the front of the pickle shop from the Peppers' humble living quarters in the rear. Molly poked her head around back and stifled a gasp. She barely recognized the place. The floor was clear and walkable—no need to climb over partially built contraptions and half-empty toolboxes. The table they used for both inventing and dining was missing all of its oil and coffee stains. Mugs and dishes were stacked neatly in cabinets, and all of her mother's inventions had been boxed up and neatly stowed on shelves. Two of the three cots were made up nicely, complete with blankets tucked in under the thin mattresses. The third cot was the only thing in the room that was even remotely messy. And that was because someone was currently snoozing on it—a pug-nosed federal agent in a long coat and bowler hat that rested crookedly over his eyes.

"What is Agent Morton doing in my bed?" Molly asked in disbelief.

"Napping," said Jasper. "He's a decent fellow, that Agent Morton. In the beginning, he just watched the store from across the street. But after a few weeks, he must've got bored from you all never showing up, 'cause he started coming in and striking up conversation. Turns out he's an aspiring piccolo player and his favorite bird is the pigeon. Anyhows, in addition to dazzling the man with my wit and plying him with free pickles, I told him how I frequently seen him nodding off against the lamppost and asked would he like to visit slumberland on a real live bed instead? He said a cot wasn't a real live bed, and I said it was better than a lamppost, and *that* he could not argue. In the end, he agreed it would be much easier to stake out the shop from the inside. He puts in a good three or four hours back there every day. He just made me promise to never tell his bosses. Agent Morton, it turns out, is not very good at his job."

"That much we knew," Molly said. When Morton had

been charged with watching their store the previous fall, she and Emmett used to entertain themselves by watching him messily eat candy apples and then attempt to clean his sticky hands on the coats of passersby. "But why'd you have to give him *my* bed? It's probably covered in caramel now."

"Never mind that, Molly," Emmett said. "Jasper, you should have told us he was back there right away. If he sees us, he could—"

"Oh, he's not waking up for at least another half hour," Jasper said. "This shop can be a pretty loud place. He's trained himself to tune out the noise."

Molly bit her lip in contemplation. The federal agent in her bed was going to be a problem. But maybe not an impossible one to work around. "So, Morton is the only one they've got watching the store?" she asked.

"Oh, no," said Jasper. "The nighttime guy is very good. You folks are lucky you did not try coming here at night or you'd already be sitting in a prison cell."

Twenty-four-hour surveillance? Molly felt a twinge in her gut. There was no use denying it: Captain Lee had been right. "We can't stay here," she said.

"Most certainly not," Jasper agreed. "That would be a terrible idea."

Molly tried not to let this news sink her spirits. They had a Plan B, after all. "This is not the end of the world," she said, to herself as much as anyone else. "Jasper, can we stay in your apartment for a few days?"

"Oh, Molly Pepper, you know if it was up to me, you folks could live at my place till the twelfth of forever," Jasper said. "But Balthazar Birdhouse is not as generous as me. And, trust me, you don't really want to share a living space with that man, anyhows."

"Balthazar Birdhouse is your roommate?" Emmett asked, aghast.

"Why do you think I've been living here at the shop for the past five months?" said Jasper.

"But—but—" Molly stammered. "Jasper, do you know anyone else who has a place we can stay?"

"Someone who won't call the police to fatten their pockets with some of that reward money? No. I don't know the best people."

"Where are we going to go?" Molly muttered, putting her hand to her chest to remind herself to breathe.

"I don't know," Cassandra said, sounding just as lost. "But we've spent too much time here already. Let's get our—"

Jasper grabbed Cassandra before she could step foot behind the screen.

"What?" she snapped.

"Morton's not gonna wake up from us just talking, but you've got some creaky floorboards back there that set him off like a rooster cock-a-doodling in his ear," Jasper explained.

Cassandra drooped. "But my Brew-Master 1900 is back there. And my Wind-Up Salad Tongs. And my Auto-Swirling Butterscotch Dispenser."

"I'm sorry, Mrs. Pepper," Jasper said.

Cassandra looked like a child who'd just been told her birthday was canceled. "Is there nothing we can take?"

Jasper darted behind the counter and pulled out a slim stack of envelopes. "Your mail," he announced, handing the pile over.

Cassandra leafed through the envelopes. "These are all bills."

"Which I have paid. Early, by the way. So I guess you don't actually need those, do you?" He took the mail back, with the exception of one envelope.

Cassandra opened the remaining envelope and read aloud: "'Has life become too hectic? Do you feel like you're always on the run?'" She glanced up at the others with trepidation before continuing. "'Make your getaway to the Hidden Hearth Inn in beautiful Petalsburg, Virginia.'— Oh, fiddle. It's an advertisement for a vacation retreat. Although Petalsburg does sound like a lovely place. The petal is the prettiest part of the flower, after all." She folded the paper and slid it into her coat pocket. "I'll hold on to this, just in case."

"This is not the time to think about vacations, Mother," Molly said.

"I know that!" Cassandra returned, a bit too harshly.

"Can't you let a woman dream?"

"I'm sorry, Mrs. Pepper," Emmett said with sympathy. "But we need to leave. I'm feeling more uncomfortable every second. Not only could Agent Morton wake up, but any of those people with their noses flattened against the windows could eventually recognize us. Also, we left my father out in the snow."

"But *where* will we go?" Molly asked. "We have to get off the street."

"I have an idea," Emmett said. "And in the meantime, at least we know that Pepper's Pickles is in good shape."

Yes, it is, Molly thought. Jasper had turned their shop into a success by changing things up in a way that she and her mother had never managed to do. He'd gained a following by doing the same thing her father used to: charming and entertaining his customers. *Jasper* was living up to her father's legacy better than she ever had. It was a rough reality to face, but Pepper's Pickles was better off without the Peppers.

Molly shook her head to clear it. Selling pickles was never what she and her mother were meant for anyway. Nor Emmett. So maybe this was all for the best. Having no shop to manage freed them up to move on to bigger and better things. More important things. After all, no one got their names into history books by selling pickles.

She took a wad of cash from the register and noticed a tall stack of yellowing newspapers in the corner behind the counter. "How far back do those go?" she asked.

"Months," Jasper replied. "I use 'em for wrapping pickle orders. You can do a lot with old newspapers. Balthazar Birdhouse once came to work in a tuxedo constructed entirely of old *New York Herald*s. You wouldn't expect it to be a good look, and it wasn't."

Molly gathered an armful of papers and asked Emmett to take as many as he could as well. It was time to stop worrying about pickles and start focusing on something she was much better at anyway: solving mysteries. And right now she was faced with plenty, starting with locating the Mothers of Invention.

"Thank you, Jasper. For everything." She hugged him as well as she could with an armful of newspapers, as the others said their farewells.

"Try not to stay away for five months again," Jasper said as he unlocked the front door.

"Okay, we'll try for eight this time," Molly joked.

Jasper opened the door and the waiting crowd cheered uproariously.

"Keep it down out there," Agent Morton grumbled sleepily from the back.

Missing Persons

DURING MOST OF his father's nearly four-year absence, Emmett lived on the streets. Miss Adelaide, the kindly old woman who operated the local bookmobile—a covered coach that functioned as a sort of mobile library—had offered to care for him. Sadly, Miss Addie passed away not long after Captain Lee's disappearance, and Emmett was forced to survive on his own. He did so by hiding the bookmobile deep in an east side ash dump and turning it into a makeshift home. It was to this small, secluded hideout that Emmett now led his father and the Peppers.

"*This* is where you lived?" Captain Lee asked, gaping at the ten-foot piles of soot and dirt that surrounded them like coal-colored sand dunes. Molly couldn't tell if he was horrified or impressed.

"For almost three years," Emmett replied. "But mostly

inside the bookmobile. I spent as little time as I could out here with the rats and shadow monsters."

"Shadow monsters?" Cassandra asked.

"In retrospect, they were probably just bigger rats," Emmett explained. "But I was young and easily frightened back then. You know, as opposed to now."

Outside the small but fully enclosed wagon, Captain Lee paused, letting Robot's crate roll to a stop in a cloud of black dust. "I'm sorry, Emmett," he said, shaking his head. "I failed you. The things you were forced to do without me here . . ."

"It's nicer on the inside," Emmett said, trying to sound upbeat.

"I thought you said it was a dank, cramped pit and that's why you never wanted me to see it," said Cassandra.

"Uh . . ."

"Wait'll you see the amazing contraptions Emmett built in there, Captain Lee," Molly interjected.

"Contraptions? Well, why didn't you say so sooner?" Cassandra said eagerly as Emmett unlocked the small door on the side of the wagon. He ducked the broomstick that swung out at head level as he opened it. Cassandra gave him a sympathetic pat on the back. "It's okay that your sweeping machine malfunctioned. They can't all be winners."

"It's a booby trap, Mother," Molly scoffed.

"Well, in that case, bravo!" said Cassandra. "The thief sees the sweeping machine and assumes he's found a nice, clean place to burgle, but he doesn't realize the sweeping machine is broken and gets scared off by all the dirt inside. Clever."

"Um, why don't you come in?" Emmett said, stepping into his former home. "You might want to watch your head, though."

"I once spent two days trapped under a very fat and lazy seal," said his father. "I will be fine." He ducked the low doorframe to climb in, as did Cassandra, the tallest of the group.

Before joining the others inside, Molly cracked open Robot's crate. "I bet you'd like to get out of there," she said.

"The person with whom you made that bet owes you some money," said Robot. "Because, yes, I would like to get out."

Molly took his cool metal hand in hers and helped him. "Hooray!" Robot said. "I am free! No more cramped, dark boxes for me!" He followed Molly into the bookmobile crawling on all fours to avoid the low ceiling. "It is cramped and dark in here."

"I can light the lamps!" Emmett said.

"Oh, this is gonna be amazing, Cap," Molly said. She flashed an enthusiastic smile toward where she thought Emmett's father was. "Wait till you see it!"

Emmett lit a candle and began turning a crank, which caused the flaming taper to move along a wire around the perimeter of the ceiling. "See, the first candle lights the other candles as it goes along the—*oof!* Sorry about my elbow, Mrs. Pepper! It's not usually this crowded in here. So, anyway, as the candles are lit, the glass jars automatically lower to—ooh, you might want to duck, Molly. *Whew!* Okay. So, the jars—*ow!* That was my foot, Robot. Can you please keep still for a—"

"Cap, your hat's on fire!" Molly cried as the sliding candle collided with Captain Lee's wide-brimmed cowboy hat. The captain yelped, tried to stand, and bumped his head on the ceiling, causing all the candles to shake. "Don't do that!" Molly shouted. "You'll set the whole place on fire!"

"Me? I'm not the one making open flames fly around in a tiny wooden box filled with paper!" the captain sputtered. Robot snatched the smoldering hat from his head and smothered the fire in his aluminum hands.

"I'm sorry, Papa!" Emmett said. "I've never used my lighting device with more than two people in here. I've never even had more than three people in here. The glass jars usually cover the candles to, you know, prevent any heads from catching fire."

"It's okay," Captain Lee said, his breath calming. "I know that coming here was a plan born of desperation."

"Desperate or not, it was still a solid plan," Molly said.

"Since none of the people chasing us even knows this place exists."

"That's true," said Cassandra. "Space may be tight, but at least we're safe." She tapped her finger against her lips. "Curtains might be nice, though. Emmett, have you ever considered putting some windows in here so you'd have a place to put curtains?"

"I feel I must announce my amazement at the number of books you have, Emmett," Robot said, looking around. What the tiny wagon lacked in floor space, it made up for in bookshelves. They ran along all four walls, show-casing everything from Charlotte Brontë's *Jane Eyre* to Jules Verne's *The Mysterious Island*. "I have never seen so many books in one place," Robot continued. "Although I have only been alive for nine months and have spent most of that time on a boat."

"Ooh, Captain!" Molly said. "Emmett's lighting system may have hit a snag, but check out his book-selecting claw! See? You use this lever here and the claw slides down the wires to grab a book for you and—" The metal claw swooped down from the center of the ceiling and rammed two of its tin talons straight up Captain Lee's nostrils. "On second thought," Molly said, "we should probably start reading through these newspapers for information about the MOI."

"Okay," said Cassandra. "But can I try the claw game first?"

* * *

"There they are!" Cassandra cried, popping up from where she'd been lying on Emmett's skimpy mattress with a newspaper over her face. Her head, and the newspaper on it, got tangled in the web of wires above, but she quickly plucked herself free. "I found the MOI!" she repeated. "Not literally, mind you. They weren't shrunken to flea size and squished inside that paper, in case that's what any of you thought I meant."

"None of us did," said Emmett.

"Not even I," said Robot. "And I take things very literally."

"Good," Cassandra continued. "But I *did* find the MOI. And the most fun thing about it? I wasn't even trying! I only put this paper over my face because I'd been angling for a little snooze."

"We know, Mother," said Molly. "You've been snoring for hours while the rest of us have been poring over every word in these old papers."

"Well, I'm sure there's a lesson in that somewhere," said Cassandra. "But I can't be bothered to figure it out, because when I opened my eyes just now, I found myself staring at an article about five women who were arrested at a South Street wharf house."

Emmett reached up and pulled the crumpled pages from the network of overhead wires. "It's from late September, so the timing would be right," he said, smoothing out the article and scanning it. "It doesn't mention the women's names, but it does tell us who arrested them: Federal Agent Clark Clark."

"That man must have had very cruel parents," Cassandra said. "Explains a lot, actually."

"It says the women were arrested for harboring fugitives who stole government secrets," said Emmett.

"Lies!" Molly said, old angers rising up. "We didn't steal anything. Those 'secrets' were ours. If anyone stole anything, it was the government stealing our right to *tell* our own story!"

"Ah! Here's what we're looking for," Emmett said. "'The women were sent up the river to Sing Sing penitentiary to await trial in the spring.'"

"At least it's not Blackwell's," Cassandra said with a shudder.

"I know, but—*the spring*?!" Molly said. "They've been locked up all this time without even getting their day in court? That settles it—we're heading straight upstate to bust our friends out."

Robot began crawling to the door.

"Oh, no, we are not," said Captain Lee. "I thought I was clear about that."

Robot crawled backward.

"Father, I think we need to at least consider—" Emmett began.

"Consider what? Making your situation even worse?

No, I'm not losing my son again." Captain Lee squeezed the bridge of his nose. "Look, maybe you're right and turning yourselves in won't win you any points with this Agent Clark, but committing an even more serious crime isn't going to make him any happier with you. Can we consider a third option? Can't someone go to the governor and advocate for their release?"

"Who?" Molly asked. "Us, the notorious fugitives who would be arrested on sight? Or you, the man who's legally dead and has no way to even prove he is who he says he is?"

"Perhaps we can appeal to Mr. Bell," the captain began.

"The man we abandoned at sea because we didn't trust him?" Cassandra said. "He and the Guild covered up the fact that they ever sent you on that doomed expedition in the first place. Publicly acknowledging that you survived is only going to put a spotlight on the majority of the crew that didn't make it back from his secret, experimental mission. I doubt the man wants that." She had dark half-moons under her eyes and lines around her mouth. It was the first time Molly had ever thought her mother looked old. "Listen," Cassandra went on, "perhaps there *is* some sort of hundred-percent safe and legal route to freeing our friends—something that involves paperwork and standing in lines at stodgy offices and waiting for men in expensive suits to make important decisions about our lives—but we don't have time for that. *I* don't have time for that. Right now, I'm going to do whatever I have to do to get all of this over as quickly as possible. We will never feel another moment's peace until we figure out a way to get the authorities off our backs. I don't know about the rest of you, but my mind is too frazzled to do that. We need more brains—and the MOI have got them in spades. We have to rescue those women because those women can help us."

"And they can help Robot," Molly added.

"Helping me is good," said Robot. "I vote for that idea."

After a short silence, Captain Lee spoke up. "I suppose I can't stop you," he said. "You Peppers do what you think you need to. We won't get in your way. But Emmett and I will not be taking part."

"Papa—"

"Emmett, I will not allow it."

Emmett looked at the floor.

Molly opened her mouth, fully intending to give Captain Lee a piece of her mind and tell Emmett they needed him, but before she could, she felt her mother's hand on her arm. She turned, and Cassandra, still looking at her, said, "Of course we understand, Wendell. You need to do what's best for you and your family."

Your family? No, Emmett was *their* family. And having him along could mean the difference between success and failure in breaking their friends out of Sing Sing.

94

Her mother should know that. Heck, *Emmett* should know that himself. Why wasn't he speaking up? Was no one on her side? She exhaled, her shoulders crumpling.

"I will go with you, Molly," said Robot.

"Actually, Robot, you should stay here with the Lees," Cassandra said. "Conserve what's left of your space rock until we get Margaret and Hertha to examine you."

Robot's neck creaked as his head swiveled to Molly. "It is okay, Molly," he said. "We will have more adventures together soon."

Molly nodded, while her mother sorted through the items in her bag. From the corner, Emmett looked over to her with eyes that said, *I'm sorry.* Or maybe they said, *You're making a mistake.* Or *I'm worried about you.* Molly looked away before the pangs in her heart grew too strong. She'd always known what Emmett was saying with his looks. Always. She couldn't bear the thought of losing that connection.

"Ready, Molls?" her mother asked, knocking several books off a shelf as she strapped a bag to her back.

"Yeah," she said. "So, what's the plan?"

"Sing Sing is up the Hudson River," Cassandra replied. "First thing we do is head back to the ferry port and get our hands on a boat."

Molly nodded. "And once we get to the prison?"

"We'll figure that bit on the way," her mother replied. "It's a long trip; what else are we going to talk about?

Emmett, dear, would it be all right if I borrowed the crank mechanism from your candle-lighting fire-setting gizmo?"

"I suppose so," Emmett said, though he couldn't bring himself to make eye contact. "I don't think I'm going to use it anymore."

"Wonderful." Cassandra took a moment to disassemble Emmett's machine and stuff the pieces in her bag. Then she crawled forward and opened the door. "Let's do this, Molls. Peppers never quit, right?"

Except her mother *had* just quit. She avoided Emmett's eyes as she followed her mother into the night.

Up the River

THE DOCKS AT the end of Barrow Street were eerily quiet at two a.m. on a cold winter night. But at least Thomas Edison's new electric streetlights allowed Molly and Cassandra to see what they were doing as Cassandra reconfigured Emmett's machine into a clockwork auto-paddler that would propel the rowboat they planned to "borrow." Of course, the lamps also put them on display for any passersby. Which is why Molly kept lookout, crouching next to her mother in the small craft, peering out at the snow-dusted piers and the bobbing boats tied to them. Every so often the clip-clopping of a horse's hooves could be heard in the distance and the Peppers would duck and hide until the sound was gone.

"Are you almost done, Mother? Someone's going to

spot us eventually. And it's cold."

"It'll take as long as it takes, Molls," Cassandra responded, bolting metallic gears to the oarlocks. "Unless you'd rather row us upstream by hand? Hold this piece still for me, would you?"

Molly did what her mother asked. "Things would be going much faster if Emmett were here to help."

"You're not the only one disappointed with the way things turned out, you know," her mother said. There was an edge to her voice that surprised Molly.

"Then why didn't you fight for Emmett?" Molly asked.

"Because it's his decision, Molls," Cassandra said, her voice softening. "If Emmett wants to stay with his father, I can't, in good conscience, tell him not to. Nor can I blame Wendell for wanting to keep his son out of trouble. Perhaps you'll understand if you become a parent someday. Pass me that wrench."

"I can understand why Captain Lee wants to keep Emmett. Emmett's great," Molly said. "But why would Emmett want to stay with him? Captain Lee won't let him do anything. He has no idea what Emmett's capable of or what he's been through in the past few years. He still thinks of his son as the quiet, cowering boy he left behind when he set sail for the South Pole. *We* know the real Emmett. *We're* the fun family! *We're* the family Emmett wants to be with."

"Have you considered that maybe Emmett wants

both?" Cassandra asked while tightening a bolt.

"Yeah, well, that's not gonna happen." Molly slumped. She watched her mother at work, twisting screwdrivers and fastening clamps with impressive speed and skill. If Emmett didn't want to be this amazing woman's apprentice, that was his loss. "You know what? Who needs Emmett and his captain?" She puffed out her chest and held her head high, trying hard to embody the feeling she wanted to have at that moment. "The Pepper ladies are back on their own, just like the old days! I was your assistant for years before Emmett came along. We're just returning to the natural order of things. Peppers don't need anyone! Isn't that right, Mother?"

"Absolutely," said Cassandra. "Even though we are on a mission with the express purpose of finding people to help us."

"The MOI don't count. They're the best," Molly said. "I haven't wanted to make a big fuss about it, Mother, but I'm thrilled that you're finally open to working with those other women." In the past, Cassandra had always been reluctant to accept help from Hertha and her crew. And she'd refused multiple invitations to join the Mothers of Invention. Molly knew her mother was jealous of what she saw as Hertha's privileged access to advanced lab equipment and a university education. So she was heartened by her mother's apparent change of heart. Because the Mothers of Invention were some of the most amazing people Molly had ever met.

Hertha Marks, the group's unofficial leader, was a genius from overseas who was full of groundbreaking ideas about energy and had been perfecting her own style of electric light bulbs independent of Edison. But there was also Mary Walton, a kindly-seeming older woman with a hidden tough side who was always seeking ways to make her inventions (and others') better for the Earth's environment. And Josephine Cochrane, the etiquette-obsessed, frilly-dressed socialite who only liked to put down her teacup if she could pick up a wrench. Sarah Goode was an endlessly optimistic young woman from Chicago with a knack for building big things that folded into smaller things and was constantly working toward her goal of earning a US patent, which would make her the first Black woman to do so. And speaking of constantly working, there was the final member of the MOI, Margaret Knight, who already had hundreds of inventions to her name and seemed to be able to create new, brilliant contraptions by the minute. If anyone could fix Robot and puzzle the Peppers out of their legal predicament, it was these ladies. They just had to free them first.

"I've been doing a lot of thinking, Molls." Cassandra paused in her work and looked up at Molly. "As soon as we free the MOI, I'm going to tell them I'm ready to accept their invitation. Well, maybe not *as soon as* we free them. I'll probably wait until we're a safe distance from the prison and don't have guards chasing us or anything. But I'm going to do it, Molls. I'm going to become a Mother of Invention."

Molly gave her a squeeze. "It's about time!"

"Well, you can thank Bell and Edison," her mother replied. "I've been resistant to joining the MOI because, for so long now, I've had my heart set on becoming the first woman to join the Inventors' Guild. But after Bell and Edison went back on their promise to make that happen, I realized I've been banking on a dream that relies on the goodwill of powerful men. I want to make history, but I've been putting my destiny in the hands of others. The Mothers of Invention are at least trying to take matters under their own control, trying to create their own futures. It's more work, but I suppose the bigger the change you want, the more effort you need to put in."

Molly wiped a tear from her cheek. Her mother was right. Hertha had formed the Mothers as a way for female inventors to pool their talents and lift one another up in an industry dominated by the all-male Inventors' Guild. Without that kind of help, what difference did it make if the Peppers cleared their names or not? They'd still have no future.

"I am very proud of you, Mother. And I will be very proud to be your assistant once again."

"Excellent." Cassandra untied the rowboat. "Shall

we go gather our team?" Molly nodded and rowed them out beyond the pier, grunting and struggling as she entered the powerful current of the Hudson River. Then Cassandra cranked up her auto-paddler and let its spring-powered clockwork arms take over the rowing duties. Soon they were chugging upriver at a steady but by no means rapid pace.

"This is going to take a while, isn't it?" Molly said. Droplets of icy water splashed into the boat and she shivered, pulling her coat tighter.

"It's not the speediest moto-thingie I've ever built, but it gets the job done," Cassandra said, admiring her impromptu machine.

"You know what? You're right," Molly said. "Who cares if a one-legged chicken could outpace us? This is a necessary step on our quest for historical significance and—oh, drat! Mother, look behind you!"

Another rowboat was headed in their direction, with two shadowy figures seated within. Away from the glow of the streetlights, Molly couldn't tell if they were wearing police uniforms.

"Could be a coincidence," Cassandra said, trying to sound unbothered. "Just another family out for a midnight row on the Hudson. Not after us at all."

"Stop!" someone yelled from the other boat.

"Okay, well, *we've* got a Patented Pepper Auto-Paddler," said Cassandra. "And *they* don't."

"Which may be why they're moving faster than us," Molly said bluntly. She glanced back at their pursuers. A thick-shouldered man was rowing vigorously, his powerful arm thrusting the small craft against the current at a surprising velocity. His smaller partner leaned forward in the bow of their little boat, calling once more for the Peppers to stop.

"Okay, this clockwork motor can't go any faster, but maybe we can if we paddle by hand like those guys," Molly said. She tried to grab the oars, but they wouldn't stop moving and rapped against her knuckles. "Ow! How do I turn it off?"

"It's a wind-up motor," Cassandra said. "It stops when it's unwound."

"Bother beans." Molly slumped in her seat. This was exactly the kind of problem that could have been solved with better planning. She could practically hear Emmett's voice scolding her in her head. No, wait—it wasn't in her head. That *was* Emmett's voice.

"Molly, stop! Wait for us!"

The other boat was just ten yards behind them now and Molly could see it was Captain Lee manning the oars. Emmett stood in the bow, waving his arms wildly overhead. Molly stood as well, nearly tipping their boat in the process. Her mother caught her and helped her regain her balance.

"You came!" Molly shouted. "Oh, thank goodness! I did

not want to be my mother's assistant again! No offense, Mother. Everything else I said was a hundred percent true."

"Why—*huff*—won't you—*huff*—stop?" Captain Lee panted as he struggled to keep his boat close to theirs.

"Clockwork motor," said Cassandra. "We need to wait for it to wind down."

"Why don't you guys just climb in with us?" Molly suggested.

"We didn't come to join you," Emmett said, crouching to keep from falling over. "We're here to stop you from making a terrible mistake."

Molly was tempted to reach across and knock her friend straight into the water. "Are you serious? It's not bad enough that you refused to help us? Now you chase us down just to keep yelling at us? Why can't you—"

"Molly, listen!" Emmett cried. "The MOI aren't in Sing Sing!"

"What?" Cassandra burst out. "Where are they, then?"

"Nowhere!" Emmett shouted. "Well, *somewhere*. But not in jail! They've escaped!" He waved a newspaper in his hand. "It's from late October. The five women arrested on South Street vanished from Sing Sing! They got *themselves* out!"

"For real?" Molly asked. "Let me see." She reached out and Emmett stretched to hand the paper to her.

"Get closer, Papa!"

"Can't we—*huff*—do this—*huff*—on shore?"

With Cassandra holding her waist, Molly stretched far enough between the boats to catch the newspaper between her fingertips and pull it over to her. "Pah! It's too dark to read!"

"Trust me, Molly," Emmett said. "The MOI are not in Sing Sing anymore."

"Those women really are quite impressive," Cassandra said with admiration.

Emmett waved a second paper. "And we know they haven't been recaptured, because this issue from just last week says the Sing Sing fugitives are still at large."

"They don't—*huff*—need to see—*huff*—that one!"

"It's okay, we believe you," Molly said. She wanted to kick herself. Of course the MOI didn't need her. They were geniuses. They were more than capable of taking care of themselves. Not only had they escaped from one of the country's most secure penitentiaries, but they'd apparently managed to hide themselves well enough to evade capture for several months now. And if the Feds couldn't find them, what hope did the Peppers have of doing so? They were on their own yet again . . . No! They weren't.

"You came for us," she said to Emmett. "You had our backs."

"Of course," he replied. "My father and I just needed some time to talk things through. Alone. There haven't been many opportunities for alone time lately."

"Tell me about it." Molly couldn't help but smile.

"Wonderful," said Captain Lee. "*Huff*—now that—*huff*—we are all friends again—*huff*—can we please go to shore?" Even in the dark, Molly could see the veins bulging in his head.

"Oh! Yeah, sorry!" Molly said. Cassandra began angling their boat toward a small dock farther up the river. Captain Lee sighed with relief. "Hey," Molly asked as the question dawned on her, "where'd you get your boat?"

"We, uh, 'borrowed' it from a dock back there," Emmett said. "I promised my father we'd return it."

"Still can't believe—*huff*—I let you—*huff*—talk me into that," Captain Lee puffed. "Peppers are—*huff*—bad influences."

Molly tried not to let the captain hear her snickering. But then she heard something that stopped her laughing altogether.

"Stop in the name of the law!" The voice was loud, easily heard over the rush of the water and the churning of Cassandra's clockwork motor. They all turned to see two more rowboats paddling up the river in their direction. A tall man in a long coat stood at the bow of one, holding a megaphone.

"Perhaps they're talking to some other boat?" Cassandra said hopefully.

"Emmett Lee! Wendell Lee! This is Agent Clark of federal law enforcement. I hereby command you to dock your vessel and relinquish yourselves into our custody!" Officers in both police boats paddled vigorously, rapidly decreasing the distance between them and their quarry. Captain Lee, on the other hand, had pooped himself out, and Cassandra's motor, which had never been exceptionally fast to begin with, was finally beginning to wind down.

"No! How did they find us?" Molly blurted. "I mean, um, *Emmett who?*"

"Too late for that," Agent Clark said through the megaphone. "A witness reported two men stealing a rowboat from the Barrow Street pier. Their descriptions matched those of Captain Lee and his son, so I was notified immediately. Molly Pepper and Cassandra Pepper, I did not expect to find you here, but you are under arrest as well," said Agent Clark. "Stop your boat immediately and await apprehension."

"I told you we were going to get caught," Captain Lee grunted, rowing harder toward the docks.

"*You're* the one who got caught!" Molly said. "*You* got seen stealing your boat; we stole ours with no problem!"

"The young lady is correct," said Clark. The tall, sandy-haired agent used his free hand to hold his black bowler hat on his head in the chill river breeze. "Although now that you've admitted to theft as well, Miss Pepper, we will add that to the list of crimes on your arrest warrant."

"Bother beans!"

"Stop your boats!" Clark commanded. "This is your final warning!"

With the commotion caused by four sets of oars, the frigid river grew rough around the tiny crafts. The federal agents were close enough now for Molly to make out their faces in the dim starlight. Clark's expression was grim, his jaw set, his mouth a flat line. He looked far more mechanical than Robot ever did.

"Apologies, Mr. Clark, but this boat is powered by a Patented Pepper Auto-Paddler," Cassandra called across the choppy water. "If you could be patient for a moment, I'll need to find the off switch!" She bent over the machine and whispered to Molly, "Jump to the other boat."

Molly's eyes grew wide with skepticism. But her mother's firm nod was all she needed to trust her. "Catch me!" she called to the Lees. "I can't swim!"

Molly swung her right foot out and took one giant step into the other rowboat. She felt an icy sting as her left foot hit the water, but Emmett, startled into action, grabbed her arms and pulled her all the way onto his seat with him.

"What are you doing?" cried both Captain Lee and Agent Clark.

"Escaping," Molly hissed softly. "Just go with it!"

"Remain in your own vessel," the federal agent called.

"Whoops! Sorry, sorry," Cassandra shouted as she leaned on the rudder and steered her boat in a wide loop around Captain Lee's, cutting within inches of the other craft.

"You're going to crash!" the captain warned.

"Yes, but not into you," said Cassandra. She overwound the crank, almost to the point of snapping, then stood and leapt across to the bow of the Lees' little boat. The craft rocked perilously as she landed. Cassandra cut off the captain's objections with, "Paddle, paddle, paddle!"

Captain Lee pumped his arms as hard as he could, while behind them, they heard the concerned shouting of government agents who now had an empty rowboat bouncing across the waves straight at them.

"Separate, men! Separate!" Agent Clark commanded. But the men paddling the police boats were too startled to react in time and the runaway rowboat knocked into both other crafts. Agent Clark fell onto his bottom and the rowers lost their grips on the oars.

"Yes!" Molly cried. "Keep going! We're almost to that dock!"

But Captain Lee paused and looked over his shoulder. "Those men could die in water that cold," he said.

"No one fell in, see?" Emmett assured him. "They're just discombobulated."

"Excellent," Cassandra added. "Then let's get back on land before they re-combobulate!"

Captain Lee brought the rowboat to the nearest pier and they all scrambled out. "This is not where we found this boat," the captain said.

"I'm sure the police will get it back to where it belongs," Molly said. She and her mother were already running east, trying to get as far from the wharf as possible before the agents reached land.

"Come on, Papa." Emmett took his father's hand and rushed to follow.

"That was the most reckless thing I've ever seen," Captain Lee said, sixty minutes and thirty blocks later, when the quartet finally felt safe enough to slow down and walk at a normal pace. "And that's coming from a man who once crossed a purple lake on a giant eel."

"Which part?" Molly asked.

"It's hard to tell with an eel," said the captain. "But I assumed I was on its back."

"No, I mean which part of *this* was most reckless?" Molly asked. "The part where we jumped between boats or the part where my mother used her boat as a weapon? Or did you mean the whole stealing boats thing in general? Because frankly, none of it felt as reckless as climbing the Brooklyn Bridge. It's a shame you weren't there for that."

Captain Lee ran his fingers through his hair. "You people are going to be the end of us."

"And yet you came to help us," Cassandra said.

"I may not approve of all your choices," said the captain, "but I will always be indebted to you for taking in Emmett when he had no one to care for him."

"Well, thank you nonetheless," said Cassandra. "Especially since we probably endangered the boy's life more than—"

"Not helping." Molly elbowed her mother.

As they neared the ash dump, they passed fewer and fewer electric streetlights. They could no longer see the tiny snow crystals whirling in the lamplight. Fewer of the thin brick tenements they passed had candles in the windows. Eventually the only sound, other than their footsteps, was that of the wind howling below elevated railway tracks.

"I can't wait to tell Robot about all this," Molly said after a time. "Was it hard to get him to stay behind?"

"We told him to guard our stuff," Emmett said. Then he paused, a strange, distant look coming over him.

"Emmett, are you okay?" his father asked.

"Yeah . . . I was wondering whether Agent Clark knew about Robot or not and a thought occurred to me. How did he know about *you*, Papa? He said the witness's descriptions matched the *two* of us. He called you by name. But he shouldn't even know you're alive. If you weren't on the wanted list, why was Clark looking for you at all?"

"Bell," Molly said somberly. "Alexander Graham Bell is definitely back by now. He must have told them everything."

"Oh, that's not good," Emmett said with dread. "Bell knows *a lot* about us. What else might he have told Agent Clark?"

That's when they passed under the train tracks and turned into the shadow-shrouded valleys of the east side ash dump. There, in the distance, they saw rising plumes of gray smoke.

All four took off at a full run, scrambling through a maze of black mounds. As they ran, they could feel heat growing on their skin and panic growing in their bellies. When they rounded the final mound into Emmett's little clearing, they skidded to a stop and raised their arms to shield their faces from the flames.

The bookmobile was on fire.

Inferno!

"ROBOT'S IN THERE!" Molly screamed as they raced to the burning wagon. Flames lapped up the sides of the wooden coach and thick smoke billowed from the open doorway, from which jutted a blazing broomstick. A man lay in the dirt, just outside the bookmobile. He wore the same kind of long black coat as Agent Clark and his men, his lost bowler hat sitting in the dust a few feet away.

"Unconscious," the captain reported, crouching to check the man's pulse. "Big bruise on his forehead. Looks like Emmett's trap took him out."

"Never mind that guy! What about—"

Molly was cut off by a figure bursting out through the smoke. Robot carried a second unconscious agent draped across his outstretched arms.

"Robot! Thank goodness!" Molly cried. "I'd give you a

hug, but you're probably very hot right now."

"It is okay. Aluminum cools very quickly," Robot said in reply. "This man is not complaining."

"Is he alive?" Cassandra asked.

"Indeed. He is in better condition than the book-mobile," said Robot. "I am sorry, Emmett, I could not put out the fire this time."

"It's okay, Robot," said Emmett. "We're just glad you're safe."

But Molly could see the distress in the way Emmett held himself; his every muscle seemed painfully taut. "What happened?" she asked.

"This fellow knocked over one of the candle lamps while he was trying to abduct me," Robot said. "He seemed to believe I was the property of Alexander Graham Bell."

"Well, that cinches it," Molly said bitterly, fuming at the cost of Bell's latest betrayal. She looked around for some way to lessen the damage. "Maybe we can smother the fire with ash," she suggested, scooping handfuls of soot from the nearest mound.

"It's pointless, Molly," Emmett said, the words catching in his throat. "The bookmobile is gone."

As if to confirm Emmett's statement, the wagon's roof and walls collapsed inward.

"We should be gone too," Cassandra said, her voice uncharacteristically shaky. "These are Clark's men. If they know about this place, so does he."

Captain Lee nodded. "Robot, please set that man down way over there, a safe distance from the fire," he said. "Emmett, can you help me with this other fellow?"

As the Lees dragged the unconscious agent to safety, Molly opened her hands and let the black dust run through her fingers. Surprised to see the tracks of tears in the dirt on her mother's face, Molly let Cassandra lean on her. Together, they watched the bookmobile burn. All those books . . . Emmett's ingenious inventions . . . the home he'd built that had kept him safe for years . . . Soon it would all be just another heap of ash in the dump.

"Okay, they're clear," Emmett said once both knocked-out officers were flopped onto a soot mound many yards from the flames. "Let's get out of here."

"And go where?" Cassandra asked, her shoulders drooping. "We came *here* because we had nowhere else to go. And all of our things were in there."

"Except the stuff we packed for the jailbreak," Molly said, patting the bag strapped to her back.

"Well, no worries, then," Cassandra said dryly. "We'll just live on rope, hammers, and potato mashers."

"Why did you pack potato mashers?" asked Emmett.

"That's not the point!" Cassandra snapped. Then she closed her eyes, her cheeks reddening. "I'm sorry, Emmett. That was uncalled for. I'm just at the end of my rope."

"I thought you just said we had rope in the bag," said Robot.

"Metaphor, Robot," Molly said glumly.

"Ah. Good one, Mrs. Pepper."

"We will make do with whatever we have," said Captain Lee.

"And whatever we don't have, we'll 'borrow,'" Molly said, making air quotes.

Her mother let out a loud sob. "I don't want to have to steal things," she said. "I don't want to have to run anymore. I don't want to keep taking ridiculous risks because we have no alternatives. We've been doing it for so long. I just want us to be able to go home."

Molly held her mother's hand. "We can't. It's nighttime and Jasper said the nighttime guy is really good."

"He is," said a voice from behind them. "As am I."

It was Agent Clark. The blond, granite-chinned agent stood in the valley between two tall mountains of ash with a pair of his colleagues flanking him. The badges on their lapels glinted in the flames as, together, the three men blocked off the only real escape route. Molly saw the others around her slump.

But she felt only anger.

"Where are my men?" Clark barked.

"They're safe." Captain Lee pointed to where they'd left the unconscious agents. "We got them away from the fire."

"Which is more than your bowler-hat buddies did for the two hundred books in there!" Molly snapped. Emmett put a hand on her shoulder, as if he was afraid she might charge the federal agents. "So many books!" she continued. "I barely got to start reading *A Tale of Two Cities*! I don't even know what the second city is yet! This is a— Hey, what are you writing?"

Agent Clark had pulled a small notepad from his coat pocket and was jotting something down. "I am adding arson and assaulting government officers to your list of crimes."

"They did that to themselves!" Emmett protested. "We saved them!"

"Look there, Agent Clark!" One of the other agents pointed to Robot. "It's Bell's mechanical man! They *do* have it!"

Robot tried to hide behind Cassandra.

"I see it, Ross," Clark said, opening his notepad again. "Aaaaaaaaand felony theft has now been added too."

Robot stood and raised his hand. "Felony theft? You are in error," he said. "They stole me, and I am not a felon. I am a Robot."

"Not helping, Robot," warned Emmett.

Robot nodded. "I will cease describing your crimes to the agents hoping to arrest you," he said. "Perhaps instead I can—"

"Whatever it is, now is not the time," Molly said.

Despite the snow, sweat dripped down her forehead. Whether it was the pressure of their situation or the heat from the raging fire, she couldn't be certain.

"Agent Clark," said Captain Lee. "You seem like a reasonable man—"

"I am not," said the agent. "Now, there are more of you than there are of us, so—"

"Sir, if you let us explain," Emmett pleaded. "There's a lot more going on here than you realize and—"

"You can explain anything you want to the judge," Clark said with no sign of emotion. "Now, as I was saying, there are more—"

"Why are you so determined to put us behind bars?" Cassandra asked with desperation in her voice. "Last year you sent me to the asylum on Blackwell's Island for attempting to assassinate the president—a crime which you now *know* I didn't commit! After that, can't you at least allow for the *possibility* that we don't belong in jail this time either?"

"I am not above admitting my mistakes." Clark flipped his pad around to show them the list he'd written. "See? No attempted assassination. I crossed that one out. But that still leaves evading arrest, breaking and entering, vandalism, violation of an executive order, illegal transit to Antarctica, theft of a nautical vehicle, arson, assaulting a government officer, and felony theft of an automaton. Now, as I was—"

"Is that all you've got?" Molly scoffed. "Because, wow, there is a whole *bunch* of stuff you're missing. Riding a train without a ticket, impersonating an acrobat—"

"Molly!" Captain Lee snapped. "I fully believe you now about the vindictive nature of this Officer Clark. But with that in mind, do you really think we should be provoking—"

"It's *Agent* Clark," Clark corrected. "Not Officer."

"Um, not to tell you how to do your job or anything, *Agent* Clark," Emmett said, the heat at their backs growing stronger. "But shouldn't one of you be getting word to the fire brigade?"

"There'll be time enough for that after you four are in custody," Clark replied. "Now, as I was saying—there are more of you than there are of us. We can't risk one of you running off while we detain the others. So you're going to have to cuff yourselves." Clark gathered four sets of handcuffs from the other officers. "Here's what's going to happen. You people are going to stay right where you are. I am going to toss these cuffs to you and each of you is going to place one cuff on your own right wrist and one on the left wrist of the person next to you."

Agent Clark threw the handcuffs. But they never reached the prisoners. All four sets stopped in mid-flight and hung suspended in the air.

"What is going on?" Clark muttered.

"Your prediction of what was going to happen was

incorrect," said Robot. His arms were outstretched and his aluminum body was humming, a dim orange glow seeping from behind his chest plate. Robot waved his hands and the iron cuffs reversed direction, flying back at the federal agents and clamping down wherever they hit. Wrists were chained to ankles, ankles to wrists. Robot swooshed his hands and the three agents' limbs were tugged this way and that until the men became one huge human knot.

"This is going to complicate things," Clark said. He was bent at an awkward angle, his head between his colleague's knees.

With a flick of his metallic wrist, Robot sent Agent Clark and company rolling up the highest soot hill in the dump.

"I didn't know he could do that." Captain Lee gaped.

"He shouldn't have!" Molly shouted. "Robot, are you crazy? Your Ambrosium!"

"I am sorry you are upset," Robot said. "But I did not want you to go to jail and I saw a way to stop that from happening. I suggest we leave now, by the way."

"You're right," Emmett said. "We can discuss your recklessness later, but right now, we need to go."

"One second," Molly said. She yanked Robot's chest plate open without asking, something she'd never done before. He flinched—as much as a mechanical man can flinch—when she did it. But she needed to know. And now that she knew, she wished that she didn't.

The little orange rock was no bigger than a domino.

"We can go now," she said, her lip quivering. "By foot only, Robot. No more powers. I refuse to lose you." She slammed his chest plate shut, and they ran.

The Call of the Tame

THEY FOUND THE agents' horse-drawn wagon waiting on the street outside the dump and stole it to get away. *What's one more entry on Clark's not-so-little list of crimes?* Molly thought. Not even Captain Lee objected.

"Where to now?" the captain asked as he drove the purloined coach through the chilly night.

Seated in the covered rear section of the wagon with her mother, Emmett, and Robot, Molly rubbed her temples and tried to think.

"Well, I suppose it might be easier to lose the police if we split up," Cassandra suggested with clear reluctance in her voice. "We can try to reconnect later—"

"No," said Emmett. "This is exactly what my father and I talked about after you left for the river. The four of us need to look out for each other. At least until we know we're all safe."

Up on the driver's bench, the captain nodded and glanced back at the others through the small window that was probably intended to allow agents to communicate with their prisoners. "My son is a very intelligent young man—not that I didn't know that already," he said. "But he made me understand the reality of the situation. And our responsibility in it. I was quick to put my son's welfare first, but this cannot be 'each family for themselves.' The Lees and the Peppers are bound to one another. Even more so after our encounters with Agent Clark."

"I couldn't be happier to hear you say it, Cap," Molly said, squeezing Emmett's hand. "But that still doesn't answer the question about where we should go."

"The MOI!" Cassandra said. "They might be able to help us, even if we don't know where they are. They have workshops throughout the city—none of which I assume they are currently using. I bet we could hide out in one of them, at least for a little while."

"Just give me an address," said Captain Lee.

The children guided Captain Lee to the facility where the MOI had first given them shelter last spring. But there were so many men in bowler hats standing outside, he didn't even slow the wagon as they drove past.

They then tried the seaport wharf house where the MOI had built their super-fast ship; it too was crawling with agents.

Desperate, Molly directed them to the tiny shed in

Washington Square Park that she thought might have been a secret MOI stash house. A guard was posted outside.

"It's no use," Emmett sighed. "Clark knows too much about us. The Feds are covering anyplace they even *think* we might go."

The sun was coming up over the Brooklyn Bridge and more New Yorkers were stepping from their apartments to begin work, walk to school, or shovel the glops of horse dung that dotted the slushy streets. More people meant more chances to be spotted.

"We need to go someplace new," Molly said. "Someplace we've never been before so they would never think to check for us there."

"What about another garbage dump?" Robot suggested. "One with less fire."

"That's not a bad idea, Robot," Molly said. "What kind of places does no one want to go to? Someplace stinky, maybe. Stables? Or a public outhouse? You think there's a hollow tree in Central Park that's big enough to—"

"No, Molly, no," Cassandra said. "I'm sorry, I can't do this anymore. Dashing from one hiding spot to the next, always looking over our shoulders. No one can live like that. Aren't the rest of you tired of running?"

The Lees both nodded.

"You want us to turn ourselves in?" Molly asked, incredulous.

"Of course not," Cassandra replied. "But we can't keep doing . . . *this*."

"I have to agree, Molly," Emmett said. "I mean, there's nothing you want more for us than success, right? You want us to become big inventors, change the world, get our names in the history books? None of that can happen while we're on the run."

"Okay, okay, I get it," Molly said, trying very hard to feel like her world wasn't falling apart around her. "We can't live our lives from the back of a stolen police wagon."

"What lives?" her mother moaned. "We've lost our home and our business."

"We can't go back to school," Emmett added somberly. "Can't find the MOI."

"We cannot fly," said Robot.

"I'm legally dead," said Captain Lee. "The only things I have left to lose are in this wagon with me."

Molly flashed him a bittersweet smile. "Aw, you said 'things'—plural."

"Yes, yes, perhaps you've begun to grow on me," the captain said, cutting her off. "My point is that any hope I had of returning to my old life has been shattered. Perhaps my best path forward is to embrace that. Maybe we all should."

"That's pretty drastic, Papa," Emmett said. "But . . . I think you might be right."

"Right about what? What are you talking about?" Molly didn't like that Emmett and his father were apparently reading each other's thoughts the way *she* and Emmett were supposed to. "Stop with the mysteriousness."

"Sorry, I'm just—thinking it through," Emmett said. "If none of us can return to our old lives, maybe—maybe we start new ones."

"It wouldn't be the first time Emmett and I have started fresh," said the captain. "Emmett was too young to remember, but when we immigrated, we got new homes, new names, new jobs. First in California and then again in New York. It's an adjustment, but you get used to it."

"You want us to go into hiding?" Molly asked. "Like the MOI?"

"Why not? It's working for them. They haven't been recaptured," Cassandra said with a hint of renewed energy. Molly did not share her enthusiasm. "Oh, Molly, think about it," Cassandra continued. "Putting all our mistakes behind us? Getting a second chance at happiness? At success? Doesn't that sound appealing?"

"Sure, but . . ." But what? Molly wasn't sure what her argument should be, but she felt pretty darn sure she should have one. Peppers didn't run and hide; Peppers fought. They had been fighting for so long, though. A break would certainly be nice. And at least they didn't have to worry about Ambrose Rector anymore. Robot was still in danger of running out of Ambrosium, but if they were living a quiet, cozy, danger-free life where Robot never needed to use his powers, that little smidgen of meteorite he had left could potentially last forever.

"We're not talking about forever, right?" Molly looked up at the others. "We can go back to being ourselves when the government finally comes to its senses and calls off its hounds?"

"That's not going to be anytime soon," Emmett said.

"But yes," Cassandra added. "If it's safe to do so, we can go back someday."

Molly shut her eyes tight, then blinked them back open. "So, where do we go?"

"We need a small town, rural," said the captain. "Preferably some distance from New York City."

"Someplace the Feds wouldn't think to come looking for us," Emmett added. "Quiet, calm, slow paced."

"Like the Hidden Hearth Inn," Cassandra said, her voice wistful.

"No vacations, Mother!"

"I know," Cassandra grumbled. "But someplace *like* that. Someplace peaceful. Not too many people. But lots of green grass and flowers and tweeting birds and maybe an apple tree. And a butterfly lands on one of the apples. And the clouds are shaped like bunnies. And the air smells like blueberries."

Molly snorted. "You should've worked on the Orphan Train, Mother."

"What do you mean?" Captain Lee asked.

"Last spring, Rector tried to get rid of me by shipping me to Ohio on the Orphan Train," said Molly. "The ladies who ran the program wanted the kids to feel good about their new homes, so they talked about how wonderfully, fantastically amazing Ohio was going to be. They made it sound just like what you all are describing."

Cassandra's eyebrows shot up. "Just like?"

"Mother, we're not—" Then she noticed Emmett scratching his chin. "Seriously?" she said.

"It would put some distance between us and Clark," he said.

"Ohio is a fun name to say," Robot chimed in. "Oh-hi-oh. Oh-hiiiiii-oh."

"Cap, please tell them we are not driving straight to Ohio," said Molly.

"Of course not," said Captain Lee. "We need to stop for supplies first. Ohio is a long trip."

"Please tell me you're all joking," Molly said. "Please tell me we're not going to Ohio."

A Whole New World
Buford's Bend, Ohio, February 21, 1884

MOLLY HOISTED THE back of her long winter coat and scratched her backside as she approached the splintery old porch of the paint-flaked gray house on the isolated dirt road in Buford's Bend, Ohio. She longed to ditch the itchy crinoline petticoat that had been driving her mad for weeks, though she couldn't deny that, as a disguise, the frilly pink dress definitely made her look like, well, *not her.* Her mother, however, was rather adorable in her gingham-clad guise as an "outdoorsy lady of the countryside." Her red-and-white checkered dress was certainly more appealing than the drab work clothes that Emmett and his father wore under their woolen outerwear.

"What do you think?" Captain Lee called as he and Robot unloaded their scant belongings out of the wagon from which they'd weeks earlier scraped off the words *Property of US Government*.

Emmett wandered the perimeter of the little one-story home, scanning the bug-eaten, frost-coated wood planks. "I'm having flashbacks to Spurgeon's place," he asked. "It's not going to fall down, is it?"

"Fixing it up will be part of the fun," said Captain Lee. A giddy grin took over his face. This was the happiest Molly had seen the man since he was first reunited with his son.

Molly wasn't sold on their new home, though. This place was so isolated. And yes, maybe that was the point—but it was going to be a harsh adjustment. Where was the constant hum of chatty pedestrians, the splash of waste buckets being emptied from third-story windows, the angry barks of coach drivers stuck in traffic? At least they still had a horse, so maybe she'd be able to re-create the smell of New York. And there would probably be new noises to replace the old, like crickets or owls or—what else made noise in the country? Angry pigs? She *hoped* there were angry pigs. That might help make this place less boring. Everyone seemed to agree, though, that they'd only live here as long as they needed to. Which was why Molly had no plans to cut off her search for Nellie Bly or the Mothers of Invention.

The frozen grass crunched under Robot's feet as he stepped from the wagon. "Oh dear, I think I broke

Ohio," he said. "You did not tell me the ground here was so fragile."

"No worries, Robot," Emmett said. "It's just a bit icy."

Molly caught herself smiling.

"This will make a perfect workshop!" her mother cried with glee from the small, ivy-strangled barn that was across the yard from the house.

"Be careful in there, Mrs. Pepper," Emmett warned. "We haven't inspected that barn yet."

"Tut-tut, Emmett," said Cassandra. "It's Mrs. Salt now, remember?"

"Still sure you don't want to rethink that pseudonym?" he asked.

"It's too late, I've already signed the lease with it," she replied. "But, look, there's already a shelf for my tools. And plenty of elbow room. You and I could swing hammers at the same time without denting each other's noggins!" She spun in slow circles, taking in the space. "We'll finally have the room—and the time—to tackle Robot's problem, Molls. And maybe a chance to rebuild my flying machine. Oh, the things we will create, children!"

Molly wasn't sold. "But there's . . . nothing here," she grumbled. "Where's all the stuff? Where are the overflowing gutters? Where are the piles of rotting trash? Where are the rats? Oh, never mind—I see one under the porch."

"This place may not have a lot of the stuff we're used to," Emmett said, "but have you seen that tree behind the house?"

"Ooh, that is a nice tree," Molly admitted. And she was sure it would look even nicer come spring when it actually had some leaves on it. "Can we hang a swing from there?"

"Absolutely," said Cassandra. "I will build you the most aerodynamic, state-of-the-art swing the world has ever seen."

Molly shrugged. "Okay, I guess this won't be the worst place in the world."

"There is the whole schooling issue, though," Emmett said with a rueful sigh.

"It might be too risky to enroll in the local school, but don't think for a moment that your education will not continue," Cassandra said with confidence. "The captain and I are each experts in all sorts of things. Classes begin tomorrow morning."

"Are you serious, Mother?" Molly raised an eyebrow. "*You're* going to teach us?"

Cassandra nodded. "See? Living in Ohio will be even better than you thought!"

"Most importantly, we will be safe here!" Captain Lee raised his arms as if he were trying to hug the fresh air. "We've done more than enough to cover our tracks in our travel from New York, and as far as anyone in town knows, this property is being rented by a recluse from Pittsburgh and her household staff."

"Yeah, no one pays much attention to workmen or servants," Emmett said. "If we can't change that prejudice, we might as well use it to our advantage."

"Believe me, we have all the privacy we need," the captain continued. "According to the man at the real estate office, our nearest neighbor to the east is an eighty-year-old woman who never leaves her house. In the other direction, there's a family with two young girls, but their house is a half mile down the road and we've got plenty of thick trees and brush between us and them. The chance of anybody recognizing us around here is—"

"Is that Molly Pepper?" came a cry from behind the captain. "Holy crow's feet! It is! Molly Pepper!"

Everyone shifted to see the two young girls who had strolled up behind Captain Lee. One was a tiny blonde with dirt on her cheeks and loose hay in her hair, the other taller, with an eagle-like nose and hair that could have been a haystack itself. Both were draped in tweed coats that hung open, unbuttoned, as if the cold meant nothing to them.

"One hundred percent?" said Molly. "Is that what you were going to say, Cap? The chance of anyone recognizing us is one hundred percent?" While the others' jaws dropped with dumbstruck fear, Molly grinned deliriously. She knew these girls. Tiny Girl and

Mop-Head—that's what she'd called them in her mind—were two of the kids who'd helped her escape the Orphan Train.

"Um, Molly, you say? Who's this Molly you're asking about?" Cassandra finally said, after clearing her throat. "There's nobody here by that name. Right, Molly? Oh, drat!"

"It's okay, everybody—they're friends," Molly said, hugging the girls. "I might never have gotten away from that corrupt Jägerman on the Orphan Train if not for these two. So, I take it you ladies got adopted? You have new families?"

"One new family," Tiny Girl announced proudly. "We're sisters now!"

"That's fantastic!" said Molly.

"Yeah, except Orla snores like an angry pig," said Mop-Head.

"Orla!" Molly said happily. "*That's* your real name!"

"They saved your life and you didn't know their names?" Emmett said.

"Hey, you're the kid from the window," said Mop-Head. "The one who was crying and hanging off the side of that crazy motor-wagon."

"Um, yeah, I'm Emmett," he replied, ignoring the look of horror on his father's face.

"We know. We heard all the stories," said Orla, shaking his hand vigorously and smiling at him as if he were a celebrity. "I'm Orla."

"Yeah, we, uh, just covered that," Emmett said.

Orla continued shaking his hand. "I'm shorter, so a lot of people assume I'm the younger sister," she said. "And I am. But only by five months."

Mop-Head pulled Orla away and nodded her own greeting. "You can call me Luddie."

"Because she doesn't want anyone calling her Ludmilla," added Orla.

Luddie kicked her sister. "You really didn't know our names?" she asked Molly.

Molly winced apologetically. "In my head, I just called you Tiny Girl and Mop-Head."

The sisters shrugged. "Can't argue with truth," said Luddie.

"Exactly how much do these girls know, Molly?" asked Captain Lee.

"Well, we don't know who *you* are, for one thing," Luddie said with her hands on her hips. "We assume the lady here is the brilliant, history-making, genius inventor, Cassandra Pepper, but you, mister, were not in any of the stories."

"This is my father," said Emmett. "Captain Wendell Lee."

Orla gaped at him. "So, is he a ghost, a vampire, or a Frankenstein?"

"I am very much alive!" said the captain.

"Technically, so was Frankenstein's monster," Luddie responded, regarding him with suspicion.

"It turned out Emmett's father was never dead," Molly said, recounting the tale with wild enthusiasm. "Just trapped in Antarctica in a cave full of giant eels and horse-sized spider crabs. We had to go there to rescue him."

"Eeee!" Orla shrieked with glee. "More story!"

"Hey, whatever happened with Thomas Edison?" Luddie asked. "Did you stop him from destroying the World's Fair?"

"Ooh! Well, it turned out Edison was really an evil madman in a mask named Ambrose Rector and—"

"Molly," Cassandra warned.

"You're still worried about those government secrecy agreements?" Molly scoffed. "We're already wanted by the police for a dozen other things."

"Eeeeee! *More* story!"

"Oh, but that reminds me," Molly said to the other girls. "We're living here under assumed names. You can't tell anyone who we really are. Not even your new parents."

"That's okay," said Luddie. "We're really good at secrets."

"Our parents don't even know about our dog," added Orla.

Molly's eyes lit up. "You have a dog?"

Luddie whistled. "Here, Dr. Stinkums! Here, pooch!"

A patchy brown mutt exploded from a nearby bush

and charged directly at Emmett. "Agh!" Emmett screamed. "It's gonna—"

Orla cackled as the dog knocked Emmett down and stood on his chest.

"Get it off! Get it—" Emmett's cries changed to giggly laughter as the dog began to lick his face. He scratched the mutt behind its ears. "Aw, you're a nice doggy, aren't you?" He looked up at the girls. "Why do you call him Dr. Stinkums? He doesn't smell bad."

"He doesn't have a license to practice medicine either," said Orla.

"Fair point," said Emmett.

"I would like to meet the dog," Robot said, plodding out of the barn to join the group. "I have never met a dog before. I imagine them to feel like hot cotton and grass clippings."

"Holy chicken lips!" Luddie shouted. "You guys *do* have a Frankenstein!"

"Oh, um, this is Robot," said Molly. "He's a metal man who was brought to life by a magical meteor."

"Eeeeee! More story!"

"Molly," said Cassandra. "Why don't you and Emmett take your friends inside and, well, tell them everything. Fill them in. Have fun!"

Molly led Emmett, Orla, Luddie, and Dr. Stinkums into the ramshackle farmhouse. *Friends*, her mother had said. They *were* friends, she supposed. Wow, she had *multiple* friends suddenly. And a dog (sort of). And her own room. And a potential tree swing. Maybe she really *could* do this, she said to herself. For as long as they needed to, anyway.

12

The Simple Life

BY MARCH, ORLA and Luddie (and Dr. Stinkums) had become regular fixtures at the Salt farm. They spent so much time there, in fact, that Captain Lee frequently questioned whether their adoptive family actually existed. He seemed particularly suspicious when the girls began showing up in the morning to join Emmett and Molly for their homeschooling.

"Won't someone be expecting you at your regular school?" he asked.

"Who knows?" Luddie said with a shrug. "But believe me, we're gonna learn a lot more from your lessons than we would at that place."

"You don't even know what I plan to teach today," said Captain Lee. "What if it's something you've already covered at your school?"

"Oh, you're assuming we've paid attention there," said Orla. "Yeah, not so much. Teach away, Professor Captain!"

Molly could honestly say it was the most fun she'd ever had at school.

With the warming of the weather, April became a time for rebuilding and remodeling. Everyone helped out, whether Lees, Peppers, or Crustaceans (the supposed family name of Orla and Luddie). There were roofs to be sealed, walls to be painted, and fences to be mended. But top priority was the barn, and in just a matter of weeks, Cassandra had the most spacious, most spectacular workshop of her career. Molly, who normally grumbled and gritted her teeth when tasked with hammer-and-nail-type jobs, found the construction process almost frighteningly enjoyable. Perhaps, she thought, she finally understood the concept of pride in one's work. That was when she spent three days turning a pickle jar lid and some loose chain links into a medallion, onto which she etched the title "World's Greatest Inventor"; she then presented it to her mother in a grand ceremony under the big tree.

Wearing her medal proudly, Cassandra wasted no time putting her new lab to use, and with Emmett's aid, she quickly lined the barn's shelves with a series of new prototype inventions. It was late May when she took her mechanical gravy press and her clockwork egg cracker into town to demonstrate them for the owner of the Buford's Bend General Store. Molly went along for the ride, eager to see her mother finally have some commercial success as an inventor. Unfortunately, there was one way in which this new country life was far too similar to their old life in the city. The store owner scoffed at "Mrs. Salt" and her contraptions, saying that if he thought he could sell the bric-a-brac that resulted from a bored woman's hobby, his own wife's crocheted nose mittens would be gracing the front counter already.

Molly was worried her mother might slide back into her Sad Place. But Cassandra seemed surprisingly undaunted. "This is a new life; I'm going to have to try things a new way," she announced when they returned home. Two weeks later, Captain Lee reluctantly went back into town under the guise of a Salt Farm employee. He took a basket of Cassandra's motorized carrot peelers to the general store and presented them as the work of his employer—the reclusive Mr. Nathaniel Salt, who was "too busy inventing to ever leave his workshop." After viewing one demonstration, the store owner agreed to put five peelers out for sale on a trial basis. When those five sold out in just two days, the man put in an order for fifty more.

It was Cassandra Pepper's first sale. And while it irked Molly to no end that an imaginary man was getting credit for her work, she couldn't deny that her mother looked more elated than she could ever remember. Her success inspired her to begin work on a far more ambitious project—a new flying machine.

With June came butterflies and woodpeckers, games of tag and nights under the stars. There were picnics, creek walks, and ghost stories at dusk. Captain Lee's silliness became more endearing. His cringe-worthy humor began to look to Molly less like an awkward attempt to win over his son and more like the product of genuine joy. More than anything, it touched Molly's heart to see the Lee men getting to know each other, not just as parent and child but as people. Emmett taught the captain how to repair a wobbly wagon wheel, and the captain took Emmett fishing (an activity Emmett participated in, even though he wilted at the sight of earthworms). The captain showed Emmett how to navigate by the night sky, and Emmett got the captain to read all one thousand pages of *Les Misérables* (a book that Captain Lee finished, even though there were hardly any boats in it).

In July, while Captain Lee tended tomatoes, eggplants, and summer squash in his garden, Molly and her friends redecorated the house they'd decorated only a few months earlier. And she announced her plans to re-redecorate before too long. "What fun is having a house if the furniture stays in the same place?" she told the adults. "Oh, and we're repainting the porch too. I'm thinking magenta will be nice for summer."

By August, it became clear that Orla fancied Emmett. Clear to everyone except Emmett, that is.

"Have you noticed how Orla always sits *really* close to me? It's weird. How can she be chilly when it's seventy-five degrees out?"

"Have you noticed how Orla sort of sings my name when she calls me? It's weird. My name's not hard to pronounce."

"Have you noticed how Orla always asks me to hand her things she can easily reach herself? It's weird."

"You think he's ever gonna figure it out?" Luddie asked Molly one day.

Molly looked over at Emmett and Orla reading *The Strange Case of Dr. Jekyll and Mr. Hyde* together under the big tree. "Wait a minute," she heard Emmett suddenly say. "If you've already read this, why are we reading it again?"

"He may invent a rocket to the moon first," Molly said.

As green leaves turned golden and crisp September air made barefoot walks less comfortable, Cassandra decided upon a name for her newest, greatest creation: the Daedalus Chariot. Her first flying machine, the Icarus Chariot, had been named for the boy in the ancient Greek myth, who, with his father, Daedalus, learned to fly on wax wings. In the story, though, Icarus flies too close to the sun, crashes, and burns, while his father follows the rules and has a smooth, successful flight. "I think it may have been a mistake to name my first flying machine after a disobedient child," Cassandra announced. "This time, I'm going with the parent who knew better."

Molly looked upon this sleeker, roomier, and supposedly faster vehicle with awe. Like its predecessor, the Daedalus Chariot had a large four-bladed propeller at the top of a tall mast in its center. But the similarities stopped there. The base of this flying machine was a repurposed sleigh (minus the horse). It had an open top, two cushioned benches, and a dashboard loaded with switches, levers, buttons, and lights. Rather than relying on pedal power, this new aircraft had a compact yet powerful combustion engine at its rear. The vehicle's lustrous red sides were trimmed with glistening chrome piping, steel gauges, and other intriguing doodads. Molly didn't know what half of them did, but she was eager to find out whenever she finally got a chance to zoom off in this work of art.

"The MOI would definitely approve, Mother," she said. And that was when it hit her. She'd grown so comfortable, so complacent with this new life of fun and ease, that she'd failed to fulfill her promise to Nellie Bly and the Mothers of Invention. It had been months since she'd done *anything* to solve the mystery of their disappearances. How could she have forgotten those women? Molly was furious at herself.

She made a vow at dinner that night, in front of the whole family: from that day on, she was going to check the newspaper daily. And she was going into town at least once a week to do research in the library. And she didn't care if anybody thought it was too risky, or if the librarian might get suspicious after a while. But nobody objected. Their new lives had given the rest of them renewed purpose—whether it was inventing or selling or teaching or gardening—but here Molly had been this entire time, relaxing and enjoying herself and simply living. All while their friends remained missing.

Molly held to her vow. She didn't stop relaxing and enjoying herself and simply living, but she also made her weekly trips to the library. And she checked the paper daily.

That's what she was doing on October 17 when she came across the article that brought her game of hide-and-seek to a sudden stop. Molly read it twice to make sure she wasn't mistaken:

DC EXPECTS BIG CROWDS FOR EDISON CAMPAIGN EVENT

The article spoke of Thomas Edison's incredibly popular run for the United States presidency and mentioned the preparations being made for a big rally in Washington, DC, later that week. But none of that was what terrified Molly. The horror lay in one sentence, buried deep in the second-to-last paragraph. "Due to Edison's immense popularity, extra crowd control officers will be on hand: 'I'll be watching Mr. Edison myself,' said the man in charge of event security, Federal Agent Archibald Forrest."

But Federal Agent Archibald Forrest was dead. Molly had *seen* him die in Antarctica. She'd touched his cold blue corpse. Whoever gave that quote to the reporter was not Archibald Forrest. And Molly knew there was only one other person it could be, only one master of disguise who knew that Agent Forrest's identity was up for grabs. Ambrose Rector was back. And he was planning something terrible in Washington, DC.

"Come on, Molly," Luddie complained. "You're it. *It* doesn't read news; *it* chases people." She and Orla swung impatiently from the porch rails. But Molly didn't pull her eyes from the paper.

"Maybe we should just hide," Orla suggested to her sister. "It's not like she's going to see us while she's got her head in that paper. She can look for us when she's done."

"Nah, we could be hiding till Election Day if we wait for her," Luddie said. "Hey, Pepper, stop looking for your old pals and start looking for your new ones! That Nellie of yours has been missing for a year now—she ain't gonna mind being missed a few minutes longer! Orla and I, on the other hand, are getting antsy-pantsy." She hopped the railing and snatched the newspaper from Molly's hands.

"Grrah!" Molly snapped at her like a starving dog protecting its food.

"Ooh, you're gonna get it, Luddie," Orla warned in a serious-yes-delighted tone. "No one comes between Molly Pepper and her news!"

Luddie stumbled backward into the porch railing. "Sorry, Molly," she said, shoving the crumpled newsprint back into Molly's hands. "It's just, you know, not all of life's problems can be solved by a newspaper."

"Like the problem of playing hide-and-seek and having no it," added Orla.

Molly took a deep breath and relaxed her tightly knotted shoulders. "Sorry," she said earnestly. "It's not you. I just saw something in the paper that set me off."

"What was it?" Orla asked.

"You didn't actually find Nellie, did you?" Luddie added. "'Cause then I'd feel like a total heel."

Molly looked past them to the little blue barn, inside of which her mother and Emmett were putting finishing touches on the Daedalus Chariot. She glanced over her shoulder to the vibrant garden where Captain Lee stooped to pluck fresh carrots from the soil. They were happy. All of them. And they were together. One big, happy family. In spite of herself, she didn't want that to end. It would feel almost cruel to tell the others about her discovery, to disrupt the happiness they'd all found with news that could mean everything was about to

147

change. Even Robot was happy.

"Hello, Molly and Luddie and Orla," Robot said as he tromped along the grass with the girls' dog yipping at his boxy feet. "I have been found as well. Dr. Stinkums is very good at this game. Every time, I stand behind the tree. And every time, he finds me. Quite impressive. Shall we play another round? I will go hide behind the tree."

"Sorry, Sir Robot, but I don't think we're playing anymore," said Orla.

"How many times do they have to tell you?" said Luddie. "He's not a knight."

"I don't care—he's wearing armor," Orla insisted.

"Technically," said Robot, "I am wearing nothing."

"Anyways, Robot, I think we might be done," said Luddie. "Molly saw something in the paper that's ruined her day."

"Oh, bother beans," said Robot. "What did you see, Molly? Was it a bumblebee that flies into your head and then buzzes around in there for hours because it cannot find its way out? I have had many days ruined by one of those."

"No, Robot, but I'm afraid the game *is* over," Molly said.

Orla shrugged. "That's okay, I'll just go hang out in the barn. Oh, Emmmmett," she sang as she began skipping off.

"Actually," Molly called out, "can you girls go home

for a while? I need to talk to my family about something important."

"Sending us back to the Crustacean house, huh?" Luddie said, looking at her askance. "Well, if that's the way it's gonna be . . ." She threw her arm around Orla's shoulders and led her sister back into the wooded scrubland between the two properties.

Molly felt bad about sending her friends away, but she saw no way around it. She knew what she had to do. "Robot, can you go get Captain Lee and meet us in the barn with Emmett and my mother?"

A few minutes later, they were all gathered around the shiny red flying machine.

"What's going on, Molls?" Cassandra asked with concern. "Did something happen?"

Molly was sure her mother could read the worry in her face.

"I found something," Molly said, folding the newspaper open so everyone could see the article in question. "And it's not good."

PART II

Everything Changes
Buford's Bend, Ohio, October 17, 1884

EMMETT PLOPPED ONTO an overturned bucket and ran his fingers through his hair the way he did whenever he was feeling overwhelmed. Cassandra began pacing in tight circles, wordlessly tugging at her "World's Greatest Inventor" medallion. Robot stood and stared blankly, save for the occasional twitch of his metal mustache. It was Captain Lee who finally broke the silence. "Well, we don't know for certain that it's Rector," he said unconvincingly.

"Who else would pretend to be Archibald Forrest?" Molly said.

"Maybe no one's pretending!" Cassandra said, her eyes alight with hope. "Maybe Agent Forrest is alive."

Emmett shook his head. "We all saw him fall into a hundred-foot gorge."

"*I* didn't," Captain Lee said with gusto, as if he'd hit upon some loophole in Emmett's argument. "And none of us saw him land, did we?"

"No, but I did dangle from his frozen corpse down in that cavern," Molly huffed. "You were *there* for that part, Cap!"

The captain harrumphed. "I had just been hit on the head. Who knows what I really saw or didn't see? In fact, are we even in Ohio right now? Maybe everything since that moment has been a hallucination. That would be more believable than some of the things we've been through."

"I saw Agent Archie in the cave," Robot said. "He definitely looked bluer than most living people. Not to mention that he was bent with one leg over his—"

"Okay, so *our* Forrest is dead," Cassandra interjected. "Maybe this is simply a *different* Forrest. It's a common surname. And that first name: Archie? How many Archies do we know, Molls? Sixteen? Seventeen? The man in that article is surely just a second Archibald Forrest. Who also happens to be a United States federal agent. With connections to the Inventors' Guild. Yeah . . . you're right, it's Rector."

The others all nodded, even if they did so with visible regret.

"Great, we all accept that Rector is back," Molly said. "So, what's our plan? What do we do?"

"*We* are not doing anything." Captain Lee scoffed.

"Rector is a dangerous criminal!" Molly exclaimed.

"Exactly!" said the captain. "Which is why we leave him to the authorities!"

Molly huffed. "Even if the Feds figure out that Rector is impersonating Forrest—which is already a stretch—who's to say they can actually stop him?" Molly said. "They don't have a great record in that department. But you know who *has* thwarted Rector's schemes multiple times? Here's a hint: their names rhyme with ours. Come on, Mother—you know I'm right."

Cassandra bit her lower lip.

"Oh, Mother. You're not seriously considering sitting it out while Ambrose Rector freezes the White House or turns the Supreme Court into jelly or whatever new madness he's planning?"

"Of course not," Cassandra said. "Except . . . Yes, I am."

"I can't believe you, Mother! I didn't give you that medal for sitting in the wings and letting other people save the day!"

"No, you gave it to me for being an inventor!" Cassandra replied. "It says 'World's Greatest Inventor,' not 'World's Greatest Rector-Stopper!' Look, I know we've gone up against the man before, but we've never really been given a choice in that." Her tone became soft, almost apologetic. "With the World's Fair, stopping Rector fell to us because no one believed us. And in Antarctica, we were literally the only ones *there* to stop him. But here? Now? The job doesn't need to fall to us every time Rector shows his waxy face."

Molly's jaw dropped. She and her mother had their differences from time to time, but never about something this important.

"Your mother is right. This is the whole reason we have police, you know," Captain Lee said. "Ask anyone— ask your little friends from down the road: Who chases criminals? Will they say inventors? Sea captains? Schoolchildren? No, they will say police."

"Orla might say dragons," added Robot. "She is very imaginative."

"We have so much more to lose now," Cassandra continued. "This house, this town, this life—they provide so much promise, so many possibilities. Here, I feel like we finally have a future."

Molly narrowed her eyes. "Look, this life is nice. It's certainly a heck of a lot less stressful than before," she said. "But do you honestly think you have a future here? You talk as if we're living our dreams, but we're all just playacting. None of us are doing what we really want to be doing. For someone who wants to be called Captain, you couldn't be farther from an ocean. And, yes, Mother, you're inventing, but no one outside this barn will ever know that! That's not gonna get you into the Guild."

Cassandra shook her head. "Oh, Molls, *nothing* is going to get me into the Guild! Just accept that they're never going to admit me. Or any woman. They've got a good thing going—why would they ever change it?"

"We'll *make* them change!" Molly said. "Let's show them up! Let's—let's do the one thing they've never been able to do: catch Rector!"

The captain sighed. "I admire your passion, but—"

"Molly Pepper," her mother said, suddenly stern. "Is this another of your get-famous-quick schemes? Are you still bent on getting the Pepper name into history books, come what may? Because after all we've been through—"

"Of course it's not about getting famous, Mother!" Molly shouted. Becoming famous heroes would mean they had no more reason to hide, and that would mean breaking up her little family, the Peppers and Lees moving on to live their own separate lives. But she wasn't about to remind anybody of that point. "I would've hoped you'd think better of me than that."

Captain Lee turned to his son. "You've been quiet through all of this, Emmett," he said. "You don't want to get embroiled in this new Rector business, do you?"

Emmett locked eyes with Molly and she instantly felt reassured. "I don't think it's about what I want," Emmett said, turning back to his father. "It's about what we need to do. Rector is dangerous, and if we're the only ones who know he's back, at the very least we need to warn people. Even if doing so puts us at risk."

Captain Lee pinched his lips closed and released a

long, slow breath from his nose. Cassandra walked off into the corner behind the Daedalus Chariot and beckoned for the captain to join her. Emmett and Molly exchanged concerned glances while their parents conferred in whispers, out of sight.

"They are telling secrets," said Robot. "Either that or they have chosen an odd moment to critique the paint job on the flying machine."

Cassandra and Captain Lee finally came back. "You're right. Keeping this knowledge to ourselves could potentially put others at risk," the captain said. "Tonight, we will compose a letter of warning, which, tomorrow, I will take to the post office for delivery."

"The post office in Haverford Hills, across the Kentucky border," Cassandra added. "So it won't be stamped with a postmark that can lead anybody back to us."

"Who are you going to send it to?" Emmett asked.

"Agent Clark," said Cassandra.

Molly winced. "He might be the government's anti-Rector guy, but he's also their anti-*us* guy."

"That's why our letter will be anonymous and untraceable," said Cassandra. "That horrid Agent Clark will receive the information in his New York office, send word to his law enforcement chums in Washington, and—voilà—our Rector problem gets taken care of. By someone else."

Captain Lee crossed his arms. "I trust this course of action satisfies everyone?"

"Not me," said Orla. "It'll be a much better story if you folks go chase the villain yourselves."

"Wh-where did you come from?" Captain Lee sputtered.

"New York, originally," Orla replied. "And Sir Robot was right, by the way. I would've said dragons." Luddie pulled her back behind the hay bale that had been their hiding place.

Molly laughed despite her frustration. "I told you two to go home!"

"Yeah, we didn't do that," Luddie said. "And once again, might I point out that, for people who are supposed to be in hiding, you're pretty stink-awful at security around here."

"Girls, please," Cassandra said, shooing them out the door.

"You should play hide-and-seek with us next time, Emmmmmmett," Orla called back as they left. "I know lots of good hiding spots around your house!"

Cassandra furrowed her brow. "Something tells me she's being very literal about that."

"You should go play with them *now*," Captain Lee said, patting his son on the back. "Go have fun. Let me and Mrs. Pepper worry about this other business."

"But how do we know the letter will be enough?" Emmett asked.

"It will," his father said, ruffling his hair. "Now, please, go be a child and enjoy your youth. That's the gift we've been given here in Ohio, after all. That's what we can't risk by going back to New York and getting mixed up in this Rector affair ourselves."

Cassandra smiled and kissed Molly's forehead, before following Captain Lee to the house to compose their letter.

Finally alone, Emmett turned to Molly. "This *isn't* just about getting your name in the history books, right?" he asked cautiously.

"No."

"Okay." Emmett nodded. "So what are we *really* going to do about Rector?"

14

A Capital Idea

MOLLY LAY CROSSWISE on her bed with her legs propped up against the bright yellow wall of her room. Her eyes followed a beetle on the ceiling, while her mind pondered a plan. The tiny red insect flew past her feet, into the dusky sky outside her bedroom window, and Molly nodded. "We need to take the high road."

"I agree," Emmett said. He sat on the edge of her bed with Robot, hunched over the open newspaper as they scoured the articles for ideas and inspiration. "I'll make no mystery of it: I like it here. Turns out I'm a lot more suited to the quiet life than I'd anticipated. But preventing Rector's next bout of mayhem is more important than that. We're the only ones who know he's out there, and that means we have the responsibility to do something about it. Whether our parents want to admit it or not."

Molly rolled onto her belly and grinned at him. "Why, Emmett Lee, are you—dare I say it—rebelling?"

"I am *not* rebelling." He sounded scandalized.

"To act in opposition to authority," said Robot. "Is that not what rebelling means?"

"Yes, Robot, that is exactly what—"

"I'm not rebelling!" Emmett repeated. "I just think our parents . . . well, they've been through a lot. Your mother has finally found some relief after a full year of running—and fighting—for her life. Not to mention her disappointments with the Guild. And my father? Well, I don't think he's gotten past the shock of being back in the world yet. Neither of them is thinking clearly about the situation. In another, less troubling time, I think they'd make a different decision. But right now, they need us to do the right thing for them. Which is not the same as rebelling."

"Whatever you want to call it, I like this feisty new attitude," Molly said. "But anyway, when I said we need to take the high road, I was being more literal. We need to fly."

"I can fly," said Robot.

"No, you can't," Molly scolded. "You'll use up the last of your Ambrosium. And that is something that will *never* be worth the risk."

"I said I *can* fly, not that I *will* fly," said Robot. "Do you like my feisty new attitude too?"

Molly made a mental note to stop sending Robot mixed messages about rebellion. "Let's focus on the plan," she said, sitting cross-legged on her patchwork quilt. "The biggest problem with warning Agent Clark by mail— other than that it relies on that stiff-wart Clark—is that it's way too slow. Who knows what havoc Rector will wreak in the week or so it takes that letter to reach New York? The Daedalus Chariot, however, should be able to reach Washington, DC, in a matter of hours."

"New York, you mean," said Emmett.

"Who cares about New York? Well, I mean—I do. New York will always be my true home. What I mean is: Who cares about Clark? Rector's in DC."

Emmett winced. "Oh," he said. "So you literally want us to go after Rector ourselves. See, I was still thinking more along the lines of—"

"Relax, Goosey," Molly said. "I'm talking about warning the person who's most directly in danger there. And a man who can probably do even more than Clark in terms of rallying forces against Rector."

Emmett glanced at the newspaper in his hands. "Edison," he said. "Edison's going to be in Washington for that rally, and he has no idea that his head of security is secretly Ambrose Rector."

Molly nodded. "I'm no fan of old Tommy Boy, as you know, but as co-chair of the Inventors' Guild, Edison practically runs this country already. If anyone can get

President Arthur to sic the army on Rector, it's him. We might not be able to trust Edison, but I think he'd at least listen to us. And he hates Rector as much as we do."

Emmett looked at the grainy photo in the paper of Thomas Edison standing before a cheering crowd with his arms raised in front of an "Edison for President" banner. "The article says he's leading in the national polls, you know," Emmett said. "Do you think he can really win?"

"Against Grover Cleveland and, uh, whoever the other guy is? I don't see why not," Molly said. "Everybody loves him. Of course, they don't know what a backstabbing liar he can be." She let out a short, caustic laugh. "And if we thought the government gave special privileges to Guild members before, just wait till Thomas Edison is running *both*."

"If he wins the presidency, he'll have to step down from his leadership roles in the Guild and his various companies," Emmett said. "Wouldn't he?"

Molly put her arm around his shoulders. "Oh, my dear, sweet Emmett. Sometimes I wish I had your innocent optimism."

Emmett frowned. "I'm going to try not to be insulted by that."

"You should not be," said Robot. "I am also innocent and optimistic. And I am quite happy."

"Back to this plan of yours, Molly," said Emmett. She could tell he was trying to hide the skepticism in his voice. "How do we convince our parents that we need to take the Daedalus Chariot to Washington?"

Molly laughed. "Oh, there's no chance of that. We have to steal it."

"Oh!" Emmett looked suddenly pale. "Oh, you want to steal . . . and sneak . . . and . . . I see . . . This is maybe a bit more feistiness than I bargained for."

"Don't worry," Orla said excitedly as she and Luddie appeared at the open window. "We'll help you steal it!"

Emmett jumped to his feet and made sure his shirt was tucked in.

"Hi, Emmmmmett," Orla singsonged.

"Hey," Emmett responded, blushing.

"Hello, Orla and Luddie," Robot said casually.

"Hello, Mr. Knight," Orla said with a wave.

"Is the dog with you?" Robot asked. "He is quite stealthy."

Molly rolled over to face the girls. "How long have you two been there?"

"How long have you been in your room?" Luddie asked in return. "It's not like we have a clock out here."

Emmett cleared his throat. "Why would you—"

"We're nosy," said Orla.

"Which you really should know by now," added Luddie. She raised an eyebrow. "Sometimes I wonder how people so unobservant have managed to be the heroes of so many great stories."

"I was going to ask, why would you help us?" Emmett clarified.

"You're our friends," Orla said plainly.

"And if this Rector guy is as nasty as your stories make him out to be, we should want him behind bars too, right?" Luddie said. "You're doing this for all of us."

She's right, Molly thought, welling with pride. It wasn't just for her own sake that she was placing herself directly in Rector's path of destruction—she was doing it for *everyone*. She was a hero! A bold, self-sacrificing, shining example to young girls everywhere. And if that didn't get her name in the history books, nothing would.

"All right, team," she said. "Let's do this."

Later that night, Emmett held his belly and groaned.

"Oh, no. Not you too?" Cassandra asked, feeling his forehead for a nonexistent fever.

"I hope it wasn't the fish," Captain Lee said, pausing his dishwashing to sniff the leftover bones of the trout they'd eaten for dinner. "Were you a tricky little tummy wrecker, Mr. Fish?" he asked the skeleton. He then answered for the dead fish in a ridiculous high voice: "Not me, Captain, I'm a good trout. Or I *was*. Now I'm a ghost trout, because you—" He cleared his throat and looked sheepishly at the others. "Sorry, old habits. It was very lonely in that cave."

"It's okay, Papa," Emmett said. "Anyway, I think it's

just—*urg*—I think maybe Molly and I both caught something."

"Yeah," said Molly. She shuffled slowly to her room, her shoulders drooping with feigned fatigue. "Dr. Stinkums was sneezing all day. I think he gave us a doggy disease."

"I don't think that's a thing that happens," Cassandra said. "But you two are obviously not in good shape. Get some rest and hopefully you'll feel better by morning."

"Just what we were thinking," Molly said. She noticed her mother had taken her medallion off. She hardly ever took it off. Even though the chain made her neck all red and ouchy-looking.

"I'm sorry, Papa," Emmett said, lurching into his room and shutting the door.

"*I'm* sorry if I was the culprit," Captain Lee called back in his fish voice.

Molly slipped into her room, shut the door, and slumped with relief. For a moment there, she'd been genuinely afraid Emmett was going to crack. Lying was not one of his strengths. Especially lying to his father.

"Ready?" Luddie whispered from where she waited in Molly's bed.

Molly nodded. "Orla all set in Emmett's room?"

Luddie gave her a thumbs-up and slipped under the heavy quilt as Molly climbed over her to the open window and slipped out over the sill.

"Good luck," Luddie whispered. And then she began howling pitifully.

"Don't overdo it," Molly cautioned. "You're supposed to be me, not a wolf."

Luddie reassured her with another thumbs-up and reduced the volume of her moans. Molly shut the window from the outside and glanced to her left, pleased to see Emmett waiting for her. Pained groans were coming from his bedroom as well.

"Think Orla's got it covered?" she whispered to him.

He nodded. "She sounds human, at least."

Together, the two dashed across the moonlit lawn to the barn, where Robot awaited them. Molly was surprised to see all the tools and scrap materials already cleared away and the Daedalus Chariot itself outside the barn's big wooden doors.

"You didn't use your magnet powers, did you?" Molly asked.

"I am still alive, am I not?" Robot replied. "Alive and feisty."

Molly shot him an icy stare. "No more, you hear me? Or you're not coming with us. I'm serious."

"I understand," Robot said softly. But he refused to make eye contact.

"Okay, get in." Molly waited for Robot to climb awkwardly up onto the old sleigh and slide onto the rear bench before boarding herself and taking the pilot's seat.

"I hope I don't regret bringing you along." She attached a tight band to the arms of her eyeglasses and stretched it across the back of her head to hold the spectacles on like a pair of goggles. Then she clicked the motor's ignition switch and hoped the sisters' moaning would keep her mother and the captain from hearing the low rumble of the engine. She turned a knob to start the four-bladed rotor spinning overhead.

"Coming!" Emmett whisper-shouted, running from the barn with a gleaming medieval knight's helmet he'd spent the afternoon crafting out of leftover scrap metal. "Can't leave without Robot's disguise," he said, climbing onto the chariot and passing the helmet to Robot. With luck, anybody who spotted Robot would assume him to be a human in a suit of armor rather than a walking machine.

"I like hats," Robot said, forcing on the tight-fitting headgear. "How do I look?"

"Anachronistic," said Emmett. "But I'd rather have people wonder why a knight is strolling the nation's capital than trying to figure out how an automaton has come to life."

"Yes," Molly said with a grin. "Plus, Orla asked you to."

"Exactly," said Emmett. "I mean, *no*. I mean— What? This was not for Orla. Why would—I mean, sure, she inspired the idea, but—it's not—it's just . . ."

"Buckle up, mateys!" Molly said, deciding to let Emmett off the hook. "I don't want to lose any passengers along the way."

All three strapped on their safety belts and Molly yanked back on the altitudinator. The Daedalus Chariot rose off the ground. "Okay, now how do I go forward?" Molly asked as she tried various levers and knobs.

"The yellow one," Emmett said, gripping the edge of his seat hard enough to make his knuckles go white.

Molly pulled a small yellow latch and a compartment fell open. A piece of paper blew out and flattened itself across Emmett's face. "The other yellow one," Emmett said, daring to let go of his seat long enough to pull the paper off his forehead.

"What's that?" Molly asked.

"That silly advertisement for the Hidden Hearth Inn," Emmett said, shoving the paper into his pocket and reclamping his hands around the seat's edge. "Your mother kept it in the chariot as inspiration. She wants to fly there someday for peace and relaxation."

"What have these past eight months in Ohio been for?" Molly rolled her eyes. "My mother needs to—"

The flying machine dipped and swerved in a powerful gust of wind before Molly righted it.

"Whee!" said Robot.

"Are you sure I shouldn't be piloting us?" Emmett asked. "You know, since I helped build it?"

"Do you get as airsick as you do seasick?" Molly asked.

Emmett swallowed hard and flexed his already sore fingers. "You're right. You drive."

In a minute's time, their little yellow farmhouse became a toy-sized box below them. "You know, even if we succeed in thwarting Rector," Emmett said, "my father is still going to punish me until I'm fifty."

"Maybe so," Molly said, settling into a seat designed for someone much taller than she. "But at least there'll be a world left to be punished in."

Off to See the Wizard
The skies over Washington, DC,
October 18, 1884

"FLYING IS NICE." In the back seat, Robot held his arms out, catching the wind as the Daedalus Chariot bobbed shakily through the clear sky hundreds of feet above southern Maryland. "I miss it."

"I, on the other hand, have discovered something I like even less than sailing," Emmett said, doubled over on the front bench next to Molly. "I'm sure my father would be an expert flier," he grumbled.

"What's that, Emmett?" Molly snarked. "I can't hear you with your head between your knees."

"He said his father would be an expert flier," Robot helpfully repeated.

"I heard him, Robot. Sarcasm."

"Ah, yes," Robot said, his knight helmet clanking as

he nodded. "You know who can be very sarcastic? Dr. Stinkums."

"The dog?" Emmett said, still refusing to look at anything other than the floor between his feet. "How can a dog be sarcastic?"

"If you could see the way he is looking at me right now, you would understand," said Robot.

Emmett instantly unfolded himself and joined Molly in spinning to face the back seat, where their friends' patchy mutt was sitting on the floor of the chariot, staring up at Robot with what, if they hadn't been so shocked, they would have admitted was a rather sarcastic expression.

"What the—? Has he been here the whole time?" Molly sputtered. "Yes, obviously he's been there the whole time—he didn't fly up here on his own. But how did we not notice?"

"I told you he is stealthy," said Robot.

The chariot banked abruptly to the left and all the passengers slid to one side of the craft, slamming into the wall. They were given a sudden, unsolicited view of tiny red and gold treetops with the blue lines of rivers snaking between them. Miniature gray squares of roofing popped up here and there on bald hills rising from the foliage. "Molly!" Emmett shrieked. "Keep your eyes on the road! I mean, the sky!"

Molly whipped away from the scenery and shifted

173

levers to right the aircraft. Having regained her ability to breathe, she glanced back again to check on all *three* of her passengers.

"I can't believe we have a dog with us," Molly and Emmett said at the same time—but with completely different intonations.

"Oh, come on, Emmett, it'll be fun to have him along," Molly said with a grin.

"Don't get me wrong—I like Dr. Stinkums," Emmett said. "I just don't think we need one more thing to worry about on this mission."

"I, for one, believe this intelligent creature will prove a valuable member of the team," said Robot. "Look at the way he is gnawing apart the leather seat, for instance. What secrets, discoverable only by a genius like Dr. Stinkums, lie hidden within the stuffing? Ah, it appears to be more stuffing."

Emmett risked a glimpse over the side at the buildings below.

"Pretty incredible, isn't it?" Molly said, the rush of cold air stinging her teeth as she smiled. Below them, bands of lush woodland began to give way to more and more smatterings of houses and streets. There were fewer pastures and silos now, more church steeples and town squares. And as they continued to sweep eastward, an instantly recognizable flash of white appeared above the trees.

"It's the capitol building! Just like it is in pictures!" Emmett said, with both awe and relief. "We're here."

Molly grinned at the grand white dome that housed the chambers of the United States Congress. Similarly majestic buildings populated the surrounding city blocks, save for one vibrant swath of nature that cut its way through the bustling metropolis. Molly had read about the National Mall, which at this time of year was a two-mile ray of multihued fall foliage stretching from the capitol steps all the way to the banks of the Potomac River. From overhead, they could see the winding paths that divided the Mall into dozens of miniature parks and the large patches of green lawn in between. And in one open clearing, a contingent of tiny men dashed around, constructing what appeared to be a large wooden stage. But it was difficult to pay attention to any of that when, erupting from the center of the great green expanse, was an immense white tower—an obelisk of alabaster marble, with squared-off corners and a pointed-pyramid capstone at its peak. The whole structure was surrounded by several stories of wooden scaffolding. "Whoa, is that—?"

"The Washington Monument," Emmett said. "It has to be. They've been building it since before the war, but I read they're about to put the finishing touches on it. President Arthur's planning a dedication ceremony in December."

"Wow, the fellas working on it must be real daredevils," Molly said. "How high up do you think we are? Five hundred feet? And I bet we could reach out and touch that thing if we get close enough."

"I'm fine not knowing the answer to that," said Emmett.

"The Washington Monument," Robot repeated. "This is a monument to the city?"

"Well, the city is named for George Washington, our first president," Emmett explained. "The monument is to honor him."

"Your first president was a tall white stick?" Robot asked. "Never mind, I will ask the dog to explain it later. You should find a place to land."

"Yeah, Washington is a busy place," Emmett agreed. "Somebody is bound to look up sooner or later and wonder why a sled is flying over their city."

"And it's not even Christmas," said Molly, scanning the area. She pointed toward a heavily wooded area southwest of the monument, near the riverbank. "Let's try down there. More squirrels, fewer senators." She twisted the descendifier and the Daedalus Chariot began to lose altitude.

"Is there enough space to—slow down! There's a *lot* of trees down there!" Emmett hung his head over the side of the vehicle, unable to tear his eyes from the rapidly approaching treetops.

"That's why we land between them," Molly said, while silently praying that was something she could actually accomplish.

"Dr. Stinkums is not worried," said Robot. "Hear him whimpering to tell us how unconcerned he is?"

Molly gripped the controls tightly as the vehicle swooped lower. The moment she was centered over a spot of grass that looked wide enough to hold the Daedalus Chariot, she switched off the forward accelerator, slammed her foot onto the down pedal, and closed her eyes. The thump when they hit the grass was more jostley than she would have preferred, but the aircraft was on the ground in one piece. The rotor slowed to a stop as Molly shut down the motor and leapt triumphantly from the vehicle. "See? Absolutely perf—" Not realizing how wobbly her legs were, she lost her balance and plopped flat onto the grass. "This is surprisingly comfy grass. Maybe just a quick nap before we save the world . . ."

"Believe me, I'd love to," Emmett said, climbing shakily from the chariot. "But let's not forget why we took this huge risk to fly here. Time could be running out as we speak."

"Time is always running out," said Robot. "Time is not a thing you can save."

"No," Molly said grudgingly, pulling herself off the ground. "But Thomas Edison is. So let's go save the big jerk."

The tip of the Washington Monument poked up above the treetops in the distance. Molly began marching in that direction, knowing it would lead her back toward the city center. Emmett waved goodbye to Robot and followed, crunching crisp autumn leaves beneath his feet.

"Arf! Arf!" Dr. Stinkums leapt from the chariot and ran alongside him, nipping at his shoelaces.

"Oh, no, Stinkums, you can't come," Emmett said, crouching before the dog. "You stay here and guard the chariot with Robot, okay? You be a good guard dog?"

The scraggly-headed mutt stared back defiantly, then trotted past him and ran ahead with Molly.

"If the dog is not staying, then neither am I," said Robot, climbing clumsily from the chariot. "I want to experience the nation's capital."

"Robot, you can't," Emmett objected. "People will see you."

"That is why you made me this knight disguise." Robot knocked on his helmet.

"I made it as a last resort," Emmett said. "So that, on the disastrous chance that someone comes upon the Daedalus Chariot in the trees, they wouldn't instantly realize that you're a living automaton!"

"It'll be fine, Emmett," Molly said, bending to scratch Dr. Stinkums's head as he circled her feet. "In fact, it might actually help us. It's like my mother's Big Hat Theory: a giant, crazy hat is the best disguise, because everyone will be too busy staring at what's on your head to pay attention to your face. As two of America's most-most wanted, we could do without too many folk examining our faces. Robot can be our big, crazy hat."

Emmett looked skeptically at Robot—a clunky, clockwork figure with a makeshift medieval helmet jammed on top.

"Do not worry, Emmett. I am not going to jump onto your head," Robot said. "I know Molly was making a metaphor."

Dr. Stinkums yipped and Emmett sighed. "Fine," he said. "But for the record, I'm against this."

"My memory imprints all things spoken in my presence," said Robot. "So, technically, everything you say around me is on the record."

"See? That kind of skill is exactly why we need Robot around," Molly said. She smiled and marched on. She knew that a big metal man clanking around with them was the exact opposite of inconspicuous, but leaving him behind felt wrong, especially when he wanted to help so badly—which was more than she could say for her mother or the captain. Besides, even without his "magic powers," Robot was physically stronger than her and Emmett combined. She just hoped that his whole "remembering everything power," which she was unaware of until this moment, wasn't also a drain on his Ambrosium. When she'd last taken a peek inside his chest compartment, the remainder of the meteorite was no bigger than an olive.

"Should I assume you know where you're going?" Emmett asked, trudging through a thick blanket of red and orange leaves.

"Following the spire," Molly replied. "We know Edison will be at his rally tomorrow, which should be smack in the middle of the National Mall. Did you notice them setting up the stage as we approached?"

"Yeah, but there's a decent chance Rector plans to strike *at* that rally," Emmett said. "We need to warn Edison beforehand, so where are we likely to find him *today*?"

"Does the Inventors' Guild have a Washington lab?" she asked as they plodded between tall trees.

"I think so," Emmett said. "Well, I don't know if it's a lab or an office or a hotel or some combination, but whenever Mr. Bell went to DC, he'd mention staying at 'the Club.'"

"The Club, huh?" Molly said. "That's vague."

"For the record," said Emmett, "I suggested stopping at a library along the way to do some research."

"It is true," said Robot. "He did."

"And I said we didn't have time for extra stops," Molly retorted.

"She did," said Robot. "Perhaps Dr. Stinkums knows where to find Mr. Edison. See how he is running ahead to lead the way."

"Stinkums is—"

"*Dr.* Stinkums," Robot corrected.

"*Dr.* Stinkums is a dog," Emmett said flatly. "He does not know who Thomas Edison is."

"Are you certain about that?" Robot asked. "He spent much of our flight reading the newspaper in the back seat. At least I think that is what he was doing with the newspaper. It was strangely soggy when he was through with it."

"Mental note," Emmett muttered. "Clean back seat of flying machine before we go home."

The odd quartet exited the thick tree coverage onto a paved walkway and found themselves suddenly in the midst of scores of meandering parkgoers. "Shh," Molly warned. "Everybody act normal."

"I fear that may be impossible for Dr. Stinkums," said Robot. "He is no normal dog."

Dr. Stinkums ate a dandelion.

Emmett's pace slowed and Molly nudged him onward. They needed to keep strolling along as if nothing unusual was happening. They needed to avoid any lingering looks. Looks like the ones they were—*sigh*—already getting. Small children were the first to take notice—stopping and pointing as their parents and nannies told them to keep moving. But it didn't take long for adult heads to start turning as well. Of course people were going to look, Molly told herself. She had a six-foot-tall metal humanoid clanking along at her side. It was only natural to look. *She* would look! But acknowledging that didn't stop her from sweating like it was high summer. And that was before she glanced at Emmett and saw enough wobble in his steps to make her worry he was about to topple over. Having to carry a swooning friend would not make it easier to flee if someone recognized them as "those kids from the wanted posters." Which felt inevitable at this point.

"Well, look who it is," said a man in a dark suit walking by them.

"Ooh, can you believe it?" cooed a woman lounging on a bench with a pink parasol. "A real live knight in shining armor."

"That is a correct assumption," Robot said as he strode past. "I am a knight."

"Is there a fair in town?" asked a bespectacled man in a straw hat.

"If there is, I would like to go," Robot replied. And the man laughed.

"Hey, it's Sir Lancelot!" called a bulky young trash collector. "Say hello to King Arthur for me!"

"I do not know the man personally, but if I should encounter him, I shall pass on your message," Robot replied. "Who should I say is—"

Molly pushed him along. "Keep moving," she said under her breath. "You're doing great, Robot."

"I am," Robot replied as two more passersby shouted about jousting and battling dragons.

Molly's apprehension began to fade. Robot was quite the spectacle for parkgoers that afternoon, but nobody seemed to give her or Emmett a second glance. "Big, crazy hat," she said to Emmett with a wink.

Just then, Dr. Stinkums took off, yapping loudly. He raced across the Mall, past a passel of food vendors, toward the tall circle of wood-plank fencing that cordoned off the construction of the Washington Monument.

"Stinkums!" Molly dashed after the runaway mutt.

"Wait! Why do we have to chase him?" Emmett called. "He's not even our dog!" Nonetheless, he followed.

A stray smear of mustard on the fence appeared to have been the source of Dr. Stinkums's urgent scramble. Molly caught up to the mutt as he licked clean the splintery plank. "Hey, Doc," she said, scooping the dog into her arms. "If you're gonna be part of this team, you can't run off like that, okay?"

"I could . . . say the same thing . . . to you," Emmett panted behind her.

She was about to respond when she heard a familiar voice. "Gently, fellows, gently! You're engaged in a historic undertaking here! You don't want to go down as the klutzes who broke our nation's greatest monument!"

Molly shoved Dr. Stinkums into Emmett's arms and got on tiptoes to peek over the fence. "Holy hopscotch! It's him!"

"Him who?" Emmett asked. "*Pleh!* Why does the dog taste like mustard?"

"Edison! He's in there." Molly began scanning the fence for an opening.

"Seriously?" Emmett asked. "That's incredible. How do we—"

Molly made sure none of the nearby vendors were staring in their direction and kicked in one of the wooden planks.

"Okay, that's one way," Emmett said as Molly squeezed herself through the opening she'd just created. He squished himself through after her, which was not easy with an armful of Stinkums.

Inside the circular construction zone, multiple brawny strongman types in blue coveralls tugged on ropes, using sky-high hoists to raise a lengthy copper tube upward to their colleagues at the top of the five-hundred-foot scaffolding. From where she stood, the obelisk seemed impossibly tall, its peak barely visible from down below.

Thomas Edison stood mere yards from them, furrowing his voluminous eyebrows as he shouted and gestured to the workers. His brown-checked suit with red bow tie and popped white collar might not have looked very presidential, but it was very *him*. Molly was shocked by their luck in finding him. She had hoped to possibly spot him over by the rally stage they were building farther down the Mall, but she'd never have thought to check the Washington Monument construction site. What was he even doing here, bossing around the workers like that?

Edison turned as Molly and Emmett approached. "What's going on back there? Hey, you kids can't—" His eyes went wide. "*You* kids!"

"Hey, there, Tommy Eds," Molly said, trying to sound far less sheepish than she felt. "So, you're probably surprised to see us."

"What in the name of Lincoln's hairy mole are you doing here?" the inventor sputtered. "How in the—" With his hands on their backs, he hurriedly steered the children to a shadowy area behind a six-foot stack of white stone slabs. "I can't be seen with you felons," he hissed. "I'm running for president! Now, what in—"

"So, I know we left things on a bad note," Molly said. "Bad note" was an understatement; the last time she'd seen Edison she'd shattered the unfinished prototype of his secret new invention. "But to be fair, you lied to us and you had it coming."

"Not helping," Emmett said, shaking his head.

"Why are you here?" Edison asked again. "And why do you have a dog?"

"Oh, this is Dr. Stinkums," Emmett said as the dog slurped his chin.

"I don't care about the animal's name!" Edison barked. "Why. Are. You. Here?"

"We could ask you the same question," Molly shot back. "You're supposed to be in town for a campaign rally."

"Oh, I didn't realize I'd hired a twelve-year-old fugitive as my new secretary," Edison snarked. "Please check my executive calendar and see what else is on my agenda for this trip, because I'm pretty sure it also says my company has been hired to install a lightning rod atop the Washington Monument."

Molly narrowed her eyes and set her jaw. "First of all—"

"She's thirteen," Emmett said. "She's going to tell you that, first of all, she's thirteen now."

"Happy birthday," Edison said dryly.

Molly huffed. "All right, secondly, we're here to save your sorry life, so you should be a little more grateful."

Edison looked too confused to be genuinely angry. He raised a scolding finger at the children, but couldn't manage to get any words out. He peeked out from behind the stone pile to ensure that his workers had things under control, then turned back to the kids. "Do you understand just *how* wanted you two are?"

"Most-most wanted," Molly confirmed.

"I could shout for the police at any moment and have you locked up for life," said Edison.

"But you haven't," said Molly. "Which means you want to hear what we have to say. I don't know if that's out of curiosity, self-preservation, or guilt because of the way you betrayed my mother, but—"

"Just say it," Edison spat. "How long do you think a presidential candidate can stay out of sight before his security detail starts getting curious?"

"That's just it, Mr. Edison," Emmett said. "One of the agents on your security detail, Archibald Forrest—he's a fake!"

"What are you talking about?"

"I'm not sure how much Bell told you about what happened in Antarctica—" Molly began.

"Why? Do you have some good dirt for me?" Edison leaned in, suddenly interested. "Because Alec Bell and I aren't exactly secret-sharing slumber party pals. I had to press him for days and I still really only know three things: he never reached the Pole, you folks ditched him in the Caribbean, and—most importantly—Rector is stranded down there."

"Not anymore!" Molly said. "Rector—he's back!"

"And he's here in Washington!" Emmett added. "Disguised as Agent Forrest! The real Forrest died in Antarctica!"

"Here's where you lose me," Edison cautioned. "Who's this Forrest person?"

"Federal Agent Archibald Forrest," Emmett said. "You know, the person heading the security detail for your rally tomorrow? He's really Rector!"

Edison blinked. "There's no one named Forrest on my security team." He squinted with suspicion. "What's really going on here?"

"We're trying to warn you that the diabolical genius

who almost killed you last year is about to try it again," Molly half growled. Edison's skepticism rankled her. "And the fake Forrest *is* on your team whether you realize it or not. He was quoted in the paper!"

"There are five men on my security detail and I know them all," Edison said. "Do you mean Foster? Agent Anderson Foster?"

"No!" Molly snapped. But then a wave of doubt washed over her. "I—I don't think so."

"It definitely said Forrest in the paper," Emmett said.

Edison rolled his eyes. "A typographical error, then. You've distracted me and put my reputation at risk over some dumb newsman's misspelling."

"No, it *can't* be a mistake," Molly said. "That would be way too much of a coincidence. A reporter puts the wrong name in his article and it just happens to be the name of a federal agent who died chasing Ambrose Rector at the South Pole? And Rector would probably get some kind of giddy thrill out of using Forrest's identity to exact his revenge too—since Forrest was a double agent who betrayed him and—"

"Aha! The traitor!" Edison threw his hand in the air. "That's why that name sounded familiar. Bell mentioned this Forrest fellow when he recounted his Antarctic misadventures to me. Ah, yes . . . now it all makes sense." The inventor leaned toward the children and glared at them. "Bell put you up to this, didn't he? He sent you here. You're working for him."

"Ha!" Molly scoffed. "We dislike Bell almost as much as we dislike you! Did he tell you we have one of his automatons?"

"Okay, I'll give you some credit for that," Edison said grudgingly. "But if he didn't send you, that just means you unwittingly fell into the trap he tried to set for me. Bell's jealous—always has been. And now that I'm winning in the presidential race, his envy has sent him over the edge. He specifically tells me about this Agent Forrest, mentions how the guy is definitely, one-hundred-percent dead, and then plants a false quote in a news article about me that makes it seem like someone has stolen Forrest's identity. He did it to scare me! He's hoping I'll be so afraid, I'll cancel my rally tomorrow. Ha! He's trying to break the unstoppable momentum of my campaign. Well, I'll show him! Anyway, this conversation has gone on too long. I've got a monument to complete and a presidency to win, which means I don't have time for prepubescent prattlings."

"But what about Rector?" Molly asked. "You're not the only one in danger, you know. You saw firsthand what he did at the World's Fair! What if he tries the same thing here? Well, I mean, he's not stupid enough to try the same *exact* thing again, but his ultimate goal at the Fair was to take over the government and here we are in the very seat of—"

"Did Bell lie to me about Rector being stranded at the South Pole?" Edison asked bluntly.

The children both shook their heads.

"Then that's where the man still is," Edison said. "And he's a corpsicle by now. People left alone in Antarctica with no gear, no food, and no transportation don't just magically appear back in the United States. They die. They starve, they freeze, and they shatter into little meat cubes for hungry walruses or something. This newspaper business you're all fired up about is nothing more than political shenanigans perpetrated by Alexander Graham Bell. I'm not going to let him get the better of me and you shouldn't either. Now, run along and, well, keep running—you are still fugitives, aren't you?"

Molly grumbled. *Fine,* she thought. *Ignore us and get what you deserve.*

"Okay, we'll leave," Emmett said. "But, um, can you maybe not tell anyone you saw us?"

Edison laughed. "You think the leading presidential candidate wants anyone to know he's been interacting with two of America's most wanted criminals?"

"Most-most wanted," Molly corrected.

A workman called for Edison from up on the scaffold. The inventor leaned down and whispered to the children. "It won't be good for either of us if people find out I've been conversing with you two. Which I'm sure you knew. So, yes, I'll keep my mouth shut for now. But understand that if I see you again, the only way I'll be able to save my own political career is to hand you two over to the Feds. Which I will happily do. So take my advice and get out of DC. Now."

He strode out from behind the stone pile, shouting up to his men. "Stop loafing! That lightning rod's not going to raise itself!"

Molly and Emmett fumed wordlessly as they squeezed back through the gap in the fence and found Robot waiting on the other side.

"I could not fit," he said. "Has Mr. Edison been adequately warned of the danger?"

"Yep, he's been warned," Molly grumbled.

"Excellent," said Robot. "I knew Dr. Stinkums would see the job performed to satisfaction."

"That's right," Emmett deadpanned. "It was all the dog." Dr. Stinkums wriggled free of his arms and ran to steal a sausage from a nearby food vendor.

"You deserve it, Doctor," said Robot. "Reward yourself."

Dejected and defeated, Molly slumped onto a park bench and shooed away some nosy pigeons.

"What are you doing?" Emmett said.

"Giving up," she droned. "Like my mother."

Emmett treated her to his most disapproving stare. "I don't believe that for a second. You're just tired and hungry, like I am. We need a break, but this isn't the time or place."

"Perhaps you would like some fruit." Robot produced

handfuls of apples and pears that they dug into eagerly.

"Where'd you get this?" Emmett asked.

"From those fruit stands," Robot said.

"Did you have money?" Emmett asked, juice running down his chin.

Robot shook his head. "Apparently, people like to give free fruit to knights."

"Yoo-hoo, Sir Galahad!" shouted a woman from across the lawn.

"You have the wrong knight!" Robot returned. "But I thank you for your greeting nonetheless!"

The children shrugged and continued enjoying their first food in hours.

"Could we actually be wrong? About what's going on here?" Molly asked, her apple-induced bliss unable to completely dispel her concerns. "Could Edison be right? Could this all be about two ego-mad inventors trying to out-flummox each other? I mean, Rector has pulled off some amazing tricks in the past, but how could even *he* escape Antarctica without a boat?"

"Maybe Rector didn't get home on his own," Emmett surmised. "Maybe he had help."

"From who? All his allies are either dead or in jail."

"Except Oogie MacDougal," Emmett said with a shiver. "He escaped from prison, remember?"

Molly shook her head. "Oogie was safely in jail when we left for Antarctica; he wouldn't even have known that Rector was stuck down there."

Emmett chuckled to himself. "Oogie's certainly not the one who was posing as Agent Forrest. Instead of 'I'll be watching Mr. Edison myself,' that quote would have been something like, 'Ach! Ah wull be peepin' the auld muckle brain maselll!'"

Molly cracked up. "Since when do you do such a good Oogie impression?"

Emmett smiled at his own skill. "I never tried before!"

"Hey, buddy, which way to Camelot?" a laughing man asked as he strolled by.

"North by northwest," Robot helpfully replied. "Three thousand, six hundred, and sixty-two miles."

"Anyway," Emmett said, chomping into his apple. "To answer your question from before: No, Edison is not right about this. It's not just Mr. Bell trying to prank his rival. If Mr. Bell wanted to spook Edison out of having his rally, he's too smart to have relied on something as chancy as Edison just happening to see one particular article in one particular paper and happening to recognize the name of a guy that got mentioned to him once, months ago."

"Yes," said Robot. "It would make more sense if someone did that to you."

Molly furrowed her brow. "What do you mean, Robot?"

"As you said, Mr. Edison did not know Agent

Forrest; he had only heard the man's name once," Robot explained. "But you spent months with Agent Forrest, and you saw him die right in front of you. If *you* saw his name in the paper, you would take note of it in a way that Mr. Edison would not. In fact, you did. That is why you are here."

Molly gasped. "Holy flapjacks, Emmett, he's right. That quote was meant for *us* to find."

Emmett started nodding vigorously. "There was no Agent Forrest, fake or otherwise. That quote was placed in the article by someone who knew it would set off alarm bells for us." His breath quickened. "Someone who knew we couldn't resist investigating the appearance of that name. Someone who wanted to draw us out of hiding."

"Agent Clark," Molly said with horror. "It's a trap."

They dropped their apple cores (which Dr. Stinkums quickly devoured) and leapt from the bench.

"We need to leave Washington," Emmett said. "Now."

"That's what Edison said!" Molly panted as the group rushed across the National Mall. "He knew!"

"Not necessarily—he could've . . ." Emmett didn't bother finishing his thought. He sped up to keep pace with Molly. They walked as fast as they could risk without attracting added attention or losing Robot, who wasn't very swift on foot. Dr. Stinkums bounded ahead, yipping, as the group entered the wooded shorelands of the park and hurried back through the trees to where they'd left the Daedalus Chariot.

"Where is it?" Molly grunted. Getting back seemed to take hours longer than their initial walk from the landing zone. Finally, they burst into the small clearing where their fabulous flying machine sat on a bed of crisp fall leaves.

The chariot was surrounded by men in black bowler hats and long, dark coats.

"Unauthorized parking of a flying machine on federal land," Agent Clark said, while writing in his notepad. "This list of offenses just keeps getting longer and longer."

The Trap Is Sprung

"BOTHER BEANS!" MOLLY cursed. Dry leaves crunched under her foot as she stomped in frustration. "I can't believe we fell into Clark's stupid trap!"

"I wouldn't call it a *trap*, exactly," said Agent Clark, tipping back his hat to give his icy blue eyes a clear look at his quarry. "You weren't difficult to locate. You flew a big red sled over the capital. It was hard to miss."

"She means the news article you used to draw us here," Emmett said. He stood close to Molly, his every muscle tensed.

"Yeah, so, congratulations, I guess. You win, Clark," Molly said through clenched teeth. "I mean, I'm angry and terrified and everything, but I've got to admit, the article was a pretty genius move. I'm a little jealous, actually."

The agent raised his dimpled chin. "As much as I'd love to take credit for this 'genius trap,'" he said, "I don't know anything about any article."

Molly and Emmett whipped their heads to face each other. "If he didn't do the article," Emmett asked, breathless, "who did?"

"Edison!" Molly growled. "I knew he was lying to us! Never should have trusted that backstabbing fiend!"

Agent Clark cleared his throat. "Hey, eyes over here! I'm the one arresting you," he said. "Now, what's this about Thomas Edison? You spoke with him? And he hasn't reported it? Hmm. That's highly problematic." He jotted something in his pad.

Molly's heart began to race—and not just from the jolt of satisfaction she felt by getting Edison in trouble. If Clark hadn't set the trap for them, that meant her original theory could still be true: Rector really could be back and on the loose in DC. This was not a good time to get arrested. But they were facing down five federal agents in a tight grass clearing surrounded by a not-so-easily navigable thicket of red oaks. Running would be pointless. There was one thing that could help them, but they absolutely could not use it. "No magnet powers," she warned Robot. Needing to break out of a federal prison was a less frightening prospect than losing her friend.

"Good call, Miss Pepper," Agent Clark said. "If the metallic fellow pulls another of its iron-bending tricks, I will see that it is melted to slag."

"I do not know what slag is," said Robot. "But I do not believe I would enjoy being melted into anything."

"You didn't say they had a knight with them, Clark," said one of the other agents.

"It's not a knight," Clark replied. "It's a . . . machine. That makes things defy gravity. I don't know how it does the things it does, but I don't like it." He reopened his pad and made another note. "I'm not sure I have jurisdiction to enforce the laws of physics, but I'm adding it to the list anyway."

"If you didn't come here to catch us, why are you even in DC?" Molly asked, hoping to buy time to formulate an escape plan. "Shouldn't you be back in New York?"

"We determined you'd left New York months ago," Clark replied. "You showing up in the city where I'm currently stationed? That's just serendipity. Get cuffs on them, men."

"Is that necessary?" asked one of the agents. "They're just kids."

"Just kids," Clark scoffed. "This is why you're still a junior agent, Slattery. Cuff them."

The men took a step toward the children.

"Wait!" Emmett said, holding up his hands. The men paused. "Don't you want to know *why* we risked everything to come to DC?"

"I admit I'm curious," Clark said flatly. "It was an

incredibly boneheaded move. I look forward to hearing your explanation in an interrogation room back at headquarters."

"It's about Rector!" Molly blurted. "He's back from Antarctica!"

Agent Clark scoffed. "Impossible. No one comes back from Antarctica."

"*We* did," Molly said.

"Nobody comes back from Antarctica *alone*," Clark clarified.

"Rector did that once already!" Molly cried.

"Nobody comes back from Antarctica alone *without a boat!*"

"Look, sir, we don't know how Rector got back, but he did," said Emmett. "He's here in the city. We think he's after Edison. We came to warn him. You can ask Edison yourself."

"I'll do that," Clark said. "Cuff them, men."

"No, wait!" Molly pleaded. She and Emmett inched back, pressing themselves against Robot's steely frame, and the men halted their advance. "Think about it, Clark," she continued. "*Someone* planted a fake clue in a newspaper to draw us to Washington—and if it wasn't you, it was probably Rector. Come on, man, Rector's gotta be the one person you want to catch even more than us."

"I would not argue with that assessment," Clark said. "*He,* however, is in Antarctica. While *you* are right in front of me, ready to be arrested. Cuff them, men."

"We'll show you the article," Molly tried. "You must at least want to see our evidence, right?" The men paused.

"No, thank you," said Clark. "Though, if you would like to tell us where your parents are, well, that might be able to help you come sentencing time."

"It'll never happen," said Emmett.

"Suit yourself. Cuff them, men," said Clark. "And stop pausing every time the children tell you to. They're the criminals."

Sheepishly, the agents advanced, steel cuffs dangling from their closed fists. But when one man reached for Emmett, there was a sudden growling at his feet. Dr. Stinkums chomped onto the agent's ankle and the man hopped back, howling in pain.

"Clark!" Agent Slattery whined. "They have a magic knight *and* a dog? You didn't tell us *anything*!"

Without warning, Robot wrapped Molly and Emmett in a dual bear hug and lifted off the ground, holding them tight to his chest. He levitated up past the treetops, soared through the open air back toward the Mall, and set down again a half mile away in the isolated garden of what appeared to be a castle.

The instant her feet were back on the ground, Molly pulled away from Robot and pounded her fists against his oil-barrel chest. "What are you thinking! You *can't* use your powers!"

"You said 'no *magnet* powers,'" Robot replied.

"Get down! Both of you!" Emmett urged. "Before they see us!"

They crouched behind a tall hedge.

"Robot just saved us," Emmett said quietly. "He pulled a really risky move to do it, but getting tossed in jail while Rector is loose and we can't even communicate with our parents? That would have been disastrous."

"Robot *dying* would be disastrous!" Molly didn't care how loud she was being.

"Of course it would!" Emmett snapped back. "Don't make it sound like you're the only one who cares about him."

"I am sorry, Molly and Emmett," Robot interjected. "But keeping my friends safe is important to me. I am willing to take risks if your safety is at stake. I understand that you worry about me, but should I not also be allowed to worry about you?"

Molly wiped the tears she suddenly realized were trickling down her cheeks. She couldn't argue with Robot's logic. Or his intentions. No matter how much she wanted to.

"Are you okay, Molly?" Emmett asked.

She was openly crying now. Not out of fear for Robot, but because it had finally sunk in that he also feared for her. "Yeah, I'm good." She wiped her nose on her sleeve and looked around. "So where are we?"

"I took us to the nearest castle," Robot replied. "Since I am a knight."

"You know, you can probably take the helmet off at this point," Emmett said.

"Incorrect. I cannot," said Robot. "It is stuck."

Molly gazed up at the red sandstone towers of the majestic building whose gardens provided their current hiding spot. There were multiple towers, some in excess of a hundred feet tall, stabbing at the sky with spear-like spires. The tallest was octagonal, housing a massive clock face halfway up and bearing a lightning rod similar to the one Thomas Edison was installing on the Washington Monument. Gothic arched windows lined the walls, but the reflections of the setting sun made it difficult to see inside.

"Hey, this must the Smithsonian Institution," Molly said with a touch of awe. "Super sciencey folks work here. I'd love to go in."

"Maybe on our next trip," Emmett said. "Now doesn't feel like the best time for a museum visit."

"Actually, the most interesting stuff is going to be in *there*," Molly said as they moved stealthily along the hedges. She pointed to the vaguely schoolish-looking building next door to the castle. More red sandstone and more towers (though not quite as tall), it was a long rectangular edifice with a colossal dome rising from its center. "The Smithsonian's Arts and Industries

Building," she said. "They've got the very first telegraph message Samuel Morse ever sent in there. You know you'd want to lay eyes on that, Emmett. They've got the desk that Thomas Jefferson wrote the Declaration of Independence on. They've got Lewis and Clark's compass, George Washington's salt and pepper shakers—"

"Molly," said Emmett.

"I know, I need to focus," she said. "But *historic salt and pepper shakers!*"

"No, Molly, look. They've got something else in there too." Emmett pointed to the banner across the front of the Arts and Industries Building, which became visible as they rounded the corner of the castle: SPECIAL EXHIBIT: 2 WEEKS ONLY! SPACE ROCKS AND METEORITES! SEE GENUINE PIECES OF ANOTHER WORLD!

"Space rocks," Robot echoed. "*I* have a space rock."

"Yes, you do, Robot," Molly said, her face lighting up. "And does that space rock in the picture look familiar to you?"

"It looks like a rock," said Robot.

"A *glowing* rock," Molly specified, grinning widely.

"Look, I don't want to get overly excited," Emmett cautioned. "I mean, it's a painting of a rock. But they did draw those squiggly glow lines around it . . . Wow, could they really have Ambrosium in there?"

"It's the Smithsonian and they're advertising space

rocks!" Molly crowed. "If there's anyplace we're gonna find more Ambrosium, it's there!"

"We have to check it out," Emmett said. "I mean, if they have it, Robot could potentially be saved! If there's any reason worth detouring from our Rector mission, this is . . . Oh."

"Oh, what?" Molly asked. "Emmett, are you okay?"

"Yeah. It just hit me that this might not be a detour. I mean, we may not be the only ones looking for Ambrosium. Maybe *that's* what brought Rector to DC."

"Oh, man, that makes sense," Molly said, her enthusiasm deflating. "But . . . but he had so much of it when we last saw him. Two huge chunks, bigger than any of the pieces he had when he attacked the World's Fair. Why would he need to steal more?"

"Maybe he used up all his space rocks getting home from Antarctica," Emmett said.

"It is a known fact that Ambrosium degrades with use," Robot added.

"All right, then." Molly stood up. "Looks like we get to visit the museum after all!"

Molly raised her leg to step over the shrubbery, but Emmett pulled her back down. "That's not what I was suggesting," he said, peering over the top of the bush for anyone who might spot them. "First of all, look—it's closed for the day."

"So . . . tomorrow?" Molly tried.

Emmett shook his head. "Agent Clark probably has every cop in DC looking for us by now. And anyway, if Rector's the one who lured us here—which I think he is—what if this exhibit is part of his trap for us?"

Molly plopped onto the grass and crossed her arms. She couldn't argue with Emmett's logic. "Okay, let's do the whole talk-it-through planning thing that always makes you feel better."

"Thank you." Emmett glanced across the lawn at the Arts and Industries Building. "We should come back in a few hours, once it's really dark," he said. "There'll undoubtedly be security on ground level. But it's unlikely a museum would bother to guard the roof . . ."

"Ooh, look at you," Molly cooed. "You're getting into it! We're gonna heist the Smithsonian!"

Robot tipped his head toward them. "There is too high a probability you will get caught while attempting this," he said. "I do not want you to become convicts for my sake."

"It's not just for you, Robot," Molly said. "If they've got Ambrosium in there, you can bet your shiny big toe that Rector is going to try and snatch it. The only way he won't is if we snatch it first. Plus, we're experienced heisters. We've pulled off riskier break-ins without getting caught. So, the pros outweigh the cons."

Robot nodded. "We will not become cons, because we are pros."

"Couldn't have said it better myself," said Molly.

Emmett held his hand at different angles, and looked through his fingers at the building. "There's a cracked window on the upper portion of the rotunda. They're casement windows, which means they'll open with a crank. I bet we could slip a hand through the missing section of windowpane to reach it. Getting up to the roof would be the issue—and no, Robot, you cannot fly us up there. If I can get my hands on some rope, though. Some pliable metal, maybe a spring or two . . . Heights terrify me—Why am I suggesting this?"

"Because it's an amazing plan!" Molly jumped to her feet. "Come on, I'm pretty sure we flew over a junkyard as we approached the city. Let's go shopping!"

"Oh, no!" Emmett said suddenly as he stood. "I just realized there's nobody chewing on my shoe. We left the dog back with Agent Clark!"

"I could not carry all three of you," said Robot. "So I chose to leave behind the one of us most capable of escaping federal custody. Have no fear. Dr. Stinkums will no doubt rejoin us soon, regaling us with tales of his daring escape. I quite look forward to it."

With their heads held low and their coat collars flipped high, they scurried off into the growing twilight.

17

Night at the Museum

MOLLY WAS GLAD to see that the streets of the nation's capital were much quieter at night. And while the moon was bright overhead, the heavy tree coverage along the Mall kept the paths and sidewalks shrouded in darkness, allowing her, Emmett, and Robot to remain unseen as they traversed the long shadowy stretches between dim corner gas lamps. It was a stark contrast to the well-lit New York boulevards they'd skulked along the previous winter. Maybe Thomas Edison's influence in Washington wasn't as strong as Molly had assumed. If the man actually took up residence in the White House, though, she was certain the Edison Electrical Company would make midnight in DC as bright as high noon.

Molly pulled her coat tight to guard against the chilly October air as they weaved among the shrubbery behind the Smithsonian's Arts and Industries Building. Molly gazed up to the edge of the roof. "Can you see your target, Robot?" she asked.

"Yes," came the reply. "I am ready and eager to try out my new toy."

"It's not a toy," Emmett said. "It's a complicated piece of mechanical equipment. That I built out of random garbage. And rush-installed into your arm in less than an hour. And have not adequately tested. You know, this is sounding less and less like a good idea."

"New toy, Robot," Molly said, jumping piggyback-style onto Robot's back. Robot raised his right arm and—*pop!*—launched his hand into the air like a rocket. The flying hand sailed upward, trailing a sturdy length of rope behind it, until its fingers clamped on to the lip of the museum roof. Robot then startled Emmett by wrapping his left arm around the boy's waist.

"Wait, don't—" Emmett began.

"New toy," Robot echoed, and the rope retracted back into his hollow arm, pulling him—and both children—up into the air. Three seconds later, they were dangling from the Smithsonian's roof.

"Woo-hoo," Molly softly cheered as she climbed off Robot onto the rooftop. She grabbed Emmett's hand and pulled him up so they could both then help Robot.

"I like toys," said Robot.

Molly was giddy, but Emmett was simmering. "I know

what you're thinking, Emmett," she said. "But what you *should* be thinking is, 'Man, I am a super-genius inventor, because I just created a way for Robot to fly without Ambrosium.'"

She couldn't be a hundred percent sure, but she thought she saw the corners of Emmett's mouth turn up a bit.

"Let's just get to that window," he said.

Moving deftly in the moonlight, they crept across a flat section of roof and then scurried along the perimeter of the massive dome, scanning the tall, arched, multipaned windows until they found the one with the broken pane. Peering in, they could see all the way down to the museum's main atrium three stories below. Much closer, however, was a railed mezzanine that girded the interior of the dome, overlooking the main hall. It would only be a three- or four-foot drop to the tiled floor of that mezzanine.

"That's promising," Emmett said.

Molly was surprised by his optimism. Because, for once, she wasn't feeling it herself. Down beyond the gilded mezzanine railing, that grand first-floor chamber housed a gridlike maze of artifacts, tall wooden cabinets, and glass showcases that were lined up like library bookshelves. There had to be thousands of items on display down there. And that was just in the atrium. The building had two more expansive wings that stretched out on either side of it for the length of a full city block. Locating a single rock among all those exhibits suddenly seemed an incredibly daunting prospect.

Molly sighed. "I guess it was too much to hope the meteorites would be directly below this window."

"It's a special exhibit," said Emmett. "I'm sure we'll see signs for it once we're inside."

Molly knelt beside the window. A portion of glass was missing from the pane in its lower right corner, the opening just large enough for her to slip her arm in. She cautiously did so, careful to avoid the sharp edge. She pressed her cheek against the glass and pushed her arm in nearly to the shoulder. Her hand finally found the interior handle. She cranked it, praying the mechanism wouldn't creak too loudly, and the window began opening outward, like a door. As soon as the opening was wide enough, Emmett squeezed through and dropped to the mezzanine floor, where he relieved Molly, easily cranking the window the rest of the way open.

Molly silently hopped down to join him. But when Robot attempted the same, his armor clanged audibly as he landed. The children both shushed him.

There was no immediate signage, so Molly led the group, on tiptoe, to the nearest of the many hallways that branched off the mezzanine. *Thunk-clank, thunk-clank, thunk-clank.*

They stopped, and Emmett gave Molly a raised

eyebrow. "Maybe the big metal man shouldn't be joining us on this *stealth* mission?" he whispered.

Molly knew there were security guards down there somewhere and that this cavernous building was basically an immense echo chamber, but knowing how worried Robot would be about them, it would feel cruel to banish him back to the roof alone.

"Hey, Robot," she whispered. "Any chance you can move more quietly?"

"Of course." He levitated a half inch off the ground.

"No powers!"

"But—"

"Softer steps! Just take softer steps, okay?"

Molly held her breath and crept farther down the corridor, with Robot taking "softer steps" behind her. His clanks and clunks were now tinks and plinks, but still audible. *Should* she make Robot wait? No. She couldn't. Because when it came down to it, she didn't trust him. She loved him, but she didn't trust him to keep himself safe when he thought his loved ones might be in danger. Suddenly, Molly had a much greater understanding of Emmett's father. She took a deep breath. Tinks and plinks would have to be good enough. At least no security guards had come rushing to investigate yet.

The trio continued down the dark hallway, poking their heads into each exhibition room they passed. One showcased skeletal wildlife, another had crafts from local native tribes, a third housed old-fashioned weaponry. This was awful, Molly thought. It was going to take them forever to find the meteor exhibit. And she couldn't even take the time to appreciate all these awesome bones and skins and swords while they were looking!

"Keep moving," Emmett whispered when she lingered too long by a fossilized beetle.

Molly huffed and moved on. "Where are all these signs you were so sure we'd see?" she whispered between clenched teeth.

"It was a *guess*," Emmett hissed back. "Did you have a better plan?"

"I thought we were being quiet," said Robot.

"We are," Molly snapped. "But—ooh!" She ran to a glass display case at the entrance of the next room.

"Ambrosium?" Emmett asked hopefully.

Molly shook her head. "George Washington's salt and pepper shakers!"

Emmett pulled her away. "Molly—"

They froze at the sudden sound of shattering glass.

"It was not me," Robot said quickly.

"It came from back on the mezzanine," Molly said. "Drat! Here we are, being so impressively stealthy, and then some other creep has to break in and be all noisy about it!"

"Who's there?" a guard called out. His footsteps were heading their way.

"Hide!" Emmett whispered.

Molly and Emmett huddled in the nearest corner and Robot stood stiff and tall in front of them. They held their breaths as a man in a blue, copper-buttoned coat stomped by, holding a lantern in one hand and billy club in the other. The guard paused in the doorway and swung his light around, shining it directly on Robot's face. He squinted at the metal man, swung the lantern to illuminate the rest of the room's memorabilia, then returned his attention to Robot.

"Huh," the guard mumbled to himself. "Hadn't realized George Washington used to be a knight."

The man turned away and continued down the corridor.

As soon as he was gone, Emmett leaned out past the doorframe and peered back the way they'd come. "Guys!" he whispered, pointing.

A man in black was emerging from a hiding spot of his own.

Molly seethed. What were the odds that some other dumb burglar would try to burgle the same museum they were burgling at the same time they were burgling it? It was ridiculously bad luck. Unless . . .

The man in black turned their way and stopped. He stood tall in a wash of moonlight that spilled in through a nearby window. His face was covered by a white mask—the warped and twisted face of Hephaestus, Greek god of craftsmen.

"Well, if it isn't my least favorite non-adults and their

pet coffee grinder," said Ambrose Rector. "At least I assume that's Bell's stolen cog puppet under that poor man's excuse for a jousting helmet."

"I am a knight," said Robot.

There was so much Molly wanted to say—to scream—but her mouth, like the rest of her, seemed to have forgotten how to work. The man responsible for her past two years' worth of nightmares was standing before her once again. The sight set astir a maelstrom of emotions within her: shock, anger, disbelief, fear. But also curiosity: Whose face was Ambrose Rector wearing under that mask? His own? Archibald Forrest's? Someone she had yet to meet?

"I must admit, you've taken me by surprise here," the madman continued. "I assumed the next time I'd see you people would be in a police notice about your arrest. I mean, credit where credit is due—you've done a better job of annihilating your reputations than I ever could have. But I assumed that meant I'd be free of you for a while. What in the world would bring you two out of hiding when— Oh, I get it. I should have expected this. You're after the same thing I am, aren't you? I bet you didn't even know I'd be here, did you? Not that it matters. Because here you are, in my way. Again." He sighed. "Of all my many enemies, why must it always be the prepubescents who get in my way? It's unfair, really. I deserve better nemeses. Or at least taller ones."

Suddenly, all the emotions fogging Molly's mind congealed into one overriding feeling: the overwhelming desire to defeat Ambrose Rector. "Follow my lead," she said, shoving herself against the nearest display case and tipping it over. The glass box hit the floor and shattered, startling everyone. From among the broken shards, Molly snatched up a pewter pepper shaker and hurled it at Rector's head. "Go, revolutionary seasonings!"

The small metal shaker thunked into the front of the villain's mask, staggering him. "Agh! It stings! How is there still pepper in that thing?" He doubled over, wiping hundred-year-old spice flakes from the eyeholes of his mask. "What did I do to deserve this? Besides all the murdering and kidnapping."

The voices of security guards reverberated from down on the first floor: "I told you it wasn't my imagination! Go! Go!"

Molly began racing for the nearest stairwell, but Emmett stopped her. "They're going to be coming straight up those steps."

"Drat." None of the exhibition rooms along this hallway had exits. They were trapped between Rector and the approaching guards.

"Ha!" Rector scoffed. "You children have gotten too cocky for your own—*ah-choo!*"

Molly caught the villain mid-sneeze, barreling into him and knocking him up against the wall so she,

Emmett, and Robot could run past, back toward the central atrium. Before they could reach the mezzanine, however, Rector drew a pistol-like armament from his coat and aimed it at Robot. Molly had seen this weapon before. Rector's rebuilt Magneta-Ray began to hum and glow with a dull orange light.

"Ha!" Molly scoffed. "Forgot Robot is aluminum, huh? Magnets don't affect him!"

Robot suddenly skidded to a stop and began a head-first slide back toward Rector.

"The helmet!" Emmett yelled. "It's steel!"

Molly and Emmett each dove for one of Robot's legs and tried with all their might to hold him in place. They crouched, grunting and sweating, their arms wrapped around his thick metal shins, while Rector pulled pack on his blaster like a fisherman trying to reel in a big catch. Robot's arms flailed until he finally managed to brace himself in the doorframe that led out to the mezzanine. With a harsh scraping sound, the helmet popped off and flew to Rector.

"I am not a knight anymore," Robot said sadly as the children scrambled to their feet.

"What's going on up here? Who are you?" yelled the bewildered security guard who emerged from the stairwell. Rector flicked his wrist and the knight helmet flew through the air, smacking into the man and bowling him over. A second guard behind him began shouting,

"We've got a man down! Get word to the police!"

Rector used his Magneta-Ray to pluck the man's buttons from his coat and pelt him with them until the guard fled back downstairs.

As Molly, Emmett, and Robot darted around the mezzanine to the other side of the atrium, they could hear more men yelling from below. "This place is going to be crawling with cops any minute," Emmett said.

"At least we've put some distance between us and Rector," Molly said, knowing full well it wasn't much of a bright side.

Just then, they heard the sound of shattering glass and Rector stepped onto the mezzanine across the atrium from them. He held his Magneta-Ray in the air. A glistening cavalry sword floated above his head. "Have you ever sneezed inside a mask?" he shouted across the distance. "It is *not* pretty!"

Then he twirled his hand and sent the saber spinning across the atrium. Molly and Emmett grabbed each other as the deadly blade came hurtling at them—

The sword suddenly froze in midair, mere inches from their heads.

"What happened?" Emmett muttered.

Robot was holding his hand out. An orange glow seeped from the seams of his chest plate.

Molly swallowed hard. "I'm, um, not gonna yell at you this time, Robot," she said.

"Ah," Rector said, leaning casually against the mezzanine railing. "So the clanky fellow still has something that rightfully belongs to me. I was beginning to wonder. I'll have to get that back before I'm done here."

There was a commotion below as a group of police officers ran into the museum. "They're upstairs!" someone yelled.

"That's my cue to exit," Rector said, putting his magnet ray back into his coat. "I've got a precious stone to snatch. Nice catching up, though." He dashed down a corridor into the east wing seconds before security guards and officers of the capitol police began pouring from stairwells along the mezzanine. They emerged from every possible entrance and began approaching the children from both directions, angrily waving their batons.

"We're trapped," Emmett said shakily. "No way down."

"Incorrect," said Robot. He hoisted Emmett into one arm and bent for Molly to climb onto his back—which she eagerly did. Then with his right hand clamped on to the mezzanine railing, he swung his gawky pipe legs to the other side and released the hidden rope in his arm. In a blink, they descended to the now empty first floor and Robot quickly reeled his hand in. Policemen gathered at the railing, scratching their heads in bewilderment.

"Ha!" Molly crowed, hopping from Robot's back. And then, "Ha!" again when she saw the sign directly in front of them: SPACE ROCKS. They'd done it! They'd evaded arrest *and* beaten Rector to the Ambrosium!

Molly raced into the exhibit and made her way down the row of display cases. A dusty black stone in the first. A dull gray one in the next. Then dusty gray. And dull black. Where was the smooth, lustrous orange of Ambrosium? Where was the glow? That sign outside showed a glowing rock! But none of the meteorites in that room were full of power; they were full of cracks and holes. "They're just rocks!" Molly barked in frustration. "That sign is a liar!"

The sound of descending footsteps reverberated from down the hall. Emmett grabbed her shoulder. "I'm sorry, Molly, but they're coming back."

Molly huffed. She would have to soothe herself with the thought that, when Rector reached that exhibit, he would be just as disappointed. Reluctantly, she joined the others, darting out through the abandoned front entrance, fleeing once more into the shadows.

Molly hunched her shoulders and pulled her coat tight, to protect herself from both the wind and prying eyes. She had a freshly pilfered newspaper rolled in one hand as she returned to the dank alley behind a condemned restaurant where they had spent the night among malodorous trash heaps. Not the accommodations she'd hoped for, but at least they'd managed to get a few hours of sleep in without being discovered.

After fleeing the Smithsonian the night before, they had trekked back into the woods to retrieve the Daedalus Chariot. Unsurprisingly, it was gone, likely impounded by Agent Clark and his men. There was no sign of Dr. Stinkums either. And so, with few other options, they fell back upon Molly's old theory of hiding someplace no one else would want to go.

"Anything in there?" Emmett asked as soon as he saw the newspaper.

"Gimme a chance to look!" Molly snapped, making him flinch. "Sorry," she said, more amiably. "I'm just tired and hungry."

"Believe it or not," Emmett said, "I didn't get the best night's sleep either, huddling between these rotting potato sacks."

"I am not hungry, as I do not eat," said Robot, who stood leaning against the brick wall. "I am tired, however. I think I am, at least. I have never been tired before. But I assume this is what tired feels like. Also, I miss my knight helmet."

Molly's brow crinkled with concern. "You're *tired*, Robot? For real? I was afraid of something like this after you used your powers last night." She handed the newspaper to Emmett and took a reluctant peek inside Robot's chest compartment. The remaining Ambrosium could barely warrant being called a nugget anymore. It was only slightly larger than a marble.

Hoping to ignore the pang in her heart, Molly turned her attention to Emmett. "What does the news say?"

He didn't have to page far into the *World*'s Washington edition to find what he was looking for. "Here it is—page two. 'Daring Theft at Smithsonian.' Aaand . . . They're blaming it on us. Of course. 'The culprits have been identified as adolescent fugitives Emmett Lee, a young man of Chinese descent, and Molly Pepper, daughter of attempted assassin Cassandra Pepper.'"

"Hey, I've broken a whole bunch of laws myself!" Molly griped. "How come I only get to be known for my mother's crime? And one she didn't even commit!"

"Yeah, well, apparently being Chinese is the only notable thing about me," Emmett said.

Molly gave his shoulder a sympathetic squeeze. "I'm sorry," she said. "You're an amazing inventor. Someday everybody's going to know your name for the right reasons."

"Thanks for the pep talk," Emmett said, "but I'm having a hard time looking that far into the future when apparently Clark *did* give our names and descriptions to every cop, agent, and security guard in this town."

Molly growled at the man's name. "Any mention of Rector in that article?" she asked.

"Of course not," Emmett said as he continued to read. "Oh! But *this* is interesting: 'Thanks to the intervention

221

of the capitol police, the criminals escaped with only two of the lauded museum's artifacts.'"

"Two? We got *nothing*!"

Emmett read on. "'One was a suit of armor'"—he paused to roll his eyes—"'the other, a large stone.'"

"What? There *was* Ambrosium?" Molly gasped. "Rector got to it first? How? He never passed us on the way to—"

"No, listen," Emmett said. "'The Star of Ceylon, which at one hundred and eighty-three carats is the largest known sapphire in the world, is a stunning loss to the museum, having been valued at over twenty thousand dollars.'"

"I do not understand," said Robot.

Molly flopped down onto a garbage can lid, dropping her face into her hands. "I do," she said. "Rector was after a rock, but not the same kind we were. He was just out to steal some big, expensive jewel! There was never any Ambrosium. In fact, there's no more Ambrosium anywhere. No more magic space rocks that we can use to save you, Robot. That tiny bit you've got left in your chest? That's all there is. Forever."

Ladies and Gentlemen, the Next President of the United States!
Washington, DC, October 19, 1884

"THE QUESTION FACING us all is this: Do we want to wait for the future? Or do we want to bring the future to us?"

Thomas Edison's voice reached even the screaming fans in the back row, thanks to the Vocal Empowernator device that amplified his speech across the entire National Mall. He paced a wide wooden stage beneath a towering proscenium arch rigged with an array of light bulbs that spelled out his name in red, white, and blue. "Some presidents are happy to stay in the present," the candidate continued. "Take Poodle-Cheeks Chester Arthur, for example. When was the last time he invented anything? No offense, Ches—you know I love you. And, hey, Arthur's better than all those presidents we've had who insisted on living in the past. Did you know that

James Madison never even *used* electricity? It's true. Not once! That's why I'm going to be a different kind of president—a president unlike any this great nation has ever seen before. Tell me, good people of America, do you want a leader who's already history? Or one who plans to write a new chapter for our country?"

Thousands applauded and shrieked Edison's name, some wobbling as if they might pass out from sheer ecstasy.

"How is he getting people to cheer for him when he's saying absolutely nothing," Molly griped.

"Maybe that's why they call him the Wizard," Emmett replied.

The two crouched beneath the stage while the vociferous candidate paced above their heads. The sea of fawning Ed-Heads on the Mall hooted so loudly that Molly wondered if they could even make out Edison's words. Still, as much as she didn't understand the wildness of the crowd, she was grateful for it. With security forces busy holding back autograph seekers, it had been shockingly easy to hop the fence into the backstage area and crawl underneath the platform.

It also helped that they didn't bring Robot with them this time. They were too afraid to. And they figured the manure-scented alleyway behind the city stables was as safe a place to leave him as any.

"But you don't even have to wait till inauguration day

to see me make my mark on Washington," Edison said to his followers. "I'll be lighting up the town in December when I crown the Washington Monument with a little bit of that Edison magic. So, remember, folks: Edison is the future and the future is Edison! And Edison is America! Edison, future, America!"

"I think he's wrapping up," Emmett whispered.

"In conclusion, let me leave you with one final thought," Edison said. "Can the other candidates do . . . this?" The rapid tapping and shuffling overhead told Molly that Edison was treating the crowd to one of his signature soft-shoe dance routines.

She and Emmett crawled to the rear of the stage and crouched by the back steps so they could catch Edison as he left. When the dance—which went on *far* too long—finally ended, the roar of the crowd made Molly jam her fingers in her ears. She only pulled them out when she saw Edison's brown-checked pant legs bound down the steps in front of her. Two men in black immediately strode over to the candidate, but Edison shooed them away. "Back off, fellas, I'm fine," he said, dabbing behind his ears with a handkerchief. "Go take a break and let me catch my breath in peace. I'm not as young as I used to be."

The men left.

"No one is as young as they used to be," Molly said as she and Emmett emerged from hiding.

"Gah!" Edison jumped. "Why do you keep doing this to me? And now at my own campaign rally? There are press people here! I can't be seen with you urchins."

"Well, Agent Clark already knows you've seen us. Because we told him," Molly said with smug satisfaction. "So . . . Who's the urchin now? Huh?"

"You!" Edison snapped. "You are the urchin! Urchins are children by definition!"

"Mr. Edison, please," Emmett interrupted. "We had no intention of bothering you again. You made your feelings pretty clear. But we *had* to tell you what happened last night. We *saw* Rector. With our own eyes."

"Look, I'm not accusing you of lying," Edison said. The crowd was still boisterous enough out front that he didn't worry about being overheard. "But you're kids—your imaginations have imaginations."

"Did you hear about the burglary at the Smithsonian?" Molly asked.

"I did," he replied.

"That was Rector!"

"Funny, I heard it was you," Edison said, crossing his arms.

"Fine, then we're done here," Emmett said, glowering at him before turning to Molly. "We did our duty, we warned him. If he refuses to take us seriously, that's on him. But *we* are not going to stand around doing nothing while a madman is on the loose, so—"

"Wait—I believe you now," Edison said.

Emmett glared. "It's bad enough you won't help us; we don't need your sarcasm on top of—"

"Stop!" Edison barked. "Rector's here! I *believe* you!"

"Really?" Emmett said with surprise. "Because I didn't think I made a very convincing argument—"

"Would you shut up! He is literally *right there!*"

Edison pointed a quivering finger at the top of the proscenium arch. Emmett and Molly spun to see the masked, black-clad figure of Ambrose Rector crouched on a pipe behind the giant letter "E." Upon realizing he'd been spotted, the villain lifted a blowpipe to the mouthhole of his mask and fired a dart at them.

"Look out!" Emmett shoved Edison to the ground and—*thunk!*—the dart planted itself into the wooden steps.

"Hurry!" Molly cried. "Call security and—"

"Don't bother," Edison said, clutching his chest. "He's already gone."

Molly spun around—the masked figure had vanished. "Yes, but your men could—"

"My security couldn't stop two little kids from sneaking back here," Edison said, brushing himself off. "They're useless. I apparently have a diabolical genius stalking me—I'm going to need *real* help."

"Are you all right?" Emmett asked him, helping the man up.

Edison nodded. "I suppose I owe you my thanks."

"This makes us even for the time I beat you up," said Molly.

"*You* didn't save me, Emmett did!" Edison countered. Then he softened his tone. "But I suppose you actually were trying to warn me of legitimate danger, so . . ." His eyes widened, the reality of the situation appearing to dawn on him. "What am I going to do? I should never have underestimated Rector. The man could be any-where! I'm a major public figure—I can't just go hide in a sewer like you two—"

"We haven't been in a sewer!" Molly said.

Edison sniffed. "Coulda fooled me," he muttered. "Look, Rector just made it clear he's out for revenge. He knows I conspired with Bell to send him on that Antarc-tic mission that nearly led to his demise, and he wants me dead for it. I don't even know how I'm going to show my face beyond this fence without putting my life at risk. You kids need to go notify Agent Clark right away."

"Us?" Molly scoffed. "Clark doesn't believe us any more than you did a few minutes ago! Besides, he'd have us in cuffs before we could utter a word. Send one of your security goons."

"What if Rector's already disguised himself as one of them?" Edison's eyes darted around in a paranoid panic. "You know how good he is at that kind of stuff!"

Molly narrowed her eyes at him.

"I'll pardon you as soon as I become president," Edison offered with a cheesy smile.

"Hold on! No one can go to the police," Emmett said. He had plucked Rector's dart from the stage steps and unrolled a thin slip of paper that was wrapped around it. "It's a message. Maybe he wasn't trying to kill anybody just now."

Edison sniffed. "Well, in that case, I retract my thanks. You wrinkled my suit for nothing."

"What's the note say, Emmett?" Molly asked, reading over his shoulder.

"'I have Bell,'" Emmett read.

"He kidnapped Alec again?" Edison said. "Sheesh. Can that guy go, like, a month without getting kidnapped?"

Emmett cleared his throat and continued reading. "'I have Bell. Speed up construction on the monument. Have it done before Election Day, or Bell dies.'"

"Okay, well, now I feel bad," said Edison. "You should have mentioned the killing part sooner. But anyway, this is all the more reason we should immediately notify—"

Emmett cleared his throat even louder and read, "'Do not involve the authorities. Tell anyone, and Bell dies.'"

"I'm just gonna be quiet now," Edison said sheepishly.

Molly looked into Emmett's eyes. She knew he was thinking the same thing she was. "It's on us again," she said. "We have to stop Rector. Alone."

"Not alone," said Emmett. He turned to Edison. "*He* has to help us."

Edison gaped. "What am I supposed to do? I'm the one being targeted. The only reason Rector hasn't killed me yet is because he knows my murder would bring the construction on the Washington Monument to an abrupt halt, and he apparently needs it finished for some devious reason. What *I* should be doing is finding a nice, cozy little safe spot. And staying there."

"Then do that and take us with you," said Emmett. "We need someplace to lie low too. At least until we can figure out our next move."

"So, where's your safe space?" Molly asked Edison. "You must have one."

Edison clenched his jaw as he mulled it over. "It's called the Club."

The Wizard's Lair

THOMAS EDISON REFUSED to leave the backstage area until he was adequately disguised. He was far from pleased, however, with the street sweeper's coveralls that the kids forced him into. And even less so with the floppy mophead they threw over his hair as a wig.

"I look ridiculous," he complained, flicking a thick strand of gray yarn from in his eye. "What am I supposed to be—a rag doll janitor? You're just trying to humiliate me, aren't you?"

"You look very *un*-Edison," Emmett said. "Which is kind of the point." Stifling their snickers, he and Molly climbed into an abandoned trash cart, which the inventor grudgingly pushed out through the crowd. And thus they made their escape.

Their first stop was the alley behind the stables, where

they found Robot *and* Dr. Stinkums waiting. "See? This dog always finds me," said Robot.

"I still don't understand why you have a dog," Edison said as Dr. Stinkums nibbled the toe of his shoe. From there, the inventor navigated them through back alleys to the rear of a classy red-brick townhouse.

"The Club," he said.

Molly peeked through ivy-ringed windows to see an extravagant hall with lush red carpeting, gold filigree wallpaper, and stained-glass chandeliers that cast twinkling colors around the room. The Guild didn't deserve all the money they had, she thought. Their "fanciness" budget had to be four times that of what they spent on equipment and research. The Mothers of Invention somehow managed to function perfectly well without velvet chairs and emerald doorknobs.

She recognized some of the men who were clinking champagne glasses and puffing cigars inside. Cameramaker George Eastman and electrical pioneer George Westinghouse were sipping drinks and laughing while Nikola Tesla juggled what appeared to be glass balls of lightning. No sign of Alexander Graham Bell, of course; Rector likely had him shackled in a dungeon somewhere. "These guys are all supposedly geniuses, right?" Molly said. "One of them must be able to help us." Personally, she was hoping it would be Tesla. He seemed fun.

"We'd be fools to trust them," said Edison. "If there's one thing you can count on your fellow Guildsmen for, it's a knife in your back. Besides, any one of those men could be Ambrose Rector in disguise. Right now, *we* are the only three people we can safely say *aren't* Rector."

"Five," Molly corrected him.

"I wasn't counting the robot or the dog." Edison squeezed the bridge of his nose like he was trying to ward off a headache. "Okay, I'm going in. That window directly above us is my personal office on the second floor. I'll enter through the front door, posing as a custodian, then go up and open the window for you."

"You must think we're fools," Molly said, stepping into his path as he tried to leave the alley. "You're just going to hide inside and leave us out here."

"If I was going to ditch you, why would I have taken you all the way here?" Edison asked with obvious annoyance. "I even detoured to find your aluminum sidekick."

Emmett and Molly exchanged glances. They didn't have much choice in the matter. "We'll be expecting you at that window in three minutes," Emmett said.

Edison hurried around to the front of the building, his ridiculous mop-yarn hair bouncing as he ran. Robot began counting as Molly and Emmett watched that second-story window. One minute. Two minutes. Four minutes. Six minutes. Molly gave Emmett a wincing look. Nine minutes. The window finally opened.

Edison bitterly threw the ragged mop-wig down at them before beckoning them up. Robot launched his hoist-hand to the sill, gathered the children and the dog, and rode the retracting rope to the second floor. They all climbed inside, ducking under heavy velvet curtains fringed with tinkling crystals.

Molly had thought Thomas Edison's private office at the Guild Hall in New York was a swanky enough place. But this DC office was a sight to behold. *I might as well be in a tsar's palace or a pharaoh's tomb,* Molly thought, gawking at the jade statuary, the crystal vases, the silver drinkware, the mounted heads of animals she couldn't begin to identify, the silken throw pillows that Dr. Stinkums had already begun shredding. "This place is so far over the top, it's come back around and hit the bottom," Molly said with disdain. "Where are the inventions? Where are the pincers, the circuits, the cogs, the wires, the sandpaper?"

"That hoohah is all back in New York," Edison said dismissively. "This is *the Club.* We come here for, you know, recreation." He sat down at his mother-of-pearl desk and pulled the chain to turn on a solid gold lamp in the shape of a unicorn.

Emmett leaned in to Molly and whispered, "You can't deny you like that lamp, though."

She couldn't.

"Now, I believe we have some business to attend to,"

Edison said, twirling a pencil.

The children sat in leather chairs across the desk from him. "Well," said Emmett, "what do we know so far about Rector's plan?"

"It has something to do with the Washington Monument," said Molly. "Otherwise why would he be blackmailing Edison into finishing it? How much work is left on it, Tom-Tom?"

"Basically just the lightning rod. But it can't be installed safely until we finish constructing the copper housing for it."

"Is Rector trying to harness lightning?" Molly wondered.

"Harness lightning?" Robot echoed. "Is that a metaphor or is Lightning a horse? Lightning would be a good name for a horse."

"Metaphor," said Molly. "A lightning rod is basically a big antenna that draws in lightning, so maybe Rector wants to suck up electricity with it, or—"

"Ooh!" Emmett burst out with excitement. "What if Rector plans to reverse the flow and use the rod to transmit energy instead of absorb it?"

Edison scoffed. "It would take a super-genius to . . . oh, that's right—he is one."

"Maybe Lightning can be the name of that unicorn," said Robot.

"Robot, we need to focus," said Molly. But focusing

was no easy task in the midst of all that fantastic gaudiness. She'd never seen so much luster in one room. The drawer pulls glistened, the chair legs shimmered, and the crystals on the curtains cast dancing flecks of light everywhere. "The sapphire! From the Smithsonian!" she blurted, her mind rushing back to the dancing lights on the walls of the Ambrosium cavern. "Rector didn't just steal it for the money; he's going to use it." She stood up, ran to the window, and pulled the curtain aside. A solitary square of sunlight was illuminated on the Persian carpet. "Look at the light coming through the window," she said. "One ray, one spot of light. But put a crystal in front and . . ." She let the curtain fringe fall into the sunbeam and, suddenly, bright shapes were flickering on every wall.

Emmett's jaw dropped. "Rector can use the sapphire to split the energy like a prism and send it out in all directions."

"What energy?" Edison asked. "Are we talking about lightning?"

"No, Ambrosium," Emmett said. "Rector's weapons *always* revolve around Ambrosium. Like the Mind-Melter, the device he used to paralyze everyone at the World's Fair. Remember how he said the Mind-Melter's rays would have been fatal if he'd turned up the intensity any higher?"

"Well, whatever he's got planned this time, he's

definitely turning up the intensity," Molly said. "Because he's transformed the whole darn Washington Monument into a Mind-Melter! Okay, not a *Mind-Melter*, exactly— I'm sure Rector isn't dumb enough to try the same thing twice—but *some* sort of giant death machine. And with that gem on the antenna, his new death machine will be able to send its lethal energy across a far larger area than Central Park. Rector will be able to zap the whole city. Maybe the entire Eastern Seaboard."

"Well, that's a humdinger," said Edison. He drummed his pencil on the desk, then stood up. "I've got to order my staff to get cracking on that monument!"

Emmett jumped up as well. "I don't think you followed what we just said."

"Yeah," Molly joined in. "Whose side are you on?"

"I'm not going to have them *finish* it," Edison scoffed. "I'm not a moron! But I'd given them the day off to see my rally. They need to get back to work. If Rector doesn't see them toiling away, he'll think I've ignored his ultimatum. Bell may be a buffoon, but I don't want his death on my conscience."

"He's got a point," Emmett said. "Rector needs to think we're playing along. Okay, do it, but make sure you tell your men not to complete the work."

"Obviously," Edison said, rolling his eyes. "Look, we're two weeks out from Election Day—stalling a construction job until then is easy. What will be difficult, though, is finding and thwarting Rector when all we've got is the three of us."

"Five," said Robot. There was a crash as Dr. Stinkums yanked down the curtain and began noisily chewing the velvet.

Edison sighed. "I'm serious, children. We can't handle this alone. Think—is there *anyone* else we can trust? What about your parents? Can you contact them?"

"Parents, plural?" Emmett asked tentatively. "So . . . you know about my father?"

"That he's alive and now a fugitive like the rest of you? Yes. What Agent Clark knows, I know."

"It doesn't matter," Molly said. "They're nowhere they can be contacted quickly enough."

"And the next time we see them, we're probably going to be grounded until retirement, anyway," Emmett added.

Edison snapped his fingers. "Say, what about those other friends of yours? Those meddlesome lady inventors? The Grannies with Hammers, or something along those lines?"

"The Mothers of Invention," Molly said sharply. "And they've got more skill in their pinkie toes than the entire Guild put together."

"They've also been missing for longer than we have," Emmett said sadly. "The police can't find them and neither can we."

"They haven't reached out to you?" Edison said. "No contact at all? Hmm, I guess they weren't the friends you thought they were."

"They would have if they could have! But it's been too risky!" Molly snapped. "I mean, what were they supposed to do? Write us a letter?"

Emmett gasped. "Maybe they did!"

"Did what?" Molly was confused.

"Sent us a letter!" Emmett rooted around his coat pockets until he found the crumpled advertisement for the Hidden Hearth Inn. "This was the only piece of correspondence sent to the pickle shop that wasn't a bill, remember?" Emmett continued. "Since when do we get vacation advertisements in the mail? What if it's really a coded message?" He smoothed out the paper and pointed to the name of the inn. "Hidden Hearth. Swap two letters and it's Hidden Hertha."

Molly jumped onto her chair, howling with glee. "It has to be! Read the rest! Read the rest!"

Robot leaned over. "Is this a riddle? I like riddles. I know a good one about a talking banana and—"

"Not now," said Molly. She, Emmett, Edison, and Robot crowded around the paper. (Dr. Stinkums snored nearby under a pile of shredded velvet.)

Has life become too hectic? Do you feel like you're always on the run? Make your getaway to the HIDDEN

HEARTH INN *in beautiful Petalsburg, Virginia. If you're feeling the troubles of the modern world* <u>encroach</u> *upon your day, you're guaranteed to find a* <u>good night</u> *here at the inn. The intersection of Shea Road and Walter Street* <u>marks</u> *the spot for a peaceful respite that will revitalize your energy and spark your creativity. The Hidden Hearth is so good for you, it should be against the* <u>law not</u> *to visit! So, stop by for a tasty beverage, put your feet up, and shake hands with Mother Nature!*

"*Mother* Nature!" Molly squealed. "That's a good sign!"

"And a very common phrase," said Edison.

"But wait. Look how 'good night' is underlined," Emmett added. "Sarah Goode, Margaret Knight. That could be their way of letting us know it's from them."

"There's more than one underlined bit, though," said Edison.

"'Marks' is underlined too," Molly said, vibrating with excitement. "Hertha Marks! How did we not notice this before?"

"Probably because of the state we were in when Jasper first handed us this letter," said Emmett.

"New York?" asked Robot.

"Our emotional state," Emmett clarified. "Exhausted, disappointed, distracted, worried—none of us were in the right frame of mind for spotting encrypted clues just then. We need to forgive ourselves for thinking this was just a silly advertisement."

"It still might be," Edison said. "Unless one of your friends is named 'Encroach,' these underlined words might be mere coincidence."

Molly racked her brain. This letter *had* to be from the MOI. But the other underlined words and phrases didn't hint to the ladies in the group. "No," she said sadly. "There's just Josephine Cochrane and Mary Walton left."

"Do riddle-makers ever misspell things?" Robot asked. "Because 'encroach' has all the same letters as 'Cochrane.' But in the wrong order."

"It's an anagram! Just like 'hearth'!" Emmett said. "Robot, you're a genius!"

"That is even better than a knight," said Robot.

"You bet your metal mustache it is!" Molly cheered. "And it explains the last underlined bit too: 'law not.' That's Walton! No denying it—this is from the MOI!"

"But what are they telling us to do?" Emmett asked.

"I think that much is obvious," said Edison. "We go to the intersection of Shea and Walter in Petalsburg, Virginia."

"Where is that? Far?" Molly asked. Edison was already unrolling a map.

"Less than twelve miles outside DC, as luck would have it," the inventor replied. "And I may have a way for us to get there. I have a regular cab driver I use when

241

I'm in Washington. Bumbles, his name is. Bit of an oaf, but he knows his way around and, more importantly, he knows how to keep his mouth shut. I know we need to watch out for possible imposters, but I can't imagine Rector even knows Bumbles exists, let alone that he has a connection to me."

"Woo-hoo!" Molly cried. "We're gonna solve a mystery! And find the Mothers of Invention! The Investigators' Guild is back!" She got suddenly wistful. "Aw, I miss Roald."

Emmett smiled. "Yeah, if he were here, he'd say, 'I am very good at finding hiding people!'"

Edison's office door flew open. "What a coincidence! *I* am also very good at finding hiding people," said someone silhouetted in the doorway.

Cassandra Pepper stepped into the light. "As evidence, I present this very moment!" she said.

Captain Lee marched into the office after her and slammed the door.

"Look, Molly and Emmett," Robot said cheerily. "Your mother and father have joined us."

"Papa!" Emmett reeled.

"What? But—Mother? What? How?" Molly stammered.

"It is a good thing you are here, Mrs. Pepper," said Robot. "It sounds like Molly is broken."

"Ah, Mrs. Pepper. A pleasure as always," Edison said

drolly. He offered his hand to the captain. "And you must be the boy's father. Congratulations on not being dead. Now, I'm going to ask the question I assume the children were attempting to spit out: How did you get here?"

"We built a motorcar," Cassandra said, as if the answer had been obvious. She focused on Molly. "Do you have any idea how many carrot-peeler motors it takes to get up to fifty miles per hour?"

"And carrot peelers do not hold up well at that speed," Captain Lee added with a frown.

"Our vehicle stopped working a few miles outside the city," Cassandra said. "And then fell apart. And caught fire."

Molly winced.

"I'm just glad you're both okay," said Emmett.

"Us? Oh, yes, we're fine," said Cassandra.

"You, on the other hand . . ." Captain Lee blasted his son with a searing glare. "Take us to the Daedalus Chariot now. We can discuss punishments on the way home. If you'll excuse us, Mr. Edison . . ." He reached for the doorknob.

"Not so fast." Edison rushed past him to block their exit. "Your little rapscallions dragged me into this colossal cluster of danger and mayhem—you don't get to just stroll out of here with them and leave me to deal with Ambrose Rector by myself. Besides, the Feds have your flying machine."

"They what?" Cassandra's nostrils flared. Until she closed her eyes and took a deep breath. "I am going to pretend I didn't hear that part. I'll have time for seething inner turmoil later. What's this about Rector? The children were right? He's actually here?"

Molly opened her mouth, but Edison cut her off.

"First answer my question," he said. "For the sake of all of our safety, I need to know how you got *here*—to this office. How did you know to find us here? The existence of this Club isn't public knowledge."

"Did the dog call you?" Robot guessed.

"No," said Cassandra. "Although that would have been fun. Wait, you brought the dog?"

Clumps of soil flew across the office as Dr. Stinkums began digging up a potted plant. Edison cleared his throat.

"Oh, yes," said Cassandra. "When we discovered you children had run off to Washington—"

"How'd you find out?" Emmett asked.

"Luddie and Orla," said the captain.

"No way!" Molly cried. "How'd you get them to talk?"

"Ice cream," said Cassandra.

"Traitors," Molly grumbled.

Edison cleared his throat again.

"Oh, yes. When we got here this morning, we saw a newspaper article about our children burgling the Smithsonian," said Cassandra.

"Oh, the punishments that are coming . . . ," Captain Lee said, shaking his head.

"We went by the museum and saw your big speechifying party out on the National Mall, Mr. Edison," Cassandra continued. "We figured our children might be with you, but you'd already left at that point. Luckily, we spotted some of your fellow Guildsmen in the crowd. We told them we were criminal fugitives who wanted to confer with Thomas Edison about his presidential campaign and they seemed quite eager to provide us with specific directions to your hideout."

Edison harrumphed. "That's what I get running an organization of backstabbers, I suppose."

Molly couldn't hold it in any longer. "Okay, enough!" she cried. "This detailed recap of how you found us is—well, it's pretty amazing, actually—but you have to save it for later! Right now, there's only one thing we should be talking about: Rector is turning the Washington Monument into a giant death ray."

"It's true, Papa," Emmett said. "Which is why I don't care how much you punish me—I'm not sorry I came here. There are too many lives at stake for any of us to sit on the sidelines. If we're going to thwart Rector's plan, we're going to need every brain we can get. That means you and Mrs. Pepper too. And the Mothers of Invention."

"You—you've found the MOI?" Cassandra asked.

"Not yet," Molly said. "But we can with your help.

Remember that odd advertisement that was mailed to us? It's a coded message from Hertha."

Cassandra bit her lip and turned to Captain Lee, who stood by silently, his jaw clenched.

"I can tell what you're thinking," said Edison. "'Why does this have to be my responsibility? I don't want to get involved.' I've been thinking the same thing. But you drove who-knows-how-far in a giant carrot peeler to get here. I'd say you're already involved."

"Only the vehicle's *engine* was made out of carrot peelers," Cassandra said. "It would be more accurate to say we drove a bathtub to get here."

"Our bathtub?" Molly gasped. "With the lion feet? I liked that tub!"

"Then maybe you shouldn't have run away," said Captain Lee.

"But your point is well taken, Mr. Edison," Cassandra continued. "Rector has made this everybody's fight."

Captain Lee sighed. "I suppose I have always wanted to meet the Mothers of Invention," he said. "I've heard many interesting stories. So, let's get to work. But not here. I'm reasonably certain those Guildsmen who directed us here also hired some reporters to follow us in hopes they might catch you conferring with fugitives. You wouldn't happen to have any hidden passages out of this place, would you?"

"We're an organization of rich, secretive men," Edison

scoffed. "*Of course* we have a hidden passage." He twisted the horn on the unicorn lamp and a camouflaged doorway opened in the wall.

"Ooh, this room has a mouth," Robot said, clambering to the passageway.

"Slow down. I've still got presidential aspirations to protect," said Edison. "In case the press is lying in wait out there, I should make sure I'm disguised."

"Here," Robot said, planting the stringy mop-wig back onto Edison's head. "You dropped this outside."

Grumbling, Edison entered the tunnel. As the others began to file in after him, Emmett grabbed his father. "Thank you, Papa."

The captain smiled and patted him on the back. "I have one important question for you," he said. "Why is the dog here?"

"I think Dr. Stinkums considers Robot his pet," Emmett said.

"Only with this group would that make sense," the captain replied as the mutt scampered past them into the tunnel, one of Thomas Edison's spare bow ties in his mouth.

Emmett and his father laughed.

"You're still getting punished when we get home."

Emmett sighed. "I know."

Return of the Investigators' Guild
Petalsburg, Virginia, October 20, 1884

"So, BUMBLES, YOU ever meet the president?" Molly asked. While her mother, Emmett, Captain Lee, Thomas Edison, Robot, and Dr. Stinkums were all crammed inside the horse-drawn carriage, Molly happily volunteered to sit up next to the driver on their ride to Virginia.

The driver seemed less happy about it.

"Why would I have met the president?" he scoffed in a British accent that wasn't nearly as fancy-sounding as Hertha's. He was an older man with a white ponytail, sunken eyes, and a cauliflower-esque odor. He picked something from his teeth and shook the reins to speed up his horses. "An' stop callin' me Bumbles."

"It's your name, isn't it?" Molly said with a shrug. She didn't care if the man wasn't feeling chatty—she was bored. They'd been rumbling down endless, identical country roads for nearly three hours now. "Anyway, Bumbles, you drive a coach around the nation's capital. It's not crazy to think you might've met the president."

"I reckon he's got his own people to ferry 'im around," said the driver.

"Well, *I've* met President Arthur," said Molly. "I've swung from his sideburns."

"Of course you have," the man droned.

"Don't be jealous, Bumbles," Molly said. "If Edison wins the election, then you'll get to say you've met the president."

"How thrilling for me."

"That's the spirit, Bumbles," Molly said. "You're from England, right?"

"Once upon a time," he said, slumping as if the conversation were sapping all his energy.

"I could tell," Molly said proudly. "I have a British friend, you know. But she's very Jane Austen-y. You've got more of a Dickens kind of thing going on."

Bumbles jerked back on the reins, bringing the horses to a sudden halt. The coach jolted and Molly almost slid off her seat. "We're here," Bumbles said with a smirk.

Molly flashed him a nasty look, but was quickly distracted by the weather-beaten road sign that read WELCOME TO PETALSBURG, POPULATION 108.

Edison leaned out the window. "Excellent, Bumbles," he said. "Now take us to that intersection we mentioned."

"Must you call me that?" the driver groaned.

As they rolled slowly along the dirt road, Molly thought about how disappointed her mother must have been by the view. Despite its adorable name, Petalsburg had more waist-high weeds than pretty flowers. The few houses they saw had boarded windows, peeling paint, and poorly patched roofs. Molly saw plenty of empty cans and broken wagon wheels, but not one of the 108 people who supposedly lived there.

After a few minutes, the coach stopped again.

"What are you doing, Bumbles?" Molly asked.

The driver pointed to the crooked, weather-worn street signs at the nearest corner. Shea Road and Walter Street.

Molly hopped down to the dusty road. Could this really be where they were supposed to go? The only building here was a tiny, run-down cube of a factory with weeds growing out of the cracks in its cement walls. She ran to peek through a window, only to find that there weren't any, just a single metal door with a sign over it that she assumed had, at one time, read STEAM WORKS (the "M" was now lying in the dirt and the first "S" was dangling upside down from loose nails).

Behind her, the carriage door opened and the passengers began stumbling out, stretching their stiff limbs. "Thank heavens! I can finally get away from that wire-haired menace!" Edison snapped. "Look at my shoe!" He lifted one foot to show everyone his big toe wiggling through the drool-coated hole in the leather. "Do you know what these shoes cost? I don't! I have an assistant to do my shopping. But I assume they're impressively expensive!"

"We, um, need to keep a low profile," Emmett warned, trying to hush him.

"Who's going to hear us?" Edison scoffed, adjusting the mop on his head. "This town is emptier than one of Grover Cleveland's campaign rallies."

"Why *have* we gotten out here?" Captain Lee asked, surveying his dismal surroundings. "This can't be the inn."

"For crying out crumpets, there ain't any inn in this rubbish hamlet," the coach driver moaned. "You're gettin' out here 'cause here's where you told me to take you. And you lot best not think you'll be stiffin' my fee on account of you ain't chuffed about the scenery."

"You talk funny," Robot said to him.

"You're a bucket," Bumbles shot back.

"I'm pretty sure the Hidden Hearth Inn doesn't exist," said Emmett, scanning the front of the dull gray building. "The letter was just disguised as an advertisement so it could lead us to this spot."

"To *this* dump?" Edison asked.

"Not necessarily this building, I suppose," said Emmett. "But there's got to be another clue somewhere near this intersection."

"Yeah, maybe this is just the first stop on a thrilling

scavenger hunt," Molly said with more than a little excitement. She pushed aside tufts of tall grass with her feet, examining the ground below. "Maybe they've left some sort of hint here that tells us where to look next. Come on, ladies. Give us a sign."

"They did," Cassandra said plainly. "Tea Works. To be truthful, I would have rather it had been the Coffee Works . . ."

Molly hopped with excitement. "Mother, you're brilliant!"

"Oh, Molly, now you're just flattering me," Cassandra replied. "It wasn't *that* good a joke."

"I don't think any of us realized it *was* a joke, Mother," Molly said. "I'm talking about what you noticed with the sign! It was broken on purpose! Tea is Hertha's favorite drink! Josephine's too! They're always *tea, tea, tea*! And they know we know that! Don't you think it's too much of a coincidence for this sign—located at the very intersection mentioned in the letter—to have accidentally spelled out 'tea works'?"

"Something tells me you'll be unhappy if I say no," said Captain Lee.

"Papa, she's right," Emmett said, unfolding the advertisement from his pocket. "We know the MOI; this kind of clue is just their sort of thing. And look, the letter even told us to 'stop by for a tasty beverage'!"

"Don't you get it?" Molly asked. "This sign is the sign!

The MOI are in there!" She placed her hand on the door handle and yelped as a jolt of electricity shocked her. She jumped back, shaking her stinging fingers.

"What happened?" her mother asked, rushing to examine her hand.

"It's . . . electrified," Molly said, blowing on her fingertips.

"Electrified?" Edison scoffed. "How? There are no poles or wires out here. Let me—" He grabbed the door handle—*zzzt!*—and leapt away, yowling.

"That was one hundred percent your own fault," said Emmett.

"Maybe I can do it," said Robot. "I have no skin." He clomped over to the door, touched one metal finger to the handle, and blew backward with a pop. Barking angrily, Dr. Stinkums leapt at the door. *Zzzzt!* The dog ran back into the coach, whimpering and smelling of singed fur.

"Okay, nobody else try to open the door!" Captain Lee shouted.

Bumbles chuckled from the driver's seat of his coach. "Barmiest bunch of blokes I ever had the displeasure . . ."

"Robot, are you okay?" Molly asked.

The mechanical man was lying in the grass, sporadically sparking. Cassandra crouched beside him and gave him a shake. He didn't move. She shook him again. And again. On the fourth shake, Robot finally sat up. "That was unpleasant," he said.

"Can we all at least agree that the Mothers of Invention meant for us to find this building?" Emmett said after a sigh of relief. "Who else is going to use electricity as a defense mechanism?"

"Maybe the letter tells us how to get in," Cassandra suggested.

Emmett went back to the coded ad. "We figured out the 'tasty beverage' part, so, after that, it says, 'put your feet up, and shake hands with Mother Nature.'"

"Put your feet up," Molly echoed. "Do we kick the door?"

"Please don't," said Captain Lee.

"Maybe they just want us to relax until we think up a solution," said Cassandra.

"I could make my feet go up," said Robot. "But that would be flying and then Molly would get angry."

"Oh, but is Robot right? Could the next clue be on the roof?" asked the captain. "Surely a little flight like that wouldn't do much damage."

"Unfortunately, a lot more damage has already been done since we left Ohio," Emmett said.

"Robot has used his powers a bunch of times to get us out of jams," Molly admitted. "We didn't want him to—told him not to—but—but—" She stammered as tears unexpectedly stung her eyes.

"But Molly and Emmett could have been hurt if I had not helped," Robot said. "You look upset, Mrs. Pepper.

But please do not be angry with Molly. She has been very protective of me. And I am protective of her and Emmett. Just as you are."

Cassandra nodded. Molly knew her mother would have behaved the same way Robot did if their situations had been reversed. Emmett probably would too. Even Captain Lee. She was suddenly overwhelmed with gratitude for having so many people in her life who cared for her so deeply. She would have pulled them into a group hug at that very moment, if not for the awkwardness of Edison and Bumbles watching.

"How much rock is left?" Cassandra asked solemnly.

Molly held her fingers a pea's length apart and her mother closed her eyes mournfully.

"But, um, hey, everybody," Emmett said, trying to break the melancholy that had fallen over the group. "Robot can get us to the roof without flying!"

Five minutes later, Robot's hand-winch had carried everyone to the roof of the Tea Works—except for Bumbles, who remained with his coach, snacking on a raw onion.

"Wow," said Molly, looking over the edge of the twelve-foot wall. "We're so *not* high up."

"This whole place is so weird," said Emmett. "I wonder if the MOI built it just as a puzzle for us."

"Or as a puzzle for *themselves*," said Cassandra. "And they made it so difficult, they couldn't find their way out, and that's why no one's seen them for a year."

"What was the next part of the letter?" Captain Lee asked. "Something about Mother Nature?"

"'Shake hands with Mother Nature,'" Emmett read.

"Well, there's a whole lot of nature on this roof," Molly said, wading through the branches, leaves, and other detritus that blanketed the tarry square. "Looks like a century's worth of autumn up here."

Edison harrumphed. "Why do these women have to make everything so difficult? What's wrong with a good old-fashioned alphanumeric code? One equals A, two equals B—easy!"

"I'm not sure *easy* is what you want when you're hiding from every law enforcement agency in the country," said Cassandra.

"We don't even know if coming up to the roof was the correct thing to do!" Edison griped. "'Put your feet up' could have meant a bazillion different things! But now we're all wandering on a roof, looking for Mother Nature! Who, I might remind you, is not a real person and, therefore, does not have hands!"

"This must not be her, then," Robot said, pulling aside a leaf-coated tarp to reveal a small statue of a pleasant-faced older woman in a flowy gown with a wreath of flowers in her hair.

"Well, that clue was more literal than expected," said Captain Lee.

Molly smiled at the statue's familiar face. "It looks like Mary Walton."

"Well, what are we waiting for?" Cassandra asked. She took the statue's hand and let out a gleeful gasp when it shifted downward like a lever. A small, circular hatch in the rooftop slid open, causing a shower of dead leaves to sprinkle down into the building. When the commotion settled, the group could see a ladder at the rim of the opening.

"I guarantee Sarah built that," said Emmett.

"Shall we?" Molly asked, already at the top of the ladder.

Edison stepped to the edge of the roof and called to his coachman. "We're going in, Bumbles! Drive back to the edge of town and wait for us there! In the unlikely event anyone should pass by, I don't want you sitting out there like a big banner that says 'something strange going on here.'"

"My name ain't bloomin' Bumbles," the driver grumbled before flicking the reins and starting his coach back the way they'd come.

Molly descended in total darkness—the factory had no windows. But the moment she stepped down from the final rung, she was suddenly bathed in warm electric light. The building appeared to be one large room, the entirety of which was now illuminated by rows of glowing bulbs that ringed the ceiling.

"What just happened?" Emmett asked, descending above her.

"Lights came on by themselves," Molly reported. "How did they do that?"

Emmett hit the ground and the room was pitched once more into blackness. "My guess is a pressure switch in the floor tile below the ladder," he said. He tapped his foot and the lights flashed back on.

Grinning uncontrollably, Molly nudged him aside and hopped on the tile. Lights off. She jumped again. Lights on. Off. On. Off. On. Off. On.

"Okay, Molly, we get it," Emmett said, guiding her away from the ladder to make way for the others.

"I remember when you used to be fun," she groused.

"What in the world was going on with those lights?" Cassandra questioned as she climbed down. The lights shut off as she stepped from the ladder.

"There's a trigger switch underneath you!" Molly joyfully explained.

"Ooh, that's clever!" Cassandra began bouncing. On. Off. On. Off. On. Off.

"Mrs. Pepper?" Emmett said.

Cassandra stopped with the lights on and joined her daughter. "I do miss our adventures," she said.

Edison and Captain Lee descended the ladder, while Robot, who could not quite fit through the hole, remained on the roof as lookout. Once everybody was down—and done jumping on the light switch—the group examined the bizarre chamber, which was definitely *not* a factory. In fact, it looked more like a café. There was a trio of restaurant-style tables and a shop counter with a paper bag sitting on it. Behind that was a wall of shelves, the highest of which was lined with porcelain teacups.

Cassandra laughed. "Ha! Tea Works, see? I was right, after all."

Then they noticed that the lower shelves were stocked with pickle jars.

"Anybody still think this might not be intended for us?" Molly said with a smirk. She got no arguments.

"But what are we supposed to do here?" Edison asked, randomly touching tables and chairs. "More riddles? Or did these women simply plan a lunch break into our wild-goose chase?"

Captain Lee looked inside the bag on the counter. "Empty," he said.

"Oh, but that's one of Margaret's paper bags," Molly said.

"You recognize a specific paper bag?" the captain asked. "They all look the same."

"No, I mean Margaret *invented* those bags," Molly explained.

"Oh, that *is* impressive," said the captain. "These are *everywhere.*"

"Yes, and that bag *must* be part of the puzzle," Molly said. "Can I see it?"

Captain Lee attempted to pick up the paper bag, but it

didn't move. "I think it's glued down," he said.

"Well, tear it free," said Edison. "Put some muscle into it, man. It's just paper!"

"Mr. Edison," Cassandra warned. "You have obviously never run a pickle shop. When you have a paper bag on your counter, you fill it. With pickles!"

Together, the Lees and Peppers began stacking as many pickle jars as they could into the bag. After the tenth jar, the weight of the pickles must have triggered another hidden switch, because the bag slowly sank into the countertop. As it vanished, a previously hidden door closed over it and a second secret panel slid open across the room, on one of the mysterious shop's little tabletops. A full place setting rose up from inside the table—china plate and crystal drinking glass, knife to the right, spoon, fork, and folded napkin to the left—all ready for a formal meal.

"Was I, uh, right about the lunch?" Edison asked.

"Maybe it's another pressure switch," Emmett said. "Take some of the pickles out and try them here."

"We can't," said his father. "They're *in* the counter."

"No, there's one left!" said Cassandra. She grabbed the final pickle jar and set it on the plate. Nothing happened.

"Empty them onto the dish," Captain Lee suggested.

"Or maybe sit in the chair," Emmett added.

"Break the plate!" said Edison.

"How about I try eating them?" Cassandra said. "I can't tell you how much I've been missing pickles. There's not nearly enough vinegar in my diet these days."

Molly shook her head in disapproval. "Do none of you see it?"

"See what?" Emmett asked.

"The place setting is wrong," she replied. "Believe me, I've heard Josephine rant about incorrect table settings enough times to know that the spoon belongs on the right with the knife." As soon as Molly reset the spoon into its proper place, they heard a click behind the counter. A miniature spotlight was shining down onto one particular teacup.

Cassandra rushed to the illuminated cup, snatched it down, and peeked inside. "Drat, no tea," she said. She tipped it to show the others some writing on the inside. "There is, however, an address. Seventy-two Phipps Lane. I think we know where we're going next."

A short pickle snack later, Molly popped up onto the roof again. Robot met her crouched at the opening, with one finger at his mouth to signal for quiet. Molly shushed the others ascending behind her. "What is it?" she whispered to Robot.

"Down on the street," Robot answered in a low tone. "The man who does not like me."

Molly peeked over the roof's edge and saw Agent Clark skulking down the block, his head turning this way and that as he scanned the area. "No way!" Molly whispered.

Emmett crawled up beside her and groaned. Their

parents and Thomas Edison soon followed, all gawking with the same disbelief.

"How is that man here?" Cassandra whispered in frustration. "How could he know?"

"Was it Bumbles?" Molly snapped her head toward Edison. "Did Bumbles betray us?"

"No, look," Emmett warned. "Clark might not be after *us* at all." Crouched among a thicket of weeds, visible from their high vantage point but hidden from Agent Clark, was a black-clad man with a Hephaestus mask.

"Clark must be looking for Rector!" Molly blurted, louder than she intended. "But why is *Rector* here? Did he follow us or—"

"Molly, shhh!"

Agent Clark's head spun up toward the roof. His sparkly blue eyes went wide upon spotting Molly and Emmett. He had clearly *not* been expecting to find them here.

"Drat," Molly cursed.

"Stay where you are!" Clark shouted up at them. "You are under—"

Molly assumed he was going to say "arrest," but he never got the chance. Rector charged him from behind and jabbed him in the back with a strange metal rod. There was an electric sizzling sound as the federal agent jolted in pain and then slumped to the grass, unmoving. The masked villain then ran off toward the edge of town.

"Did Rector just . . . save us?" Cassandra asked.

"I don't know if he even saw us," said Emmett. "Clark did, but Rector never looked up this way. Maybe he thought Clark was talking to him."

"Who cares?" said Edison. "We're in the clear now. Let's scamper off while we can! You, Can-Head, lower us down!"

"Hee hee, that is not my name," Robot said with a sound that approximated a laugh. "You are silly, Mr. Edison."

Once the whole team was back on the ground—and it was determined that Rector was no longer in the vicinity—Emmett rushed to check on Agent Clark.

"Still breathing," he reported.

"I suppose it was only a matter of time before Clark caught on to his schemes," Edison said. "The old boy's been pretty active over the past forty-eight hours or so."

"Okay, so maybe Clark followed Rector here, but why did Rector come to Petalsburg in the first place?" added Molly. "Has he been following *us*? Or did Rector have his own business here?" She gasped. "Do you think he could be tracking the MOI too?"

"If there's even a chance of that, we must locate your friends first, no?" said Captain Lee.

"What about him?" Cassandra asked of Agent Clark, who was splayed out in the dirt beside the road.

"Eh, he'll come to eventually," said Edison. "And I'm

guessing you people don't want to be around when he does."

"No," said Molly. And the group headed off on foot in search of Phipps Lane, checking over their shoulders the whole time.

Petalsburg was a ghost town. For the life of her, Molly couldn't figure out what would have brought Rector here if he didn't know about the letter from the MOI. But she didn't have long to worry about it.

"It's here! Seventy-two!" Captain Lee called out just a few blocks later. The house in question was a standard colonial-style home in no better shape than the rest of the town. The brown paint was chipped, the roof tiles curled, the lawn overgrown, and the window shutters hanging askew. Molly walked up to the cracked wooden door, but stopped before grabbing the knob.

"Um, anybody else wanna try opening this one?" she asked.

Before anyone could answer, the door opened from within.

"No worries, love," said Hertha Marks, standing there in a glorious lavender dress with peacock feather fringe. "We've been watching for you ever since you triggered the alarm in our puzzle room."

Molly threw her arms around the woman.

"I missed you too, Molly," Hertha said. "Now, if everybody would come inside quickly—this is a *secret* hideout and we prefer not to have large crowds standing outside our door in broad daylight."

The rest of the group hurried in and—shuffling awkwardly because Molly's arms were still clamped around her—Hertha locked the door. Molly finally let go when she realized how amazing the interior of the house was. The dilapidation outside was all a smoke screen. Inside, the MOI's hideout was sparkling clean, its walls lined with all manner of tools and engineering implements. Electric lamps illuminated metallic worktables, on which were displayed the many intriguing gadgets the Mothers must have been hard at work on over the past year. Most excitingly, the rest of the team was there too.

Molly, Emmett, and Cassandra exchanged warm greetings with everyone.

"I knew you'd solve our puzzles," Sarah Goode said, beaming. She wore a bright green blouse with a blue kerchief around her neck, and brown pants. Molly was happy to see that she too had discovered the benefits of wearing trousers for work. "Hertha very wisely suggested that we not put clues to our specific location in our letter to you, in case someone else intercepted it. So we came up with the factory idea—only someone who knew us would be able to solve it! Even still, we had to make the puzzles really challenging to keep away any unwanted so-and-sos. But I knew they wouldn't stop you. I believed in you!"

"Oh, hush, Sarah," Mary Walton scoffed good-naturedly. "We all knew they'd figure it out."

"Well, okay," said Sarah. "But I said it most."

"You certainly took your time getting around to it, though," Mary added. The older woman had her wild gray hair tucked under a floral knit cap. "But, hey, better late than never. And we certainly are happy to see you all."

"The pickle puzzle was really clever," Emmett said enthusiastically. "And so was 'feet up' to tell us to go on the roof. And the sign that said 'Tea Works.' And—"

"Just please tell me one thing," said Josephine Cochrane, buttoned up in a formal black dress, as usual. "Who figured out the table setting?"

Molly took a bow.

"That's my girl," Josephine said proudly. "But, please, dear—curtsy. You're not a butler."

Just being in Josephine's presence, Molly stood a little bit straighter. "I should've figured you'd still be all gussied up in frills and corsets and such," Molly said. "Even though you're living in hiding and literally no one is going to see you."

Josephine raised her chin. "It's teatime, darling, why would I wear anything less?"

"Yeah, I dressed up for you too." Margaret Knight, clad in grease-spattered coveralls, chuckled as she removed her goggles. The pink rings around her eyes were the only clean parts of her face. She set down the gizmo she was building and shook hands with Cassandra. "Working on anything exciting?" Margaret asked.

"The captain and I rode two hundred miles in a bathtub powered by carrot peelers," Cassandra said.

"I'd like to see that," said Margaret.

"It exploded," said Cassandra.

"Makes me even more interested," said Margaret.

Hertha shook hands with Emmett's father. "This must be the mysterious captain of which you speak."

"Oh, yes!" Emmett said, remembering himself. "Everyone, this is my father, Captain Wendell Lee. He's, um, back from the dead."

"Or, as most people call it, Antarctica," said the captain.

"You must have some amazing stories to tell," said Sarah.

"That's what the children say," said the captain.

"Oh, Robot's here too," Margaret said, giving a hug to the metal man.

"That is very observant of you, Miss Knight. I am indeed here," said Robot. "Unfortunately, the most fascinating member of our party, Dr. Stinkums, is still hiding in the coach."

"A doctor?" Mary asked.

"He's a dog," said Molly. "But that's not important now. We need your help."

"We assumed," said Hertha. "Since you finally came out of hiding to seek us out. Does it have something to do with you two burgling the Smithsonian Institution?"

"Well, yes," Molly continued, speaking rapidly. "We thought there might be Ambrosium in there, but there wasn't, and Robot is running out of his, because it degrades every time he uses his powers, and we need you to figure out how to stop it and save him."

The women's concern showed on their faces. "We will spare no effort to help a friend," said Josephine. "Even one held together by bolts and screws."

"Oh, but that's not all—" Molly began.

"Very clever window design here," said Edison, who'd been quietly examining the room. He still had the mop on his head. "Soundproof, I assume. Are they airtight as well?"

"Of course," said Margaret.

"Perfect," said Edison, running his fingers around the doorframe.

"And, um, who is this final member of your little squad?" Hertha asked.

"Oh, yeah—the wig! Don't worry, that's just Thomas Edison," said Emmett. "Mr. Edison, you can take off your disguise now."

"Oh, I think I shall," Edison replied. He began chuckling. "You know, this whole time there was a little part of me holding out hope that one of you would set me up with a perfect line like that. But I never want to get too hopeful with you mudskulls. Just leads to disappointment most of the time."

Everyone stared in confusion as Edison tossed his mop-wig to the floor. "But thank you, Emmett," he continued. "Because 'you can take off your disguise now'—I mean, wow, it's not going to get much more perfect than that, is it?" He peeled off his fake eyebrows, plucked off his fake nose, and scraped away his fake chin. "And wow again, because—look at your faces. I have to say, I don't know if you're more stunned by me revealing myself or by your own stupidity, because I cannot believe you fell for this *again*! Same disguise! Same impersonation! At first, I said to myself, no, don't try Edison *again*—that's way too obvious. But then I was like, no, let me do the thing they'd *most* expect and see if it fools them. And it did!"

"But—but—" Molly stammered.

"Sorry, kid, no time for mumbling," said Ambrose Rector. "Because you've done me the favor of getting me into a room with literally every person who has ever thwarted me in the past. Time for—"

Hertha snapped into action. "Ladies, Plan Twelve!"

The women each began to step off in different directions, but Rector was too quick. He whipped a small glass vial from his pocket and shattered it on the floor. A noxious scent instantly filled the room and people began collapsing. Molly grabbed her mother's hand and started for the door. Before she could take two steps, she felt the tug of her mother dropping to the ground. Molly tried to scream, but couldn't find her voice. The room grew blurry around her. She saw Emmett stumble into the wall. Molly tried to take another step, but her feet were too heavy to lift. And she was so, so tired. She fell, first to her knees, then onto her side. The last thing she saw was Ambrose Rector's pasty face smirking down at her.

"The thing I'm happiest about"—his voice sounded like it was underwater—"is that you never, ever learn. Good night, Molly Pepper."

PART III

21

A Dastardlier Plot
Undisclosed location, October 21, 1884

THE FIRST THING Molly saw when she opened her eyes was bars. *I'm too young to have woken up in this many prison cells,* she thought. She was in a freestanding cage, a cramped cubicle of iron bars with barely enough space to curl up on its cold metal floor. She gently lifted her pounding head and tried to scope out her surroundings. But she could not shake the blurriness from her eyes.

"Your spectacles, Molls," she heard her mother say from somewhere nearby. "They're on the floor by your knee."

Molly felt for her glasses and put them on. With her vision back in focus, she saw that Cassandra was in a separate cell a few feet away from hers. Captain Lee, in yet another cell beyond her mother's, greeted her with a sad little nod.

"Rector," Molly muttered as she suddenly remembered what had happened. "I don't understand. How could Rector be Edison? We saw Rector and Edison at the same time. Rector tried to *kill* Edison right in front of us."

"Rector's got an accomplice, someone pretending to be him, while he pretended to be Edison." The response came from Emmett, caged on the other side of whatever room they were in. "It's the only explanation. The masked man at the rally never spoke. It could have been anyone."

"Bumbles," Molly spat. "No way that guy isn't evil." She stood and gave her cell door a shake.

"Save your energy, love," said Hertha. "He's got us all locked in tight."

Molly rose and looked around as her eyes adjusted to the dimness. She could see now that the large room was almost entirely filled with prison cells. There were fifteen freestanding cages just like hers, arranged in a three-by-five grid, with narrow paths in between them. Most of the cells had occupants. Emmett was locked up on the opposite side of the room, already busy checking every inch of his cell for a flaw he could exploit. Many of the cages in between him and Molly held members of the Mothers of Invention, each detained individually. Sarah waved, while Mary worriedly wrung out her knit cap and Hertha tried to find a comfortable sitting position on the floor of her cell, a feat made impossible by her big-bustled skirt. Josephine was using a handful of feathers (presumably plucked from Hertha's dress) to dust her cell, and Margaret was patting herself down, checking the many pockets on her coveralls. "That scallywag took all my tools," she grumbled.

Molly's gut churned. Everyone who could have conceivably come to her aid was locked up with her. And she didn't even know *where* they were being held. Rector could have taken them anywhere while they were unconscious. The walls and floor around them were bare gray concrete, devoid of any identifying characteristics, save the metallic panel lined with toggle switches mounted next to the door. Other than that and the cells, the room contained only some shoddy wooden chairs and a table, upon which a large, lumpy something-or-other sat covered by a white sheet.

"I'm sorry," Molly said, the weight of her guilt forcing her back to the floor. "This is all our fault. You ladies managed to avoid detection for a *year*. Then, three seconds after you open your doors to us—*slam!*"

"Rector used you to get to us," Hertha said in a tone that was probably meant to make Molly feel better, but didn't.

"I, for one, am glad for the company," said a familiar male voice. Molly peered toward the back of the chamber. In one of the farthest cells sat Thomas Edison.

"Don't panic," said Mary. "He's the real thing."

Molly squinted at him. "Tell me something only the real Edison would know," she said.

Edison fumbled around in his coat pockets and pulled out a handful of loose gears and broken metal rods. "You broke this," he said bitterly. "I'm still trying to remember how it goes back together."

"Trust me, it's him," said the man in the cell next to Edison's. "Just as annoying as ever."

"Mr. Bell!" Molly exclaimed. "So the bit about you being kidnapped was true?"

"Sadly, yes," said Alexander Graham Bell. He slumped in the corner of his cell, his suit wrinkled and his beard haggard. "You know, if you hadn't abandoned me on that ship, none of this might have—"

"Oh, quiet down," Cassandra snapped. "You know full well you were going to turn us in when you reached New York."

Bell lowered his head. "I wouldn't say *full* well," he grumbled. "Half well, maybe. I hadn't decided yet. It was a tricky situation. But I know for certain that if you hadn't run off, I would never have agreed to meet up with that ersatz Edison when he offered to help me find you."

"So, you got yourself captured trying to capture the Peppers?" Sarah said. "I officially take back the sympathy I gave you."

Emmett paused his search for hidden escape routes. He looked suddenly queasy.

"Are you all right, dear?" asked Josephine.

"Yeah, I just . . . um . . ." Emmett turned to the men in the rear cages. "Mr. Edison, how long have you been here?"

Edison counted silently on his fingers, then looked up. "I've lost track. Is it eleven or twelve?"

"Days? Or weeks?" Hertha asked with concern.

"Months," came the answer.

Molly's mouth grew dry. "We've been working with Rector this entire time?" she squeaked out.

"So this is the first time I'm meeting the actual Thomas Edison?" Captain Lee asked, scratching his head. "Hmm, not sure which one I like better."

"I'm confused," said Cassandra. "What about your presidential campaign?"

Edison's thick eyebrows shot up. "I'm running for president?"

"Technically speaking," said Hertha. "Though, as it is now patently clear, it's Rector who has been running under your name."

"Me as president?" Edison laughed. "Well, that's all the proof we need that the man is a lunatic. I'm not even a politician. Why would anyone consider voting for me?"

"You're winning," said Josephine.

Edison leapt to his feet with renewed vigor. "Get me

277

out of here—I'm going to be president!"

"Sit back down, Tommy Boy." The room's thick steel door swung open and Rector strode in.

Molly scowled at the villain. He wore no mask this time, no makeup—just his own pasty, sweat-glistened face. He'd changed clothes, though, from his brown-checked "Edison" outfit to his preferred long-tailed black suit. In his right hand, he casually twirled what looked like a two-foot-long aluminum baton—the mysterious weapon that had zapped Agent Clark into unconsciousness. "You're not going to be president, Tommo," Rector continued. "You're not going to be anything, because you're never leaving that cell. But, hey, at least you won't have to endure it much longer. Why's that, you ask?"

"I didn't," Edison said dourly. "I'm assuming it's a death threat."

"It is," Rector said plainly. "I've only been keeping you alive long enough to witness my ultimate triumph. And like the racing aardvark whose impressive tongue crosses the finish line long before his feet, I can taste victory already."

"I see your analogies are as sharp as ever," said Molly. She might be behind bars, but she refused to act like this man's prisoner. She stood tall—chin up, shoulders back—and stared him in the eye.

"As, I see, is your sarcasm," Rector returned with a devilish grin.

"Molly," Captain Lee warned from his cell.

"How are you even here?" Cassandra asked, voicing a question that was probably running through most of the heads in that room. "We left you in Antarctica. With no food, no shelter, no transportation. How in heaven's name did you get back?"

"That, um, that would be my fault," the real Edison said sheepishly. "You see, my buddy Bell here wasn't the only one who built a secret ship for a covert voyage to the South Pole."

"You what?" Bell glared at him from the adjacent cell.

"Oh, come on, Alec," Edison said. "Do you honestly think that, after finding out you were defying presidential orders to sneak off and find the South Pole, I wouldn't take a stab at getting there before you? Friendly competition! It's the Guild way!"

"Yeah, how'd that work out for you?" Margaret snarked.

"Well, for your information," Bell huffed, his face up against the bars of his cell, "I wasn't going against presidential orders! *I* had a secret deal with President Arthur!"

"Of course you did!" Edison snapped. "Well, let's see how many secret deals you make with the White House when I'm president!"

"You're not going to be president!" Rector shouted. "I am! Let's bring this back to me! Although I suppose I should thank you, Tom-Tom, for the ride home. You see, Mrs. Pepper, you did indeed leave me in a sorry state down there. But I didn't have to wait even a week before Edison's expedition arrived upon those snowy shores. Then it took me about—what would you say, Tom? Five minutes—to capture his crew and commandeer his ship. Once I sailed back to America with Edison as my prisoner, it felt like the situation was practically begging me to assume his identity again. It's poetic, isn't it? That I will end up taking over the United States government with the same disguise I used on my first attempt?"

"So, you're now hoping to become president *as* Edison," said Mary.

"Dear me, no!" Rector said. "When I rule this country, it's going to be as me, not this thistle-browed miscreant. And I'm going to take control the good old-fashioned way—by force! I don't even care about the election. I only decided to run for president because I was spending so much time in Washington and I couldn't bear all the attention going to those other two fools who are running. Seriously, have you seen those guys? Grover Cleveland is nothing more than a shrugging mustache. And who even is James G. Bland?"

"James G. *Blaine*," Sarah corrected.

"My point exactly!" Rector shouted. "If I hadn't forced myself into the mix, America would end up voting for one of those losers to rule them. Pah! You people don't deserve democracy. But deciding to throw myself into the competition has had scads of benefits for me. It's given me access to just about anywhere I want to go in this town. Plus, as it turns out, campaigning for president is fun. You get to hold big rallies, hear thousands of people screaming your name—"

"Pretty sure it was Edison's name they were yelling," Molly taunted. "Nobody even knows *your* name."

"Shh!" Captain Lee hissed. "Don't antagonize him!"

"Sheesh, Wendell," Rector said, turning his attention to the captain. "After three years in an ice cave, I figured you'd be better at keeping cool. You get it? 'Cool'? Because you were in Antarctica?"

Captain Lee gripped the bars of his cell with such intensity that Molly wondered if he might actually rip them loose. "That was your biggest mistake," the captain sneered.

"The 'cool' joke?" Rector asked. "I mean, it wasn't my best, but—"

"Leaving me alive in Antarctica. *That* was your mistake," Captain Lee said, seething. Everyone else fell silent. "You stole everything from me in that moment— my livelihood, my dreams, my *son*," the captain continued. "Keeping me from my boy for so long, forcing me to miss so much of his formative years, preventing me from seeing the man he would become, all while knowing he was missing me, assuming I was dead? That was a fate worse than death. But you underestimated me, Ambrose. Because I'm back now—three years stronger, three years smarter, and three years angrier. You should have taken me out when you had the chance."

"You realize I have the chance again *right now*, don't you?" Rector said. He waltzed up to Captain Lee's cell.

The captain stood firm at the bars, refusing even to blink.

Rector raised high his metal baton.

"Papa, no!" Emmett cried. "You don't need to do this! Back down! Please! I need you!"

Rector lowered his weapon. "Well, isn't that sweet?" he said. "Relax, Emmett, I'm not going to kill your father. *Yet.* I don't want his death to upstage my big moment, and I wouldn't put it past you people to still be crying over it then."

Emmett melted against the bars of his cell.

"Ha," Molly scoffed, hoping to break the tension. "We should've figured you wouldn't hurt any of us. No, you want to force us all to watch you erupt a volcano under the White House, or whatever it is you're planning. Your ego won't let us miss it."

"First of all," said Rector, "you talk about my ego like it's a bad thing. No one ever conquered the world without believing they could do it. Secondly, you're right—I can't wait to torture you all with screams of mind-melted Washingtonians. I want to see you all crushed by the

282

knowledge that you couldn't stop me, that your last acts on this Earth were an abysmal failure. It is almost as important to me as taking over the country. Why do you think I went through all those Machiavellian machinations to bring you all together? It would have been much simpler to kill each of you where I found you. But I need you all to be here for this, all of you who've bested me in the past. And for the record, that does *not* include Bell and Edison. Those two clodpoles have never bested anybody. I kidnapped them strictly for the torture and humiliation."

"Wait a minute. Did you say 'mind-melted Washingtonians'? You actually built another Mind-Melter?" Molly laughed. "I can't believe you really *are* using the same exact plan again!"

Rector scowled. "Do you have any idea what a challenge it was to stay in character while you were going on about that back in Edison's office?" he said. "Because it's *not* the same plan! This is the *new and improved* Mind-Melter! It's on top of the Washington Monument! And the Star of Ceylon will amplify its signal throughout the nation's capital and beyond!"

"But it's still a Mind-Melter!" Molly snickered. "That big brain of yours couldn't come up with something different?"

"Why would I need something different," Rector retorted, "when I'd already devised the perfect plan for the World's Fair last year?"

"Do you own a dictionary, love?" Hertha asked him. "I think you need to check the definition of 'perfect.'"

"Yes, I'm not sure how something 'perfect' can be 'improved,'" added Cassandra.

"That's because you lack imagination," Rector said, sniffing haughtily.

"Well, *I* was under the impression that 'perfect' plans generally worked," Josephine taunted.

Rector's nostrils flared. "It *did* work! Until it was thwarted!" he said, his face taking on an unhealthy level of pink. "That's why I owe my perfect plan a second shot at success!"

"Are you even listening to yourself?" Margaret asked.

"Enough!" Rector shouted, kicking the bars of Captain Lee's cell. "I made *one* mistake at the World's Fair!" he shouted. "One mistake!"

"You underestimated us," said Molly.

"No! My mistake was taking hostages in New York, as if the venal dimwits in Washington would care about anyone other than themselves!"

"No, I'm pretty sure it was underestimating us," Emmett said, joining in.

"Grrrrahh!" Rector lifted his silver baton and lurched forward, as if he were going to charge straight across the room to Emmett's cell. But before he could get anywhere, Captain Lee reached out and grabbed the villain's coat collar. He yanked Rector backward, slamming him into the iron bars. The madman was caught off guard, but quickly recovered and rapped his silvery baton across the captain's hand. There was a sizzling sound and sparks flew as the baton hit. Everyone gasped as Captain Lee yanked back his scorched, red hand and fell to his knees, grimacing in pain.

"I guess it was you who was wrong, Molly," Rector said, jaw tight and shoulders heaving. "You said I wouldn't hurt anybody yet."

"Papa!" Emmett called out. "Are you okay?"

"I . . . I'll survive," his father replied, his voice strained. "I'll always . . . always keep you safe."

Molly tried to stop her legs from shaking. In the past, she'd used Rector's fragile temper against him. Needling him with frustrating questions and snarky barbs had become a kind of game to her; eventually Rector would lose his composure and make some grievous error. She'd used this tactic to escape from him multiple times in the past. But she'd forgotten just how dangerous the man could be when pushed too far. And now Captain Lee had suffered for it.

"Fine, Rector," she said solemnly. "You've won."

"Tell me something I don't know." Rector laughed, brushing off his coat and straightening his collar. "Now, listen closely and perhaps there will be no more . . . accidents. Tomorrow, when I go back to the National Mall for the monument's dedication—"

"Tomorrow?" Cassandra blurted. "It can't be Election Day already. Have we been unconscious for two weeks? But . . . Oh. No, of course you didn't *actually* command the crew to stall their work."

"Ding, ding, ding!" Rector sang out. "Yes, that was just a lie for you folks. Election Day is still weeks away. But, you see, Chester A. Barfer got a very *different* version of the ransom note; his said the process needed to be *sped up* or Bell would die. So, while you were running around, solving puzzles in crud-town Virginia, President Sheepdog has been scrambling to put together an impromptu dedication ceremony for tomorrow afternoon. And guess what? All the presidential candidates have been invited—Cleveland, Blaine, and, of course, yours truly."

"I think you mean 'me truly,'" Edison said smugly.

Rector stared. "There was more wrong with that sentence than I care to correct. But suffice it to say, I will be melting the brains of Washington tomorrow and you will all be stuck here, forced to listen to it. You see, I won't be foolish enough to have you at the 'scene of the crime,' as it were." He reached into his pocket and showed everyone what looked like a dotted black egg. "But I will be bringing this mobile version of my Vocal Empowernator, which will be beaming all the terrifying sounds back to this speaker box." At the table by the wall, he pulled back the corner of the sheet to reveal a large gray metal case with a phonograph-type horn. "And don't waste your time contemplating escape. I believe you'll find your cells quite unbreakoutable. Though, just to be safe, I won't be leaving you alone."

"Aha! We knew you had an accomplice—someone wearing that mask and pretending to be you!" said Emmett. "So where is Mr. Bumbles?"

A tall, lanky redheaded man in a bright green suit poked his head in from the hallway. "Nae! Tha wid hae bin maself!"

Oogie MacDougal—the infamous chief of the Green Onion Boys, the dangerous fugitive at the top of the government's most wanted list, the Scottish maniac who'd had it out for Emmett for years—strutted into the room and flashed a sneering grin. "Guid day, Emmett, mah wee jimmy. Lang time, na see. A've bin keekin tae th' future fer anither meetin atween th' twa o' us."

An uncomfortable silence followed, until Captain Lee finally broke it. "Who is this man, Emmett? What did he say? Was that a threat? Was that English?"

"'Tis Scots!" Oogie barked.

"He was greeting your son," said Alexander Graham Bell, whose childhood in Scotland gave him a slightly better understanding of Oogie's thick brogue.

"But none too kindly, I suppose," said Cassandra. "This is the crime lord Emmett stole those loads of guns and cash from."

"Not *stole* exactly," Emmett sputtered. "That was, you know, just a bit of . . . Did we *have* to remind him of that?"

"Ah didnae forget!" Oogie snapped.

"All right, all right," Rector said, patting the red-faced criminal on the back. "I've already told Mr. MacDougal no killing until after the dedication ceremony."

"Oogie MacDougal," Molly breathed, still not quite able to believe it. Another of their oldest foes back for vengeance. "So it was you we fought at the Smithsonian."

"Nae, tha Rector wis Rector," said Oogie. "Bit ah wis Rector whin Rector wis shooting darts at Rector whin Rector wis Edison." He scratched his head. "Ah've ne'er bin Edison, far as ah recall."

Molly frowned. "So Bumbles wasn't involved? Feh. I'd been *sure* that stale old grumplebum was a bad guy. He even *smelled* evil."

"Oi! Once a man reaches a certain age, 'e can't be held accountable for 'is natural aroma!" The white-haired coachman raged into the room, spittle foaming at the corners of his mouth. "And for the last time, my name ain't Bumbles! It's Grimsby! Uriah Grimsby!"

Emmett and Molly looked to each other in horror. They'd heard that name before, but never had a face to tie it to until now.

"That's who you are?" Molly snapped. "You're the man who trapped Nellie Bly in Barbados?"

Grimsby let out a phlegmy chuckle. "Trapped? More like recruited."

"Bumbles! You spoiled my surprise," Rector chided. "Oh well. Guess I might as well introduce you to the final member of my little team." He leaned through the doorway and called down the hallway. "Ah, there you are. Come, say hello to your former friends."

No, Molly said to herself. *No, this cannot be what he's making it seem like it is. It can't be.*

But it was. Nellie Bly walked through the door, and Molly nearly squeezed herself through the bars in a fit of fury. There she stood: the young reporter whom Molly had trusted enough to tell all of her family secrets, the woman who'd befriended them, survived a shipwreck with them, who had fought to help them escape Rector's ship in the Caribbean. And now she was standing at the right hand of their archnemesis. And it was definitely her—same old threadbare tweed dress, same reporter's notepad tucked into the pocket of her skirt.

"Oh, Nellie," Cassandra sighed mournfully.

"Nellie, this can't be," said Emmett. "What did he—"

"How could you?" Molly screamed at her. She couldn't hold back her rage. "You're working with him?"

"Oh, Miss Bly has been a far bigger asset than either of these other goons," said Rector.

"Oi!" complained Grimsby.

"The young lady is quite a skilled researcher," Rector went on. "I might never have known about the Star of Ceylon without her. Or the location of the Guild's Club! Can you imagine how embarrassing it would have been if, as Edison, I didn't know where my own secret hang-out was? Oh, and I can't begin to tell you how much easier it's been to avoid police detection with Nellie here, keeping tabs on law enforcement activity for me. She's been invaluable, really." He put his arm around Nellie's shoulders and the young reporter didn't so much as flinch.

Molly was aghast. "How could you do it, Nellie?" she screamed. "*Why* would you?"

Nellie gave a haughty sniff. "Money," she said. "A lot of money."

"And an offer to be my official state journalist, running all of the nation's press after I take over," Rector added proudly. "What ambitious young reporter could turn down a position like that?"

"One who wanted to be an *actual reporter!*" Molly clenched her fists so hard it hurt. "We went back looking for you, you know!" she yelled at Nellie. "I never stopped looking! I've checked the papers every day!"

"And you never saw my name in there, did you?" Nellie fired back. "Well, Mr. Rector is going to change that for me. It's nothing personal, kids. This is me fulfilling my lifelong dream. You can't say you didn't see this coming. I told you back when you first invited me on your Antarctic expedition that I was only coming along to record the story. I warned you back then that my career would always be my number one priority. That hasn't changed."

Molly slumped against her cell door and squeezed her eyes shut to keep from tearing up. It was true; Nellie *had* said as much. But by the time they'd parted ways in Barbados, Molly had truly believed their relationship had grown into something more, that Nellie had come to put their friendship ahead of the Almighty Story. She had looked up to Nellie, wanted to be like Nellie. Now that very thought made her queasy.

"I thought so much better of you, Nellie," Hertha said with disgust. "It was your passion for shedding light on the truth that led me to take you under my wing. Now you settle for being private scribe to a dictator, writing whatever this madman tells you to?"

"Simply getting your name in the papers is that important?" Emmett asked. He sounded more hurt than angry.

Nellie looked down her nose at them. "I've made my choice. I'll live with it. Now, if you'll excuse me—"

"No!" Molly screamed in fury. "You don't get to stab us in the back and just walk away! We were a team! Robot nearly died saving you from Rector's ship! Me and Emmett almost . . . Wait. Where is Robot?" She couldn't believe she hadn't noticed his absence until then.

"Ah, yes, that would be some more of Miss Bly's handiwork," said Rector. "See, I ran into a little problem back on Phipps Lane: your robot wasn't affected by my knockout gas. And that mechanical monstrosity had a rather negative reaction to seeing all his friends incapacitated on the floor around him. For a second, I thought I might actually be in danger. Luckily, I had my minions waiting nearby to help me load your bodies onto the coach. Miss Bly ran in and gave Robot a zap with my Sizzle-Stick." He waved the metallic baton he'd used on Captain Lee. "The unfortunate bit is that she miscalculated the level of charge to use."

"I'd seen him get shocked by the door of the Tea Works," Nellie explained apologetically to Rector. "I assumed he'd get up again. I'd never used the Sizzle-Stick before."

"It's okay, Nellie," Rector said, patting her on the back. "Your heart was in the right place." Rector turned to the table and pulled back the rest of the sheet. Robot lay there motionless, black singe marks at his joints and loose springs poking from between the metal plates of his torso. "It's a shame, though," Rector continued. "There were all sorts of experiments I'd planned to perform on this guy. They'd be pointless now that's he just a lifeless hunk of aluminum." There was nothing Molly could do to hold back the tears.

"You monster!" Cassandra cried.

"You—you—you're worse than Rector!" Molly shouted at Nellie. "Robot saved your life in Barbados! And you *killed* him? He might have been made of metal but he had more humanity than you!"

Nellie cast her eyes to the floor. "I don't need to take this abuse," she said. "I did what I had to do. And you'll all see soon enough that *I'm* the one who made the right choice." She marched out.

Oogie MacDougal chuckled and nudged Grimsby with his elbow. "She's up ta high doh, thon ane," he said.

The old man squinted at him. "Whuzzat?"

"Ah says the lass is doin' her dinger, eh?"

Grimsby stared.

"Whit's off?" Oogie frowned. "Ye hae a bum lug?"

Grimsby scowled. "I ain't takin' this abuse neither!" He stomped out after Nellie.

"Henchmen," Rector huffed, rolling his eyes. "You can scram too, MacDougal. As for the rest of you, enjoy your perfect prison. You'll only be spending the one night in it." He followed Oogie into the hall, then popped back in a moment later. "Because tomorrow you'll be—"

"Dead, yes," Hertha said flatly.

"Oh, good, you got that," Rector said with a grin. "In that case . . . ta-ta!" He slammed the door.

For a long time, none of the prisoners spoke. They didn't even make eye contact. What was there to say? Molly couldn't stop staring at Robot's silent metal frame, draped across the tabletop, his left arm dangling awkwardly over the edge. She longed to press her cheek to his. If Robot had conked out while flying them to safety when Agent Clark was chasing them, or if his final mote of Ambrosium had turned to ash while he was magnetically hurling artifacts at the museum guards, then at

293

least he'd have gone out a hero. But he had been *murdered*. By someone they all thought was a friend! It made the pain—and anger—even worse. She didn't care if their cells were "unbreakoutable," she was going to get free somehow. And when she did, she was going to get her revenge. On Rector. On Oogie MacDougal. On Nellie Bly . . . That one still hurt so much. She couldn't believe Nellie had done what she did to Robot. And then she apologized to *Rector* for it? Molly would never forgive Nellie. Or forgive herself for trusting her. She should have believed Nellie when she said she'd always put her career first and . . . Molly gasped.

"Molls, are you all right?" her mother asked. "Why are— Are you . . . smiling?"

"Nellie was a stowaway," Molly replied, feeling a surge of renewed hope. "We never invited her on our expedition. In fact, we weren't very happy to find she'd snuck along. We had a whole big back-and-forth about it! So why say we invited her? Why lie about an insignificant detail like that, when we'd obviously know it was a lie?"

"What are you saying, Molly?" Captain Lee asked.

"Nellie's still on our side," she replied. "She was giving us a signal!"

Traitor!

Long into the night, Molly stood in her cell, her fingers gripping the bars and her eyes focused on the door as if the power of her stare could will Nellie Bly back into the room.

"I'm worried about you, Molls," said Cassandra.

"She's coming back for us," Molly said for the sixth time that hour.

"I'd love to believe you," her mother replied. "But . . . she *destroyed* Robot, Molls."

"And I'll never forget that," Molly said, her eyes staying on the door. "But maybe it really *was* an accident. Maybe that apology to Rector was secretly meant for us."

"I hope you're right, Molly," Emmett said, working at his cell's lock with a loose button from his coat. "But you standing there, staring like that, is actually kinda distracting."

"That line about us 'inviting' her *wasn't* an accident," Molly insisted. "It was something she knew we'd recognize as an inconsistency, but that Rector would have no reason not to believe."

"Or maybe the woman's been lying to so many people for so long that her tall tales have gotten tangled in her head," said Edison.

Bell tugged at the gold chain in his lapel pocket and checked his watch. "It's two a.m., girl," Bell said. "At the very least, sit down and get some rest."

"Rest for what?" Hertha interjected, her tone sharp. "So we're all perky and refreshed before being executed? She should be helping us work on an escape, just as you should! We've got a dozen crackerjack minds here; we should be putting them all to use."

"I think I'm making progress here," said Margaret. She was on her knees digging at the hinges of her cell door with her stubby fingernails.

"You can do it," Sarah cheered, while toying at her own lock with the corner of her shirt cuff. "I believe in you!"

"If you could believe some tools into our hands, that would help," said Margaret.

"Mr. Edison," asked Captain Lee. "You had some shards of metal in your pocket. Perhaps the women could use those?"

"No way," Edison said, huddling to protect his broken

gizmo. "This is my next big invention. I need each and every piece."

"Unless it's a cell-door opener, I don't know how it could possibly be more important than what we're doing," said Mary.

"It's a pile of scrap," Josephine scoffed. "You don't even know how those pieces go together."

"But when I do figure it out . . . you're all going to be wowed," Edison said. "This invention is going to turn the world upside down."

"Ooh, is it a shoe that you wear on your head and hats that you put on your feet?" Cassandra asked.

"Of course not," Edison replied.

"So . . . that one's still up for grabs?" said Cassandra. "Excellent! I know what my next project is! After we escape, that is."

"Which will be any minute—you just watch," said Molly. *Come on, Nellie,* she continued in her head. *Please let me be right about you. I need to know there are people out there who can be trusted.* "Believe in Nellie."

"I believe in her," said Sarah. "But I also believe in myself, which is why I'm not going to stop trying to pick this lock."

"Molly," said Emmett. "Even if Nellie is some kind of double agent, that doesn't mean she'll be able to free us. What if she never gets the opportunity? What if Rector has already sniffed her out as a spy? What if—?"

There was a click and the chamber door opened. Everybody hurriedly stopped fidgeting with their locks and dropped their hands to their sides.

"I knew it," Molly announced triumphantly. And then quickly deflated when she saw Grimsby's pale, wrinkled head poke into the room.

"Knew what? That it were me?" the old Brit asked, looking uncomfortable. "You know, that smell ain't coming from me proper. It's the garlic bulbs in me pockets." He patted his hip. "Hold on. These pants ain't got no pockets. So, where did I put that garlic?" He scratched his blotchy scalp.

"Is there something you want from us, Mr. Grimsby?" Hertha asked.

Grimsby stopped feeling around for his missing garlic. "Not unless any of you been up to something needs punishing," he said with a sneer. "Anybody 'ere need punishing?"

The prisoners remained silent, their faces solemn.

"Shame, that," said Grimsby. "But you never know when I may pop in again for another look-see. Maybe I'll get me chance next time." He grunted and left, shutting the door once more.

Molly leaned against the bars and slid to the floor, allowing herself to sit for the first time in hours. It felt like a good time for crying, but she couldn't work up any tears. Her body was too dried out. Or maybe too numbed by disappointment. "I'm sorry," she said, to no one in particular. "I just . . . I so wanted to believe that Nellie didn't go bad—*couldn't* go bad."

"We understand, Molls," her mother said softly. "We *all* wish that had been the case."

"But, you see . . . holding on to that hope let me hold on to the hope that we might get out of this somehow," Molly continued. "And the hope that we can still stop Rector. And that we can save our reputations, get some recognition, stop hiding, get to live our old lives again. Or new ones, better ones." She dropped her head to her chest. "But without hope for Nellie, I'm not sure I can hold on to those others. I don't want to give up, Mother. But—"

The chamber door clicked and inched open again.

"Get out, you mangy old yeast-fly!" Molly snapped.

Nellie Bly slipped inside and eased the door shut behind her. "Okay," she said sheepishly. "I suppose I deserved that."

Molly jumped to her feet. "I thought you were Bumbles."

Nellie frowned. "Well, now I'm insulted."

"What do *you* want?" Hertha asked.

"If I said, 'to get you out of those cells,' would you all start being a little nicer to me?" she replied.

Molly danced around with as much celebratory vigor as her cramped little cell would allow.

"So, you *are* on our side?" Cassandra asked, hesitant to sound too hopeful.

"Of course!" Nellie replied, and then began

shushing the words of gratitude from around the room. "Do you think I'd actually align myself with a maniac like Rector?"

"Well, you certainly put on a good show, dear," said Josephine.

"Acting!" Nellie said with a flourish.

Emmett seemed unimpressed. He glared at Nellie with an anger he couldn't hide. "But . . . But you killed Robot."

"What?" Nellie sputtered. She spun to face the table where the metal man lay motionless. "Oh my goodness. Robot! Why are you still lying there? Get up!"

Robot sat up with a creak.

"You're not dead!" Molly cried.

"Acting!" Robot said with a flourish. He climbed down stiffly from the table and shuffled to Molly's cell. The girl reached through the bars and squeezed his thick aluminum fingers.

"Sheesh, Robot, you've been lying in here with us for hours," Emmett said. "You could've said *something*."

"I was waiting for Nellie to tell me it was safe," said Robot.

"I did!" Nellie said. "Before I left earlier, I said that whole bit about how they'd 'soon see that I did the right thing.' That was me telling you to let them in on our secret."

"Oh, well, that was very vague," said Robot. "You

should have said something like, 'I am going to leave now and when I do, Robot will show you he is not dead.'"

Nellie threw her arms up in resignation.

"I am sorry to have frightened you," Robot said to the others.

"We're just happy you're still with us," Cassandra said with a tear in her eye.

"Well, I'm *also* sorry to have put you through all that, but if I hadn't pretended to kill Robot, Oogie or Grimsby would have done it for real," Nellie said. "And then we had to make sure Rector believed he was out of commission, so I told him to play dead until I gave the signal."

"And then her signal was too vague," said Robot.

Nellie rolled her eyes.

"Well, thank you, Miss Bly," said Hertha, "for not ruining my reputation as a good judge of character."

"What I don't understand is why you're still here," said Captain Lee. "If you've been faking loyalty to Rector, why have you stayed with the man for months? Why haven't you escaped or called the police or—"

"I'm a news bear!" Nellie flashed Molly a sly grin. "I will go *anywhere* and do *anything* for a story. So when the most devious criminal of our time invites me to be part of his inner circle, you bet I'm going to play along with that. Plus, it's been a lot easier to keep an eye on Rector's shenanigans from the inside. I've been getting the scoop, while at the same time doing whatever I could to gum up the gears of his operation and slow his progress. I had to do little things here and there to actually help him—like pointing him toward the Star of Ceylon—so he'd believe I was truly on his side. But I've been working against him wherever I could. I kept lying to him about 'heavy police activity' in areas he wanted to go. I even sent an anonymous message to Agent Clark about a 'Rector sighting in Petalsburg,' hoping he might keep the bad guys busy long enough for me to warn the MOI before fake Edison got to them. That one didn't work out as planned. But my main priority was keeping him from enacting his plan until I'd found all of you! I didn't want to turn on him until I knew all of you were safe. But, wow, you folks are good at hiding!"

"So you were looking for us while we were looking for you?" Molly said. "Why didn't you try to send us a message or something?"

"Who do you think put that article in the paper about Forrest?" Nellie said. "I tried putting all sorts of hidden messages into news articles. Most of them were just trying to let you know I was alive, but I realized that even if you saw those, you'd have no way of responding or finding me. So I decided to put something out there that would draw you to Rector, knowing that if you found Rector, you'd also find me. I knew there'd be a risk of you getting captured, but I also knew I'd be here to get you out if that happened."

Molly beamed.

"This is all quite interesting and I'll adore reading more about it in a bestselling book someday," said Josephine. "But right now, I think we'd all rather see you pull a key ring from one of those skirt pockets."

"Oh, I don't have keys," Nellie said.

"That seems like a flaw in the escape plan," said Cassandra.

"There are no keys," Nellie explained. "The locking mechanisms on these cells are electronically operated. They're opened by flipping those switches on the wall in a specific pattern. That's why he's been calling his prison 'unbreakoutable.' Well, that and his disregard for the English language."

"All righty, then," said Mary. "Get flipping!"

"Oh, I don't know the combination either," said Nellie.

"I stand by my previous comment about this escape plan," said Cassandra.

"But you have *some* way of opening these cells, right?" Molly said.

"Of course," said Nellie. "Go to it, Robot."

Robot leaned over and whispered to Nellie, "I do not know the combination either."

"No, you big goof," Nellie said. "Use your magnet powers. Rip those bars open like you ripped open Bell's ship."

"Oh. I see," Robot said slowly. He raised his hands tentatively.

"Robot, don't!" Molly warned.

"The bars are iron," Nellie said. "They should be no trouble for—"

"Nellie, you don't understand," Emmett said. "Robot can't use any of his special powers. It eats away his Ambrosium every time he does."

"And he's only got like a grain of rice's worth left!" Molly added.

Nellie winced. "I—oh, I'm sorry. I had no idea."

A solemn silence followed.

"No one wants Robot to die," Hertha finally said, but her disappointment was evident. "We'll find another way out."

"I sincerely doubt that," Rector said, throwing open the door. He, Grimsby, and Oogie MacDougal surged into the room. "I knew you'd turn on me eventually, Miss Bly. That's why I've had Bumbles keeping tabs on you."

"You know, they know my true identity now," said Grimsby. "You got no reason to keep callin' me—"

"Quiet, Bumbles!" Rector snapped. He returned his attention to Nellie, who slowly backed away while struggling to keep a brave face. "I've been aware of your treachery for quite some time, Miss Bly," Rector continued. "Like the underpaid carnival worker who can't afford a home of his own and needs to live in the house of mirrors, nothing happens behind my back without me knowing about it. Believe me, you would never have gotten that little piece about Forrest into the papers if it hadn't suited my purposes and helped bring more of my enemies to me. And do you think you could have gotten that Morse code message out to Clark through *my* telegraph lines if I hadn't allowed it? But I knew that, for these fools behind you, it would help further the idea that Rector and Edison were two different people, so I didn't stop you. You've been working for me all along, Nellie, whether you knew it or not."

"Okay," said Nellie. "But did you know that I secretly told Robot to play dead?"

"No, that one's on Bumbles," said Rector.

"Me?" blurted Grimsby. "Why is it my fault?"

"Cuz yer a scabby auld walloper," Oogie chuckled.

"No, because you were supposed to be keeping an eye on Nellie, Bumbles," Rector said. "Or is that what you just said, MacDougal? Doesn't matter. But speaking of Robot . . ." He drew his Sizzle-Stick from a slot on his belt and handed it to Oogie. "Shut him down for real, won't you?"

Oogie grinned wickedly as sparks flickered from the tip of the metal rod.

"No!" Molly screamed. "Robot, defend yourself!"

Oogie raised the baton, but Robot caught his arm.

"Let gae, ye boxy bampot!" Oogie snarled. But Robot twisted the gangster's hand back upon itself. The Sizzle-Stick made contact with Oogie's chest, shocking him.

The gangster yowled and stumbled into Rector. More crackling sounds rippled through the air, and Rector howled in pain as well. Both men fell in a heap and the baton clattered to the ground.

"Two down!" Molly cheered.

Grimsby was the only villain left standing. He and Nellie both dove for the Sizzle-Stick, but the reporter's hand scooped it up first. The white-haired henchman grinned awkwardly. "Ah. Yeah, so . . . I ain't never 'ad nothin' against you personally," Grimsby said. "In point of fact, I, uh . . ." He dove for the door, but Robot slammed it shut in front of him.

"I do not revel in violence," Nellie said, closing in on her former captor. "But you—you nasty, garlic-reeking old git—you kept me locked in a stable until your boss showed up to offer me a job, so . . ." She jabbed the baton into his belly. He sizzled and fell.

Nellie threw the stick down on the table and crouched by Oogie's fallen body. "Robot, help me search him," she said with urgency. "He's got the switch positions written down—I've seen him check the paper while he—"

Everybody in the cells started yelling.

"Hush up," Nellie said. "I'm going as fast as I can!"

As Robot bent to search Oogie, an electric zapping sound echoed through the room, and the metal man toppled over, thumping across the unconscious gangster. Rector stood behind him with the Sizzle-Stick still smoking. "Acting!" the villain said with a flourish.

Nellie stood. "Ah, good," she said. "So, you know I was, uh, faking on these prisoners, right? Pretending to be a traitor to you so I could—"

Zzzap!

Nellie collapsed.

"I'd say 'good try,'" said Rector. "But honestly, it wasn't very good." The people in the cells stood in silent shock as the villain, whistling cheerily, began flicking a series of switches on the wall. "And to think MacDougal told me I was building too many cells. At least I think that's what he told me. It was more like, 'tae minny soles!' So, who knows—maybe he was saying his boots were too small. Doesn't matter. I've proven myself right yet again: it is always better to have more than not enough. That's also true for appetizers at cocktail parties." He continued flicking switches until the doors to two of the unused cells swung open. "See? Room for everybody."

23

An Inescapable Dilemma

THIS LATEST DEFEAT sucked all the life and energy from the room. All the manic attempts at lock-picking and intense searches for ways to dismantle their cells had come to an end. All the prisoners simply sat and stared. Not even Margaret was tinkering. Save for a brief moment of relief when Robot blinked back to consciousness again, the atmosphere was one of utter despair.

"This is all my fault again, isn't it?" Molly said eventually. She assumed it was almost morning, but there was no way of knowing in the windowless chamber. "Everyone was hiding out safely and happily. But I couldn't leave well enough alone. And now look . . ."

"If it's your fault, then it's my fault too," said Emmett. After everything, he was still quick to jump to Molly's defense. "You and I *both* decided to run off after Rector."

"As did I," added Robot.

"I appreciate the solidarity, guys," Molly said. "But we all know that neither of you would have done something as rash and risky as this on your own. I'm the bad influence."

"I do what I want," Robot retorted.

"And I'm perfectly capable of making my own terrible choices," Emmett said. "Just ask my father."

"It's true," said Captain Lee. "Sometimes I think I wouldn't even need Rector's machine to melt my brain; all I need to do is listen to my boy tell me about the crazy things he has done. But I've made mistakes too, Emmett—things I thought were for the best, but which only served to drive a wedge between us." He dabbed the corner of his eye. "In case we truly don't have much time left, I want you to know that my deepest regret is not being there for you, to see you become the person you are today. What I have learned of you in the past year has astonished me and amazed me. You are brave and clever and loyal. You have accomplished things I would never have dreamed of attempting. Even when you make choices I don't agree with, I can't help but admire the reasons for which you make them. You listen to your brain *and* your heart. And most of the time, you even manage to figure out which is giving the better advice. It's a remarkable talent. But I've never just come out and told you. So, before it's too late: Emmett Lee, I am proud to be your father."

Emmett wiped his eye.

"And I would like to add that as far as we're concerned, the both of you, Emmett and Molly, have been tremendously *good* influences on us," said Hertha. "The entire reason we got together as a group was to fight the establishment, to play against their rules and pave a more promising path for future inventors who might not be born into the privilege the Guildsmen enjoy. You two have repeatedly shown us that the future is worth fighting for."

"Hear, hear!" Sarah cheered, and the other members of the MOI nodded and applauded.

Cassandra stood. "Well, Molls, I need no more inspiration than *this*." She reached into the collar of her dress and pulled out her "World's Greatest Inventor" picklelid medallion. Molly smiled. Then Cassandra flipped the medal over and held it out for Molly to read the new inscription she'd etched into the opposite side: "World's Greatest Rector-Stopper."

Molly suddenly felt warm all over. *That's the despair melting away*, she thought.

Thomas Edison cleared his throat. "So, um, do Bell and I have to say something nice about the kids now? That seems to be what's happening . . ."

"Oh, uh . . . yes," said Bell. "The children are . . . very . . . challenging. But that's good, I suppose. Everyone needs to be challenged sometimes."

"Okay, people, I don't know how much time we have,

but probably not much," Molly said, putting the men out of their misery. "So, let's put our talented heads together and figure a way out of here."

Nellie pointed to the panel of switches by the door. "I don't suppose any of you happened to see the switch pattern when Rector opened the cage to put me in?"

Josephine shook her head. "The brute purposely stood in the way to block our view."

"And I believe each cell has a different combination anyway," added Mary. "He clicked those switches twice—once for your cell and once for Robot's."

"Well, there are only twelve switches and a limited number of up-and-down combinations to set them in," said Sarah. "So, we should eventually be able to figure out at least one of the patterns. If we can free even one of us, that person could get out a call for help."

"Righto!" Cassandra said with excitement. "Let's start with up-down-up—"

"Excuse me, but aren't we getting ahead of ourselves?" Bell asked. "Unless one of you can stretch your arm a good fifteen feet, we've no way to reach that panel."

"Robot can!" Emmett said.

Robot extended his right arm between the bars and launched his hand at the panel. It flew through the air, punched at the switches, and then fell to the ground. He reeled it back in. "I do not suppose we can place a little pedestal in front of those switches, so my hand has someplace to sit while it does the flicking?"

"I'm afraid not," said Mary.

"If I use my magnet powers—"

"No."

"Molly's cell is closest. What if we built a really long stick that could reach the switches from there?" Cassandra asked.

"Build a stick out of what?" asked Edison.

"Whatever we can find," said Cassandra.

"There's nothing in these cells with us," Edison continued. "Literally nothing."

"Except *everything on our bodies*," said Hertha. "Cass, that's a brilliant idea."

"Of course it is," said Cassandra. "Ooh! Course it is . . . course it . . . corsets! Ladies, you know what to do!"

Hertha smiled. "Gentlemen, put your jackets over your heads."

"What? Why?" grumped Edison.

"Common decency," Josephine scolded.

"Just do it," Captain Lee urged the other men. And when they all had their faces covered, Cassandra, Hertha, Josephine, and Mary began digging down into their underclothing to tear free the long stiff wires that gave shape to their corsets.

"This is the first time I've ever been glad to be wearing one of these torture devices," Mary said, ripping free a long strand of wire.

"Society forces us to squeeze into these things," said Hertha. "It's about time we got something out of the deal."

Within a minute's time, they had harvested several handfuls of sturdy, bendable wire. But just then, there was a click at the chamber door. The ladies quickly shoved the wire bits under their skirts. "What in my name is going on here?" Rector asked. He was dressed in his Thomas Edison disguise again.

"Excuse us!" Josephine snapped as she and the others speedily rebuttoned their dresses. "Can we please have some privacy?"

"No," said Rector. "You're my prisoners. Now, explain. What's with the guys under the coats? Are they dead?"

"Just showing some discretion while the ladies adjust their garments," Captain Lee said from beneath his jacket.

"Womenswear is not designed for lengthy imprisonments," said Hertha.

"Or anything, really," added Molly.

"Fine, pretty yourselves up for doomsday," said Rector. "And men, stop playing ostrich. I'm about to go to the Washington Monument and I want all ears uncovered to hear the screaming."

"Hurry up and do what he says," Molly urged, not because she wanted to obey the madman but because she was eager to get him out of the room so the women could assemble their switch-flipping pole.

Captain Lee's head turned back and forth between their captor and the real Edison. "The resemblance is uncanny," he muttered.

"There's a reason he's managed to fool us so many times," said Emmett.

"No shame in being tricked by the best," Rector said proudly. "In fact, you should feel privileged. It's not just any so-and-so who gets to be gulled by the greatest actor to have ever walked the face of the Earth."

"You *are* quite good," said Cassandra. "Have you given any thought to, oh, I don't know, returning to acting? Say, instead of violent conquest?"

"Never," said Rector. "Blame society; I've chosen the path that is far more socially acceptable." As he fiddled with knobs on his big gray Empowernator box, his henchmen strolled into the room.

"Morning, ye doaty dobbers," Oogie said with a wicked grin as he menacingly twirled the gleaming Sizzle-Stick. Behind him, Grimsby grumbled something unintelligible.

Rector cleared his throat and tapped the strange black egglike device that was now pinned to his lapel. "Testing, testing." His voice came from both his mouth and the Empowernator's speaker. "Perfect!" He smoothed the wrinkles on his coat and straightened his bow tie. "Well, ta-ta, nemeses! Enjoy the program. I hope you're all adequately traumatized by the time I come back to kill you." And with that, he left.

Sighing, Grimsby shut the door and sat in one of the rickety chairs by the wall. Oogie set the stun baton down on the table and took a seat next to the old man—directly in front of the cells' control panel.

"Bother beans." Molly frowned. How were they supposed to break out with these two goons chaperoning them?

Rector's voice suddenly crackled through the Empowernator. "As you've probably noticed by now, I am not leaving you unattended. I learn from my mistakes. In fact, they're the only things I learn from. No one else has anything to teach me that I don't already know, so if I'm to learn anything else for the remainder of my life, I have to rely on myself to teach me. Ah, the perils of being a super-genius. Are you grousing and grumbling? I bet there's all sorts of grousing going on right now. Drat, I should have made this a two-way talking *and* listening thingie."

"That's called a telephone!" Bell cried. "I already invented it!"

"But that would be too much like Alec's silly telephonic whatsit," Rector continued. "As if those are ever going to catch on. Am I right?"

Edison chuckled. "Heh. Totally."

"Anyway, I can't keep talking the entire trip," Rector

went on. "Well, I'm sure I *could*—but I won't. I've got a country to take over. I will, however, be updating you from time to time. And, of course, you'll hear when I start my speech at the ceremony. In the meantime, you will be properly supervised by those two fine fellows before you. Well, one fine fellow and one pungent scarecrow. Ta-ta!"

Oogie glanced at Grimsby. "Ah'm the fine fella," he said.

Grimsby rolled his eyes.

Molly's mind was reeling. They might have collected enough wire to construct a reaching arm, but how could they put it together without being seen? And even if they could, there was now a criminal maniac sitting in front of the switches. Molly looked across the room to Emmett and made a flicking motion with her finger. Emmett shrugged. Running his fingers through his hair—a sure sign that he was devolving into panic—he began looking around the room. A bit too frantically.

"Havin' a fit there, boy?" Grimsby asked. "It's best none of you try fakin' any medical ailments. I seen enough of that pish-posh from captives in my day and I won't be fallin' for it."

"Ach, Emmett isnae fakin'," said Oogie. "Tha bairn is nae but a wee feartie."

"A what?" Grimsby snapped. "For cryin' out loud, man, speak the Queen's English!"

"Hello, friends and enemies—mostly enemies,"

Rector's voice rang from the speaker. "Wow, if you could see this crowd. This is without a doubt the biggest crowd of people that has ever gathered on the National Mall. Seriously, this is amazing. I'm going to melt so many minds!"

"He's there already?" Sarah said. "It hasn't been but ten minutes. We must be very close."

"This bunker's built right into the banks of the Potomac," Nellie explained. "Even on foot, you could reach the Mall in—"

"Quit yer clyping, lassie!" Oogie warned her. "Rector wants ye alife, bit he ne'er said naethin' abit not hurtin' ye."

Nellie, who must have witnessed Oogie MacDougal's temper in her months undercover, quickly quieted.

"I think we're just surprised Rector would build his hidey-box within the Mind-Melter's danger zone," Cassandra said to the guards. "But I suppose you two are protected with those itty-bitty earplugs that keep the rays from reaching your brain."

"Dornt need 'em! Ma lugs huvnae e'en a wee chuckie in 'em," said Oogie.

"I have no idea what this tooty tartan just said, but none's got those earplugs but Mr. Rector 'imself," said Grimsby. "He filled us in on what you lot did last time. So if you 'ad any plans for swipin' our plugs—we ain't got any!"

"Then you'll be paralyzed by the Mind-Melter just as we will," Mary said. "What kind of spell does Rector have you under that you'd be willing to sacrifice yourself to—"

"Nah, we're all in the clear down here," Grimsby said, slapping the wall behind him. "Boss tells us 'is melty rays don't get through concrete."

Oogie sneered at him. "D'ye caa me tooty, ye bowfy auld footer?"

As their jailkeeps traded incomprehensible insults, Molly spotted Emmett waving to get her attention. He surreptitiously motioned toward the Sizzle-Stick lying on the table outside Molly's cell. With his back to the bad guys, he pointed to the stick, made a poking motion, and mimed opening a door. Molly instantly knew what he was getting at and had to stop herself from yelping with excitement. A surge of electricity from the Sizzle-Stick could short-circuit the electronic locks on their cell doors.

"You're a genius," she mouthed back to him. But they still had a big problem. No matter how far she stretched her arm, there was no chance of her reaching a table six feet away. She pointed to her arm and then held two fingers close together to indicate "too small."

"Psst!" Emmett got Nellie's attention and pantomimed writing with an invisible pen. Nellie pretended to scratch an itch as she covertly pulled a pencil and notepad from her hidden skirt pocket.

Oogie's eyes appeared to catch the movement as Nellie slid the pad from her cell to Emmett's and Molly quickly spoke up to draw the gangster's attention. "Hey, Oogie!" she called out. "What's it feel like to go from big, bad crime boss to groveling henchman?"

The gangster turned on her with a fiery fury. "Haud yer wheesht, lassie! Nae a body tells Oogie whit ta dae but Oogie."

Grimsby looked on eagerly, ready for a show. "That's right, mate," he encouraged. "Teach that jabberin' brat a lesson. Assumin' that's what you were doin'."

Oogie stood, glaring at Molly, and Hertha jumped in. "Well, it's obvious who the boss is in this room," she said casually. "I mean, between a Scotsman and an Englishman? There's no question."

Both men took the bait. They began jabbering at each other, Grimsby declaring things about "his proud Saxon heritage" and Oogie barking words like "dunderheid" and "numptie," which Molly assumed to be insults. But neither of their captors seemed to notice as the prisoners passed, from cell to cell, the note that Emmett had just written. By the time Molly got to read the note, which asked for all the loose corset wire to be passed to Emmett, most of the women were already doing so. Any time either Oogie or Grimsby began to glance toward the cells, someone would quickly toss out a new comment to keep their argument going.

"Well, it's clear which one of you has more years of experience," said Nellie at one point. To which Oogie responded by howling, "Aye! This minger's aulder than ma granda's ashes!"

A few moments later, Margaret helpfully pointed out, "He's also the only one who hasn't been previously trounced by any of us." To which Grimsby responded by scoffing, "S'true, MacDougal, I 'eard you got your scrawny tail stomped by this bunch at the World's Fair!"

Holding the paper out of sight, Molly read the rest of Emmett's note, which also asked for pieces of metal that might be used to fashion a clamp, and anything that could be used to tie pieces together. Without turning away from the bickering henchmen, Molly began unlacing her boot and watching, from the corner of her eye, as Mary unraveled yarn from her knit cap, Bell removed the chain from his pocket watch, and Margaret shook out her boot to find a handful of loose bolts in there. In the back row of cells, Thomas Edison stared wistfully at the broken collection of gears and springs in his hand until Bell finally reached over and gave him a shove. "Oh, just give it to them, Tom," Bell whispered. And Edison rolled his gadget bits into the next cell.

Molly carefully reached out to hand her unthreaded bootlace to her mother, but paused when she saw Cassandra take off her "World's Greatest Inventor" medallion.

The elder Pepper looked into her daughter's eyes and raised her brows as if to ask, "Is this okay?" Molly nodded. Her mother believed in herself—and believed in her. She didn't need a medallion to show it.

As all of the scavenged items were stealthily passed from cell to cell over to Emmett, the Empowernator's speaker crackled back on. It was not Rector's voice they heard, but that of President Chester A. Arthur as he made opening remarks to the cheering crowd outside the Washington Monument. "Thank you, ladies and gentlemen, for joining us on this historic occasion. Here with me today are the three men who will be vying for my job in a fortnight—Governor Grover Cleveland, Secretary of State James G. Blaine, and inventor, entertainer, and all-around amazing guy, Thomas Alva Edison. But the contest to see who will become our next president can wait, because today we gather to honor our *first* president, George Washington. And I think old George would be proud, because you lucky folks are about to bear witness to the lighting of the world's first *electric* monument. That's right, in a surprise move—a surprise even for me; I only learned about it this morning—this big, pointy . . . honor spear is going to be illuminated, from top to bottom, with state-of-the-art electric light. Yes, it's true. And that bit of spectacularity comes to us, of course, courtesy of Mr. Edison, who is far more than just a political candidate."

"Hey," objected Grover Cleveland.

But President Arthur just continued. "In fact, you folks all the way in the back can hear me right now, because I'm speaking to you through Mr. Edison's magnificent Vocal Empowernator! Incredible, isn't it? Sounds like *someone's* got a bit of an edge in this race, eh?"

"Hey!"

In the secret prison, the president's speech became increasingly difficult to hear over the rising volume of the spat between the jailers. Oogie was threatening to "skelp yer foosty face!" as Emmett sat hunched over in his cell, furiously bending, twisting, and arranging the odds and ends that had been passed to him.

"And now," they heard President Arthur say through the speaker, "the candidates and I will make our way to the top of this towering . . . tower, where we will flip the switch to shine our beautiful light straight into the eyes of President Washington's ghost up in heaven!"

Rector was moments away from activating the Mind-Melter. Molly tried to imagine any scenario in which they'd make it there in time to stop him, but she came up blank.

Luckily, the walk up the stairs inside the Washington Monument must have been a long one, because for minutes on end, the only sound coming through the speaker was footsteps and panting. Grimsby was bragging about how he'd been committing crimes back when Oogie was the size of a chicken's toenail when Emmett began sneaking his completed invention over to Nellie in the next cell. It wasn't easy to stealthily pass a five-foot-long wire arm with a trigger on one end and a clamp at the other, but Nellie managed to get it to Hertha, and Hertha to Josephine, without attracting any undue attention. But as Cassandra reached out and grabbed it from Josephine, the long rod clanked noisily against the bars of her cell.

Grimsby's head turned. "Oi! What's going on over there?" he snapped.

But Oogie MacDougal, his ire fully sparked, was in no mood to disengage. "Dinnae ignore me when Ah'm haverin' at ye, auld man!" And with one powerful blow to the side of the skull, he laid Grimsby flat. The elder henchman's white ponytail flopped onto his face as he hit the ground and lay utterly still.

Several of the prisoners gasped.

"Did he just—did he kill Bumbles?" Emmett sputtered.

That was when Oogie, shoulders hunched and chest heaving, noticed the long, bizarre rod in Cassandra's hand. Fast as she could, Cassandra whipped the gadget through her cell and out the other side to Molly. Molly grabbed it and thrust it out between the bars of her cell door, reaching for the table by the wall. She squeezed repeatedly on the cog-wheel trigger, snapping open and closed the bent jar lid that functioned as a makeshift

323

clamp. On the third squeeze, just as Oogie leapt for it, the clamp caught hold of the Sizzle-Stick and Molly yanked the weapon back into the cell with her. Wasting no time, she flicked it on. Sparks flew from the tip as she jabbed it against the lock and, with a whiff of smoke, her door cracked open.

She was free! And Oogie was fuming. He flipped the table over in anger, knocking the Empowernator speaker to the floor as he charged toward Molly's cell. Molly waited until he was only a few inches away before swinging the door open and smashing it into his face. She leapt out and turned to zap open her mother's cell, but Cassandra waved her off. "Get Emmett next," her mother said.

Oogie had already recovered and was running at her again. But he took a tumble over Cassandra's outstretched foot and skidded onto his face as Molly dashed across the room and sizzled the lock on Emmett's cell.

Emmett jumped free as Molly turned and raised the stick to fry Nellie's lock, but before she could bring her weapon down, Oogie's hand clamped around it. He pulled, trying to pry the Sizzle-Stick away from her, but Emmett wrapped his hands around Molly's and together they engaged in a tug-of-war with the seething, red-faced crime lord.

"Ye're deid, bairns," Oogie hissed through clenched teeth. "Deid."

Cheers of encouragement roared from the cells as Molly and Emmett bent their knees and pulled with all their might. But they could not get the Sizzle-Stick away from Oogie.

"Molly," Emmett panted. "On three."

Molly nodded. "One, two . . ." She and Emmett simultaneously released their grip and Oogie's own momentum sent him stumbling backward. The Sizzle-Stick flipped through the air and smashed against Robot's cell door, cracking in half with a shower of sparks.

Molly scrambled to snatch up the pieces of the broken stick, but it was obviously dead. No more opening the cell doors. And nothing to keep Oogie at bay.

The gangster stood up and wiped a trickle of blood from his swollen lip. "Nae too toof noo, are ye, lassie?" Oogie said as he walked, slowly and menacingly, toward the children. Molly and Emmett held hands, trying desperately not to falter as the murderer approached.

"Oh, look," said Robot, "the Sizzle-Stick unlocked my cell before it broke."

The metal man shoved his door open into Oogie's face and grabbed the staggering gangster by his shirt collar. Oogie squirmed as Robot lifted him off the ground and hurled him across the room into the center of the grid of cells.

Flat on his back, Oogie woozily lifted his head. "Ah'mno fallin' frae fistycuffs with a teapot," he groused.

But before he could even attempt to stand, Captain Lee reached through his bars and grabbed Oogie's right wrist. Then Alexander Graham Bell promptly seized the villain's left arm. Sarah grabbed his right ankle, and Margaret the left. And there the four held him, spread-eagled on the concrete. No matter how he writhed, Oogie could not pull free. "Agh, Ah'm fair puckled."

"We'll hold him," said Captain Lee to his son. "You get the cells open."

Emmett ran to the control panel and started randomly flicking switches, while Molly tried fruitlessly to shock open her mother's cell with the broken stick.

"Stop, children—listen!" said Hertha.

Everyone paused to hear the speech coming through the Empowernator. With all the commotion, no one had realized that Rector was speaking again. ". . . find out two weeks from today, when this nation chooses its next ruler. But let's be honest—it's going to be me."

"Hey!" said Grover Cleveland.

"And I must say," Rector continued, "I do like the feel of looking down upon all you little people from way up here. Figuratively, of course. But I am basically on top of the world up here, which I think we can all agree is where I belong. And I'll prove it to everyone when I turn this bad boy on in a moment, but first, let me tell you a little bit about my road to awesomeness . . ."

"He's launching into one of his villain speeches,"

Hertha said. "That could give us a good ten, fifteen minutes."

"I'll work fast!" Emmett said, madly flipping switches.

"No! Molly, Emmett, Robot—you need to go and stop him," Cassandra urged. "You're our only hopes!"

"Maybe," Edison said skeptically. "But if they stay here in the bunker, at least they'll be shielded by the concrete."

"Unless Mr. Rector was lying about that too," said Robot.

"It might not be my place to butt in," said Hertha, "but if Rector takes over Washington, and then the country, and then the world . . ."

"MacDougal's got the combinations in his jacket!" Nellie reminded them.

"Heh! Nae anymore," Oogie snarled from the floor. "Rector said they doors wid ne'er needs be open agin, sae Ah et it! Tha' wee piece o' paper is in mah tummy."

"I, um, I can keep guessing at combinations," Emmett said.

"That would only waste more precious time," Cassandra said. "Children, you can do this. Hand me that Sizzle-Stick; I'll fix it and get the rest of us out. But you three need to go. Now. You're our only chance to stop Rector."

"But . . . how?" Molly asked.

"Any way you can," her mother replied.

"Son," Captain Lee called from the next cell. "I know you're hesitating because you're thinking I would not want you to do this. And you're right. Why would I want you to do something so crazy and dangerous? But this is bigger than my feelings. Make me proud, Emmett."

Emmett nodded.

Molly handed the broken stun rod to her mother. "Don't worry, everybody!" she called as she, Emmett, and Robot rushed out the door. "We'll save the world!"

"Head due east out of the woods from here until you reach the Mall!" Nellie said.

"Use anything you see to get you there faster," Hertha urged. "A wagon, a horse, anything!"

"Believe in yourselves!" Sarah yelled.

The freed trio rushed down a cement corridor, scaled a flight of steps, and burst outside into a grassy clearing surrounded by trees. The sun was bright and the children had to squint until their eyes adjusted. Behind them, they could hear the rushing waters of the Potomac River, while the roaring of the crowd at the monument could already be made out in the opposite direction.

"I don't suppose we'd be lucky enough to find Grimsby's coach sitting out here for us," Emmett said.

"Better than that," Molly replied, unable to believe her eyes. "Look! It's the Daedalus Chariot!"

She ran to the gleaming red vehicle. She had no idea how her mother's flying machine had appeared at the riverside outside Rector's secret bunker, but she didn't care. Then she saw who was sitting in the pilot's seat.

"Well, this is fortuitous," said Agent Clark. "Molly Pepper, you are under arrest."

Dogfight

"AGENT CLARK!" MOLLY shouted. Her heart was pounding. "Believe it or not, we are so glad to see you! I'm not even angry that you've stolen my mother's flying machine! Listen, Rector is disguised as Thomas Edison *right now*. He's at the Washington Monument with President Arthur and he's going to—"

"Tell me whatever stories you'd like while we're on the way to city jail," the federal agent said, unclipping a pair of jangling handcuffs from his belt.

"Sir, you don't understand!" Emmett said. "Rector has turned the entire monument into a giant version of his Mind-Melter from the World's Fair! He's about to use it on the crowd and—"

"I'll be happy to take down your report at the station." Clark stood, ready to disembark from the chariot.

"If you are not interested in the exploits of Ambrose Rector," said Robot, "perhaps you would like to go inside this odd little building and arrest the criminals in there."

"Yes! Oogie MacDougal is right down those steps!" Molly shouted as Clark approached. "You know, the most wanted man in America? Besides us. He helped Rector kidnap all of us. Our parents and the MOI are holding him down in there, but—"

"Your parents are here as well?" Clark said. And Molly saw, for the first time, something on his face that could possibly be called a smile. "And the Mothers of Invention? Well, I believe I have, as those of the gambling persuasion say, hit the jackpot. Let's get you cuffed and we'll all go inside together."

"We're losing precious time!" Emmett pleaded. "Every second we waste talking about this is one second closer to Rector turning on his death machine."

"You've been chasing Rector for a year!" Molly said. "Now we're telling you where he is and that he's about to *kill thousands*—and you don't want to stop him?"

"Oh, I'll get Rector too," Clark said, holding the cuffs open and ready to slap across a set of child-sized wrists. "But later. You're here now."

"Incorrect! We are not," Robot said. He pulled Molly and Emmett close, one in each arm, and, with a rumbling hum, lifted off the ground.

"Robot, set us down, now!" Molly said, her stomach

clenching from both the panic and the bumpy ride. She pulled on his neck, trying to steer him downward. "You're too important to lose!"

"So are you," said Robot, ducking a terrified pigeon.

"Molly, you're going to make him drop us!" Emmett warned. "But Robot, she's right, this is—"

"This is silly," said Robot as they zipped under wispy white clouds. "You said it yourself: every second we waste talking is one second closer to Rector turning on his machine. I have a way to get us there fast. It is silly for me to pretend I cannot fly, when flying can potentially save you and thousands of others."

They'd been in the air for barely a minute and already they could see the towering white obelisk rising above the trees.

"I know you want to help," Molly said as they swooped over rooftops. "But you can't put yourself at risk like this!"

"That is the same argument your mother made back in the barn when you told her you wanted to go after Rector," Robot said. "Everything is on the record, remember?"

Emmett looked into her eyes and nodded. They both knew Robot was right.

"Besides," Robot continued, "Agent Clark is a very stubborn man. The only way we were going to get him to pursue Rector was to lead him to the villain ourselves."

"Wait, what do you mean by that?" Emmett asked. He and Molly cautiously twisted their necks to peer behind themselves. The Daedalus Chariot was bobbing shakily in the sky not fifty feet away, Agent Clark scowling at the wheel.

"Disobeying a direct order from a law enforcement agent," he shouted over the wind. "Evading arrest. Reckless flying of an unregistered automaton. So many crimes for the list."

"That man really needs a hobby," Emmett said.

"I think we are his hobby," said Molly. She yelled back at Clark, "You don't know how to fly that thing! If you break my mother's flying machine, I am going to be so mad!"

Agent Clark pulled furiously at knobs and levers, and the chariot jolted forward, increasing its speed. The whole vehicle was shaking, but the agent was nearly side by side with the children now. He leaned out and took a swipe at Emmett's foot.

"Hold on," Robot said.

"You're the one with your arms around us!" Emmett sputtered, tucking his legs up to his belly. "*You* hold on!"

Robot dove downward, then swooped back up, looping upside down, and leveled out again behind the Daedalus Chariot.

While Molly whooped with glee, Emmett shut his eyes tight. "You can't save us if we're dead!" he squealed.

They zoomed over the red stone towers of the Smithsonian, and the flying chariot banked hard right, swerving to circle back around behind Robot again. Below them, the crowd on the National Mall suddenly came into view. At least no one was writhing in pain yet. Rector was, blessedly, still chattering away, his voice echoing through multiple Empowernator speakers positioned around the Mall. But Molly knew he could pull that lever at any moment and she would start feeling the paralyzing agony of the Mind-Melter. As they closed in on the monument, they could make out the tall antenna rising from its peak—and the bluish glint of the stolen sapphire way at the top. Molly wondered if Robot could get close enough for her to reach out and snatch the gem from the tip of the lightning rod, but even if she managed to pull off that extremely risky stunt, that would only diminish the effects of Rector's machine, not stop them.

".. . is the duty of every American to make a sacrifice to his country," Rector was saying. "And for those of you gathered here today, the exact nature of that sacrifice will soon become clear. Just remember, everything we do today, we do to forge a better America! And so, in closing . . ."

"Run, people, run!" Molly tried shouting down to the happily ignorant spectators. Several people saw them flying overhead and began pointing. And applauding.

"They think we're part of the show," said Emmett.

"Well, that *would* be a pretty great show," Molly said.

"This is your final warning!" Agent Clark shouted. "Land your flying tin man this instant!"

"Can't you hear Rector?" Molly screamed. "He's going to turn on the machine *now!*"

"Wow, you folks sound really excited about making this sacrifice," Rector said, responding to the roar of the crowd. "I bet you neither of these other candidates would get a reaction like that. Eh, Arthur?"

President Arthur chuckled. "Heh heh, I think not!"

"Hey!"

Outside the peak of the monument, Clark swooped at the flying children from a high angle. He glared sternly until he realized he was on a collision course with the people he was pursuing. His face was suddenly awash with fear. Robot rolled to the side just in time to avoid a midair crash. The crowd went wild.

"All right, people, that's enough," said Rector. "I'm beginning to think there's something else going on out there. Best to just get on with it. Shall we, Chester, old pal?"

"We're out of time!" Emmett cried. "We need to get in there *now!* Robot, can you fly us straight in through those windows?" At the pinnacle of the monument, just below the pyramid-shaped capstone, were several large openings that led into an observation chamber. It was in that marble-encased room, five hundred and fifty-five feet above the National Mall, that President Arthur and the candidates stood unwittingly with Rector around his doomsday device.

"I will try," Robot said, aiming himself at the obelisk's south-facing window. But as he approached, he began losing altitude.

"You're too low, Robot," Molly said. "Pull up!"

"I am trying," Robot said. "I . . . I am tiring."

Oh, no, Molly shouted internally. *This is it—he's out of Ambrosium.* But he was also their only hope of stopping Rector. "You can do it, Robot!" she cried.

Emmett joined in. "I believe in you!"

Straining, Robot rose higher, arcing back up to the height of the window. And then he kept going. Straight past the monument.

"You missed!" Emmett cried.

"I noticed that as well," Robot said. "I am sorry. Hold tighter."

Molly didn't question the order. She wrapped herself around Robot's torso as he loosened his grip on her and launched his detachable right hand at the open window. The aluminum fingers clamped on to the edge of the opening and held tight as the rope connecting hand to forearm stretched fully taut. Tethered to the obelisk, Robot whipped wildly around the monument. The children screamed with terror. The crowd screamed with delight. And the momentum hurled Robot straight through the window into the observation chamber. The metal man clattered onto the marble-tile floor, letting go of both kids as he landed. Molly and Emmett rolled, in unintentional somersaults, directly to the feet of President Chester A. Arthur, who was draped in furs and sporting bushy, badger-like sideburns. He gawked at the children with dismay, while behind him, bulldog-cheeked Grover Cleveland and a sad-eyed man who must have been James G. Blaine, leapt into each other's arms.

Rector, however, seemed unaffected by the sudden entrance of these newcomers. He stood confidently beside a glistening chrome device lined with blinking electric lights of various hues. He still looked uncannily like Thomas Edison as his hand rested on the machine's big red lever. "A good seventy-eight percent of me expected you kids to show up here somehow," he said. "I'm not sure how you escaped my unbreakoutable prison, but—congratulations! Now you get to witness America's doom up close and in person."

With that, he pulled the lever.

25

At the Apex of Disaster

MOLLY KNEW THAT when faced with a dilemma, Emmett's natural inclination was to pause, examine all relevant factors, and weigh the pros and cons of any potential outcomes before determining the best course of action. At that moment, however, in the observation chamber of the Washington Monument, with Ambrose Rector pulling the lever that would signal not just Emmett's doom but the doom of all those around him, she saw her friend defy his own instincts. Before the lever was even halfway to the on position, Emmett threw himself at the villain, growling like a rabid chipmunk.

As shocked as Molly was, she was more than happy to follow Emmett's lead. In a blink, both children had Rector pinned to the floor, his hand safely torn away from that deadly red lever.

"Police! Police!" President Arthur shouted. "They're attacking Thomas Edison! They're trying to take out the next president before he even wins!"

"Hey!"

There were no guards or federal agents up in the observation chamber with them, however—probably by Rector's design. And it would take several minutes for anyone to run up all those steps. In the meantime, while Robot stood by the window and reeled in his hand, Molly and Emmett continued to kneel on the villain's chest and pin his arms down.

"President Arthur, it's us!" Emmett said. "Emmett Lee and Molly Pepper! We're here to save you again!"

"This isn't Edison!" Molly said, ripping at the rubbery nose and false eyebrows on the imposter's face. "See? It's Rector!"

Cleveland and Blaine gasped.

"Again? You have got to be kidding me," President Arthur muttered, running his hands down his furry face. "Can I manage to preside over one single ceremony without it being ruined by this disguised megalomaniac?"

"How do you think I feel, Chester?" Rector said, struggling beneath the children. "At least your plans get thwarted by a devious genius—mine get scuttled by babies!"

"That machine was never going to light up anything,

sir," Emmett said to the president. "It's another of Rector's Mind-Melters—the lightning rod up top is an antenna that is going to transmit the machine's rays all over Washington."

"*Was* going to," Molly specified. She gave Rector a sly grin. "But we stopped you. We win, Rector."

"Um, does anybody else see the giant wind-up man over there?" Blaine asked, rubbing his eyes. Robot waved hello with his reattached hand.

On the floor, Rector laughed. "This isn't over," he said.

"Yes, it is," Molly insisted. "We're not moving until the police get up here."

"Oh well," Rector said smugly. "I guess all three of us are about to go boom, then."

"What?" Emmett turned his head. "Molly! Look out!" He grabbed her and dove to the side. Rector rolled off in the opposite direction, getting clear just as the Daedalus Chariot slammed violently into the window frame it couldn't begin to fit through.

Arthur and the others dropped for cover as Agent Clark, tossed from the pilot's seat, came flying into the chamber along with various flaming bits of flying machine. While Clark moaned on the floor, Molly skittered back to the window and peeked out to see, hundreds of feet below, the bulk of the Daedalus Chariot on the ground in a smoldering ruin. "You broke my mother's invention!" Molly shouted at Clark, who was staggering to his feet, his suit torn and singed.

"And you let the bad guy get free!" Emmett added. Rector was climbing over hunks of wreckage toward the stairwell.

"Agent Clark?" President Arthur sputtered from across the room, where he used a windowsill as leverage to get himself back onto his feet. "What is the meaning of all this?"

"Those children are wanted criminals," Clark replied groggily.

"Never mind them, you ninny! Stop Rector!" the president shouted.

Clark did a double take, noticing Rector for the first time. But it was Robot who stepped in to block the madman's exit.

"I am sorry, Mr. Rector," Robot said proudly. "But I have caught you."

"You want to catch someone, Tinpot?" Rector said, spinning on his heel and stepping back to grab the president by the lapels of his sable coat. "Go fetch!" And Rector shoved Chester A. Arthur out the window.

"No!" Clark cried. But there was nothing he could do; the president was already plummeting down toward a screaming crowd of spectators.

Without wasting a second, Robot flew out the window and zoomed down after the falling president.

Breaths halted in the observation chamber until the

cheering outside told everyone that Arthur was safe. Robot had saved him.

"I just can't get a break today, can I?" Rector groaned.

The pause gave Agent Clark just enough time to leap over the wreckage and face down the villain. "Ambrose Rector, you are under arrest," he said. "For murder, theft, trespassing, breaking and entering, multiple attempted assassinations, disturbing the peace, consorting with known felons, falsifying documents, extortion, fraud, kidnapping, resisting arrest, more kidnapping, impersonating an inventor, destruction of property, arson, trespassing, building an underground bunker without the proper permits—"

"Back to plan A," said Rector. He lurched for the Mind-Melter, but Clark tackled him. Cleveland and Blaine cowered in the corner as the madman and the federal agent wrestled at their feet.

"Should we help him?" Molly asked.

"He's got that," Emmett replied. "Let's get this." He lifted a long piece of iron sleigh rail from the chariot's debris and began beating the Mind-Melter with it. Molly hoisted a heavy propeller blade and joined him in pummeling the doomsday device. They pounded the lever until it snapped clear off; they shattered the flashing lights; they dented the chrome panels, pried them open, and ripped loose handfuls of sparking wires. In less than thirty seconds, the death machine was reduced to a fizzling lump of scrap metal. Molly and Emmett dropped their implements of destruction, and smiled even as they panted for breath. The Mind-Melter was dead. Rector couldn't hurt anyone now.

"Look out," cried Blaine. "He's got a thingie!"

The children turned to see that Rector had drawn his Magneta-Ray. The weapon hummed and a broken hunk of chariot hurled itself into Agent Clark, knocking him over. The attack bought Rector enough time to race into the far corner, where he retrieved a strange backpack from a shadowy hiding spot. Molly immediately recognized Rector's antigravity pack. The cretin was going to fly off to freedom just like he had in Antarctica.

"That's another count of assaulting a federal officer," Clark said, standing back up. "Drop your weapon, Rector. I can do this all day."

"He really can," Emmett added.

"That backpack makes him fly!" Molly cried. "Don't let him use it!"

"Enough out of you!" Rector screamed. "You think my Mind-Melter can't hurt anybody anymore?" He waved his Magneta-Ray and the banged-up death machine, now with jagged bits of metal peeled back into dangerously sharp blades, began floating in the air. It hovered for a second before hurtling itself directly at Agent Clark's head.

"Look out!" Emmett cried. He dove, plowing into the

agent's side, and knocking him out of the way. A sharp corner of shrapnel slashed Emmett's shoulder as the Mind-Melter flew past him and sailed out through the window.

"Emmett!" Molly cried as her friend hit the ground, gripping his bleeding arm.

"I'll live," he said through gritted teeth. "Stop Rector!"

The madman had powered up his antigravity pack and was already hovering several inches above the floor. He took the time to give Molly a sarcastic salute before floating out the window.

No, Molly thought. *You do not get away again.*

Molly charged after him. She leapt up, bracing one foot on the windowsill, and pushed off, launching herself out into the clear blue sky.

Breaking the Cycle

FOR A MOMENT, Molly was flying. No chariot to sit in, no Robot to be held by, just her—soaring through the air all on her own. And then, of course, gravity took over. Luckily, Molly had leapt with enough momentum to reach her goal. She caught Rector's feet before he could hover out of reach.

"What the—?" Rector yelped, obviously not expecting to have a passenger dangling from his brown leather loafers. He looked down at Molly and laughed.

That was when Molly began to question her strategy. Or whether it could even be called a strategy.

"So, here we are again," Rector said as they soared above the gawking crowd. Molly would have liked to glare up at him defiantly, but she couldn't seem to tear her eyes from the swirling mass of dots down below that she knew were confused, terrified people. Her mind flashed back to the World's Fair, when Rector had taken her hostage as he flew to freedom in the stolen Icarus Chariot. She'd escaped that time by leaping down into her mother's arms—a trick she couldn't possibly pull again here. At the Fair, they had been flying no more than fifty feet in the air; they were ten times that height now. It was impossible even to make out individual faces on the people below. She wondered if her mother was among them. Or Captain Lee, or any of her friends.

"See how history repeats itself, Molly?" Rector said. A flock of chittering sparrows parted around them. "I bet that even in your precarious situation, you still think you can best me. And who knows, maybe you can. Probably not. Definitely not. But the point is, even if you do somehow win the day here, how will that change things for you? Let me give you a hint: it won't. It won't change a thing. You've quote-unquote 'stopped' me twice before. Has anything changed for you, your mother, or your friends? No. You always end up right back where you started."

One of Rector's shoes began to slip and Molly had to switch her grip to his ankle. But then his thin black sock began to slide too.

"Think about it, Molly," Rector continued. He circled the monument in long slow loops, keeping them over the crowd that was helpless to interfere. "If you come out on top today, do you think they're suddenly going to change their minds? Tell everyone the truth about what you did? Do you think you'll ever get any credit for saving the world from 'Crazy Ambrose Rector'? Do you think anyone will ever listen to you and your insufferable band of overachievers?"

"Yes," Molly sneered back. "Because all those people down there? They heard the fight over the Empowernator. They heard everything! They know . . ." But even as she said it, she realized that none of their words were currently echoing through speakers down below.

"Oh, you poor, naive little thing," Rector replied. "You sound so proud of yourself, it almost feels cruel to point this out, but you must not have noticed our good friend President Arthur flick off the Empowernator the moment you crashed into the room. The oaf had no idea what was going on, of course, but if there's one thing the man knows how to do, it's avoid bad press. He jumped to it on pure instinct, protected my anonymity without even knowing it. So, no, I'm sorry, but nothing has changed and nothing will. You can't fight the system. The system always wins. That's why I'm going to replace the system, *become* the system."

Molly clenched her teeth as she fought to hang on.

"You're a clever girl, Molly," Rector continued. "I complain about you, sure—"

"And try to murder me," Molly snapped.

"And try to murder you a little bit too, yes," Rector went on. "But only because you're such worthy competition. Look, I feel that sock sliding. We don't have much time for parlay here. What I'm trying to say is that if you keep fighting me, even if you win today, you'll end up back in the same place you were before—in the back of a smelly old pickle shop, unknown and unappreciated, no matter what you do. As for me, I'll escape—I always do. But you never will. You won't escape the fate society has assigned you. Your mother will continue to languish in obscurity, your friends will still be stymied by a world that doesn't appreciate them and continues to present them with nothing but obstacles to their success. You will never get credit for any of the feats you've accomplished, any of the battles you've fought. And why? Because of this system. The system you're always fighting so desperately to stop me from taking down! You protect your own oppressors!"

Molly said nothing. Her wrist felt like it was about to snap.

"You know I'm right, Molly," Rector continued. "If you win, you end up back in the same place you were a year ago. And the same things will come from it. Your frustration will build until you eventually do something desperate, anger the powers that be, and end up on the run again. Until my next dastardly plot. Which we all know is coming. And then we'll end up doing this all over again, Molly. Again and again and again."

Molly swallowed. She knew Rector liked to play mind games with her. But deep in her core, she knew there was truth to what he was saying. Her fingers started going numb. She couldn't hold on much longer.

"The only way to break the cycle is to do something different," Rector said. "Change the rules of the game, Molly. Join me. Just give in. It's either that, or wind our clockwork lives back up and start all over again. Hey, maybe next time, I'll escape with you on a rocket to the moon. That could be fun, eh?"

Molly shivered in the biting autumn air. Rector was right. But he was also wrong. The system *did* feel rigged against her—against lots of people. It *was* a broken, unfair system in which so many were set up for defeat from the start. The system *did* need changing. But not like this. Not Rector's idea of change. Creating real change would take time and effort, and it might be thankless. The people who do the hard work might get no credit, no recognition, no reward other than knowing they've made a difference. It was a daunting thought. But Hertha's words rang through her head: *the future is worth fighting for.*

She craned her neck to look Rector in the face, but peering up at him, all she could see was his dark silhouette against the sun, directly overhead. Her left hand gave out. It slipped free and hung limply at her side, tingling with pins and needles. She tried to tighten the grip of her right hand, but the cramps pulsing through her palm made it beyond difficult.

"Okay," she said.

"Okay what?" Rector asked. "I want to hear you say it."

From the corner of her eye, Molly caught a glint of gleaming metal, soaring through the sky.

"Okay, I'll beat you again," she said, grinning as Robot swooped up and grabbed her by the waist. "I'll beat you every time, if that's what it takes."

"I believe," Robot said, "that Miss Pepper is not enjoying this ride. Shall we go to the ground, Molly?"

For once, Molly was not upset about Robot breaking the no-flying rule. "Yes, Robot," she said. "We've already thwarted Rector's little plot. All that planning and scheming, and, look, he's on the run yet again, flying off with his little backpack, foiled once more by a couple of nosy kids. Rest with that thought until next time, Ambrose."

With his arms around Molly's waist, Robot angled to fly downward, but Rector had other plans. He grabbed Molly's arms and tried to yank her back to him. "No!" he shouted. "She does not get to run away this time! We are not going through this dance again in six months! Or ever! The cycle ends today!"

"Let go!" Molly cried as Robot and Rector both began

spinning in the air, playing a vicious tug-of-war with her.

"I tried to make it your choice, Molly! But if you won't break the cycle, I will!" Rector snarled. "I'll change the game by taking you out of it!"

"Hold tight, Molly," Robot said as the fliers began spiraling out of control. Molly smacked at Rector's arms and shoulders in an attempt to make him let go. Robot joined in, daring to release one of his arms from Molly in order to whap the villain in the gut. But Rector struggled even harder. As the three figures tumbled through the sky in high-altitude somersaults, people began to scatter, afraid to be directly under the midair confrontation.

"No more, Molly!" Rector cried. "This ends now!" He let go with one arm and reached back, patting around on his antigravity pack. He was looking for something. His fingers found his Magneta-Ray, but that apparently was not what he'd been seeking. He hurled it angrily into the trees, and immediately went back to feeling around the backpack. Molly finally spied what he was reaching for—another Sizzle-Stick, protruding from a pocket on the side of the pack. He was planning to shock Robot out of the sky.

But caught as he was in a dizzying spin, he seemed unable to find his weapon. With increasing panic, Rector ripped open one pocket after another, tearing at any strap or button he could touch. Eventually, his fingers found their way around the thick black cord that held down the flap to the backpack's main compartment. He yanked it, releasing the flap, and the antigravity device inside—a skull-sized, circuit-covered metal box that housed a chunk of Ambrosium—floated out. The small machine drifted straight up into the atmosphere until it vanished from sight.

Molly gasped. But Rector didn't seem to notice what had happened. He pulled his hand forward, having finally located his Sizzle-Stick. "Aha!" he crowed, raising the weapon overhead in both hands like a victorious king on the battlefield. Then he finally felt the tug of gravity. Ambrose Rector's eyes went wide with horror as he plummeted helplessly to the ground, five hundred feet below.

Molly closed her eyes, but she could still hear the screams. And the thud.

"He's—he's—"

"He is gone," Robot confirmed.

Molly hugged Robot tight as they finally began to descend unimpeded. But Robot didn't float straight down.

"I am trying to take you farther away," he said. "I do not want you to have to see what has become of Mr. Rector."

"Thank you, Robot," she replied. "But you're still going . . . What do you mean, 'trying'?"

They began descending faster than they were moving

forward. "I cannot . . . keep myself . . . aloft," Robot said. His voice slowed with every word. "I think . . . maybe, Molly . . . I am done too."

"No, Robot, no," Molly said. "Just land, okay. Land and we'll—"

"Thank you . . . for being . . . my family."

Robot's body shook as he struggled to slow their descent. His feet thumped down hard on the lawn of the National Mall. He bent to set Molly gently on the ground, then collapsed onto his back. "Thank . . ."

And then he was silent.

"No," Molly cried. "Robot! Robot!" On her knees beside him, she threw open his chest plate. Inside, she saw gears, springs, bolts—but no Ambrosium. The chamber was empty.

After the Fall

"THAT WAS QUITE a show!"

"Well, until that one actor accidentally died."

"Oh, yes. Tragic that."

As she sat on the grass, cradling Robot's lifeless aluminum body, Molly listened to the murmurings of the slowly dispersing crowd that filed past her without acknowledgment. It was true: the president had shut down the Empowernator. The spectators outside all thought it was a performance. None of these people even heard Rector's name. Molly laughed, an ironic chuckle that slipped out between tears. Rector had become a criminal because his father wouldn't let him be an actor—and now he'd died with people thinking he was one.

"Hey, is that the girl from—"

"Shh! Don't bother her. I think she's still in character."

"Or she could be, you know, mourning the death of her costar."

"Either way, let's not get involved."

"Yeah, you're right . . . Hey, all those different flying machines were pretty amazing, though, right?"

"Yes! I had no idea Thomas Edison had invented such incredible things! That man's definitely got my vote."

Molly wiped her face on her sleeve. She would be furious about that later. Right now, she didn't have the capacity for anything beyond sorrow. She stroked Robot's smooth metallic head. She wished she had a hat for him. Any hat. She'd told him he could wear a hat when he . . .

"Molly! Thank goodness!" Her mother pushed through the crowd and dropped to her knees to embrace her.

"It's over, Mother," Molly said softly as Cassandra caressed her head. "It's all over. And Robot is . . ."

"Oh, Molly." Cassandra hugged her daughter tighter.

Captain Lee appeared at their side a second later, with the rest of the former captives right behind him. He looked around anxiously. "Where's—"

"I'm here, Papa!" Emmett came running from the direction of the monument. He immediately threw his arms around his father. Then he looked down. "Oh, no. Robot?"

"I'm sorry, son." Captain Lee closed his eyes as tears

ran down his cheeks. "But he was a hero. Just like you. I'm so proud of you, son."

"You should be proud, sir," said a deep voice. President Arthur, surrounded by an entourage of federal agents, walked up and cleared his throat. "This is the second time now that these children have been instrumental in, well, saving my life."

Agent Clark, out of breath and looking more of a wreck than the Daedalus Chariot, pushed his way to the front of the agents. He surveyed the group before him: the Peppers, the Lees, the entire MOI. "Excellent, you're all here," he said. "Men, put these people under arrest."

The Mothers immediately began protesting, but it was President Arthur's words that got the agents to stop advancing. "Did you not just hear me say they saved my life?"

"But, Mr. President," said Clark.

"I just saved *your* life!" Emmett said to Clark.

"Potentially," the agent replied. "We have no way of knowing for sure whether that machine would have killed me or not. And, actually, we don't know where it landed. By pushing me out of the way, you might have allowed someone else to be squashed by that thing."

Emmett went pale. "I . . . um . . ." He looked up to the window of the monument and raised his hands in an L shape to calculate the angle. "Excuse me. I'll be—um, I'll be back." And he ran off.

One of the agents made a move to follow, but President Arthur stopped him. "Look, I'm still president for a while longer, and I'm hereby pardoning all these people of any crimes they may have committed," he said. Smiles began to spread across the faces before him and he quickly added, "Crimes committed *up to this point,* that is. Understand that those secrecy agreements you signed are still in effect, and if any of you choose to once again break those contracts, this government will have no choice but to prosecute you to the fullest extent of the law, whether it be me or Mr. Edison there."

"Oh, yeah," Edison said, a smile coming over his face. "I guess I'm going to be president. Since no one will ever know it was Rector who's been running and not me. Neat."

"As president of the Inventors' Guild, I look forward to working closely with you, Mr. President," Bell said, shaking Edison's hand and giving him a sly wink.

Molly slumped into her mother's arms. Rector had been right. Everything he'd said, it was already coming true.

"Well, I didn't sign anything," Nellie Bly said, waving her very full notepad. "And I think the American people will be very interested to hear about—"

"Nothing," Clark said. "They will hear about nothing. Because neither you nor Mr. Lee are leaving this area until you've signed the same agreement as the others."

He turned to the president. "I can at least do that, right?"

President Arthur nodded. "The nation needs to keep its secrets."

Clark sent someone to retrieve paperwork for Nellie and the captain. "No mention of Ambrose Rector, Ambrosium, or the incident at the World's Fair. The official stance is that none of those things ever existed. Are we clear?"

"Let me get this straight," Nellie said. "If I don't sign away my rights, you'll toss me straight into jail?"

"This is criminal," said Mary.

"Utterly unfair," said Sarah.

"Positively ghastly behavior," Josephine scolded.

Molly yelled at all of them. "Yeah, it's awful! *They're* awful. Did you expect anything less? But none of it matters anymore. Robot is *dead*. He's never going to make another terrible metaphor. He's never going to juggle pickles again. Never going to twirl his silly metal mustache." Her words faded as she buried her face into her mother's shoulder.

"We are so terribly sorry," Hertha said somberly. "It is a terrible loss. Come, ladies, let us give the family some space to mourn." She shot a stern glare at the president as the women walked off.

"Oh, um, yes," President Arthur sputtered. "Us too. We shall let the Peppers, um, cry for a bit. Don't worry, Clark, we'll make sure those other two sign their papers." Bell and Edison followed as the president ushered his gang of federal agents back to the monument where a group of reporters awaited the "official" story of what had happened that day.

Only Captain Lee stayed with the Peppers. He crouched by them and peered into Robot's empty chest compartment. "Are we certain he's—?"

Molly nodded.

Cassandra ripped off a strip of her skirt and held it for Molly to blow her nose into. "His Ambrosium was going to run out eventually," she said. "He chose to use the last of it to save your life. I will be forever grateful to him for that."

Something caught the captain's eye. "Um, Cassandra, didn't you once say you might be able to try a—what did you call it?—a transplant? If we found more Ambrosium to put into him?"

"Yes, but— What are you looking at?"

"That dog. That ridiculous, wonderful dog." Captain Lee stood and pointed to Dr. Stinkums, who was trotting around the Mall, growling and gnawing at the silvery blaster between his teeth. The dog noticed the captain and padded over, the ray gun in his mouth glowing a faint orange.

Molly jumped up. "Rector's Magneta-Ray! There's Ambrosium in there! Oh, Dr. Stinkums, Robot was right—you *are* a genius!"

The dog shook his head and snarled, crunching down on the ray blaster until it cracked in half and a walnut-sized, glowing tidbit of Ambrosium plopped onto the grass.

"Good show, Dr. Stinkums!" Cassandra cheered.

"I would never have believed it if I hadn't seen it with my own eyes!" said Captain Lee. "That dog might just have saved the day!"

"Good puppy!" Molly cooed.

And then, in one gulp, Dr. Stinkums ate the Ambrosium.

"No! Drop it, drop it!" Molly tackled the dog and stuck her fingers into his drool-slick mouth, feeling around behind his teeth and under his tongue until the dog made a very unpleasant noise. She let him go. "It's gone."

"I would never have believed it if I hadn't seen it with my own eyes," Captain Lee said.

Cassandra winced. "Is Dr. Stinkums going to become an evil genius now?"

"That little shard was our last chance to possibly save Robot," Molly said.

"We don't know for certain if the transplant would even have worked," Cassandra replied.

"But we could have *tried*," Molly said. "With that rock we wouldn't have had to just sit back and accept things the way they were. That rock could have changed everything! But now it's . . ."

She froze, a cascade of intriguing thoughts rushing through her mind.

"Molls? Are you all right?"

"Yeah," she replied. "I just . . . I had an idea." She looked into her mother's eyes. "It might not be over."

"Excellent," Cassandra replied. "What might not be over?"

"Everything," said Molly.

"Are you sure you're all right?" asked Captain Lee.

"Absolutely," Molly said. "I thought we were stuck, trapped in this cycle. But we can break it, we can try something new. I can't believe I'm saying this, but I have to do what Rector said. Not killing people or any of that stuff—don't worry. I have to change the game."

"Wonderful," said Cassandra. "Because whatever game we've been playing, I don't like it."

On her tiptoes, Molly looked around for Nellie Bly. She spotted the young reporter signing papers amid a group of black-suited men, and beckoned her over. Nellie finished signing, shoved the documents angrily at the men, and jogged over to Molly.

"What is it?" Nellie asked.

"Are you ready to write the biggest story of your career?" Molly asked.

"Well, having just signed away my ability to do so without getting tossed in prison . . ."

"No, listen," said Molly. "You may not be able to write

about Rector, but there's an even better story that's just waiting to be broken—about corruption at the Inventors' Guild. And that topic isn't covered by any secrecy agreements."

Nellie pulled out her notepad. "Go on."

"Where do I even start?" Molly said. "With the Guild covering up the failed expedition that killed twelve people and stranded Captain Lee for years? Or how about the secret backroom deals President Arthur made with Bell and Edison allowing them to send expeditions to Antarctica after he'd declared it illegal for other explorers to do so?"

"Ooh, and don't forget how the Guild bribed the World's Fair Planning and Preparatory Committee to reserve all of Inventors' Alley for its members," Cassandra added.

"This is . . . wow," Nellie said, writing feverishly. "The news bear strikes again!"

"Oh, we're just getting started," said Molly. "I can tell you about hidden labs, spying, stealing ideas from one another, the Guild's secret Club in Washington, DC, where they blow all their government funding on fancy napkins and gold unicorns . . ."

Emmett ran up and leaned against Molly, doubled over and panting.

"Oh, hey, Emmett," Molly said. "We're helping Nellie write a scandalous exposé to sink the Inventors' Guild!"

"That's great," he said, catching his breath.

"Son, are you okay?" his father asked. "Did you find that machine? It didn't squash anybody, did it?"

Emmett nodded. "I found it. I found the Mind-Melter. And the good news is that, no, nobody was hurt. It landed off in the woods back toward the bunker."

Molly winced. "What's the bad news?"

"Oh, sorry—there is no bad news!" Emmett said cheerily. "Just more good news. Because I also found *this* inside of it . . ." He opened his coat to reveal what he'd been hiding:

The Mind-Melter's former power supply, a bowling-ball-sized hunk of Ambrosium.

And the Winner Is . . .
New York City, November 4, 1884

"EXCUSE ME, EXCUSE me!" Molly nudged her way through the crowd of eager, hungry customers jamming Pepper's Pickles. She squeezed over to the wall across from the counter, which she'd been decorating, day by day, with front-page articles from the *New York World*.

DECEPTION, TREACHERY & ABUSE OF POWER

AT THE INVENTORS' GUILD

A STARTLING EXPOSÉ

BY NELLIE BLY

TIES TO GUILD CORRUPTION SPELL TROUBLE FOR

PRESIDENT ARTHUR

CAN HIS SIDEBURNS SAVE HIM?

BY NELLIE BLY

PUBLIC OUTCRY LEADS GOV. CLEVELAND TO

SHUT DOWN INVENTORS' GUILD

FAMED NYC HEADQUARTERS TO

GO UP FOR AUCTION

BY NELLIE BLY

Molly pasted her latest favorite at the end of the line.

MIRED IN SCANDAL, EDISON ENDS

BID FOR PRESIDENCY

INVENTOR'S NAME TO BE REMOVED FROM BALLOT

BY NELLIE BLY

"Our friend has certainly had a busy couple of weeks," Cassandra said, tossing an unsealed jar of Hungarian Half-Sours to a customer and splashing brine across the first several people in line. "And it's all thanks to you, you know."

"Oh, pshaw," Molly said with overplayed modesty.

Emmett worked his way through the packed shop to restock tins of salt on the shelf next to her. "Seriously, though, Molly," he said under his breath. "Does it bother you that your name isn't in any of those articles?"

Molly shook her head. "It can't be. I knew that full well when I pushed Nellie to write about the Guild. I mean, sure, it would have been nice to be as famous as

365

she is right now—and technically speaking, we deserve it—but seeing the impact her stories have had already . . . Yeah, sure, it bothers me. I haven't become a different person suddenly! *But*—at the same time, I am ecstatically happy that the truth is finally out there. Some of it, anyway. To be honest, I'm mostly shocked that she got her exposé published in the *World*. It was her editor there who turned her in to the Feds last year when she first tried to write about you-know-who."

Emmett shrugged. "I guess the *World*'s new publisher—I think his name is Mr. Pulitzer?—is more open to muckraking stories like the ones Nellie writes."

There was a commotion as someone squeezed in through the packed doorway. "Make way! Pickle seller coming through!" Jasper Bloom called out as he sidled into the room. The customers all cheered. "Hello, pickle lovers of New York! I have returned! I am sorry to have been absent for such a lengthy length of time, but, as you all know—you'd *better* know—today is Election Day. I had to do my civic duty and cast my vote for president. But apparently, everybody else in the city decided to do so at the exact same time—"

"Not *everybody* else," Cassandra said pointedly.

"Someday," Molly said to her.

"—because the only lines longer than the ones here are the lines down at the ballot boxes. I tried to tell them folks that I had pickle people waiting on me back here, but they made me stand in line just like everyone else. Balthazar Birdhouse wouldn't've waited, I can tell you that much. He'd've run screaming if he saw lines like that. The man's got no patience. Not that it would've mattered—Balthazar Birdhouse only votes for himself anyways. Every election, he writes his own name in. Doesn't matter if it's for president or dogcatcher, he thinks he's the one for the job. And speaking of jobs . . . Mrs. Pepper! Thank you for taking my place while I was out being a good citizen, but I'm ready to slip behind that counter again, so you can go take it easy."

"Oh, it was no problem, Mr. Bloom," Cassandra said, absentmindedly noshing on a pickle she had pulled for a customer. "Honestly, I think Robot could have handled the task by himself."

"Thank you, Mrs. Pepper," Robot said with a tip of his dashing gray fedora. "But as the newest, least experienced employee of Pepper's Pickles, I am happy to remain Mr. Bloom's apprentice until I have mastered all the skills necessary for this position." He leaned over the counter, lowering his big-eyed metallic face toward that of a small child waiting with his mother on the other side. "What can I get for you, human youth?"

The boy squealed with delight. "The toy man's talking to me!"

"I am not a toy," Robot said cheerily. "Nor a man. But you are tiny and presumably uneducated, so call me what you wish. I like children. And dogs. Isn't that right, Dr. Stinkums?"

The scruffy pooch did not respond. He was too busy stealing pickles from a customer's bag.

"How the heck did that dog get in the store?" Molly gasped.

"Never mind that—how did he get to New York?" Emmett asked, gaping. "I thought we'd lost him again when we left DC!"

"I am not surprised he found his way to us," said Robot. "Dr. Stinkums is a genius, after all."

Molly crouched down and scratched the pooch's matted fur. She couldn't help but wonder if the Ambrosium he'd ingested had finally turned Dr. Stinkums into the genius Robot always thought him to be. Was it her imagination, or could she actually see a spark of intelligence in those big brown eyes? The mutt looked her in the eye and nodded his head, as if he could read her mind. Then he coughed up the pickle he had apparently tried to swallow whole. And tried to swallow it whole again.

"I think Dr. Stinkums should be my apprentice, just as I am Mr. Bloom's apprentice," said Robot.

Emmett laughed. "The only problem is that Dr. Stinkums doesn't live in New York," he said. "He belongs back in Ohio with Orla. And Luddie. We should probably take him back there."

"Ah, I see what's going on, Emmmmmmett," Molly said with a playful smirk. "You're looking for an excuse to go see Orla again."

"What?" Emmett protested. "You think I *want* to— That's not— I mean—"

Molly laughed.

Over at the counter, a woman asked for some dill pickles and Robot thrust his hand directly into a brine-filled jar to retrieve some. "Won't you rust?" the woman asked.

Robot knocked on his chest, which glowed with a faint orange light. "Aluminum," he said proudly. "I cannot rust. I can, however, do this." And he began juggling the pickles to raucous applause from the customers.

Molly smiled. She'd always said Robot was meant to be an entertainer.

With all the cheering for Robot's circus act, Molly almost missed the entrance of Hertha and the Mothers of Invention, and Captain Lee right behind them. Hertha stood tall and raised her hand above the crowd to point toward the cordoned-off rear area of the store. Cassandra nodded.

"You have the helm, Mr. Bloom," she said to Jasper before joining the children, Captain Lee, and the MOI in the living space behind the privacy screen.

"All right, Robot," said Jasper. "Let's sell some pickles. And don't be afraid to throw in some stories about old Balthazar Birdhouse—these folks really seem to like getting educated about that fella."

"I have never met the man," said Robot.

"And you should pray you never do!" said Jasper.

In the back, Cassandra greeted Hertha, Sarah, Josephine, Mary, and Margaret with a warm smile. "Well, look at this," she said. "You're all here. To what do we owe the pleasure?"

"We're celebrating!" Sarah said gleefully.

Hertha raised her hand and dangled a jingly set of keys. "Guess who just pooled their funds and became the new tenants of the building formerly known as Inventors' Guild Hall?"

Cassandra narrowed her eyes. "If you say it's anyone other than you, those keys will have been cruelly misleading."

"It *is* us!" said Mary.

"I can't wait to clean the place up and finally make it presentable," added Josephine. "If we were to melt down all that gold, we'd probably have enough to buy the theater next door as well."

Molly and Emmett hugged each other, giddy with happiness for their incredibly worthy friends. "Finally," Molly said. "We'll finally have a Guild that's all women!"

"Oh, no, dear, we're not that petty," Hertha said. "This new enterprise of ours will have quite a different goal from that of the old Inventors' Guild. We plan to dole out resources, workspace, and mentoring to promising inventors who may not have had access to such things in the past. We're looking to give a boost to craftspeople whose enormous potential has been stifled by lack of opportunity."

Cassandra grinned contentedly, but said nothing.

Margaret nudged Hertha. "You might want to tell her who you're talking about."

"Oh, quite." Hertha pulled a shiny bronze key from the ring and held it out to Cassandra. "No one as brilliant as you should be stuck in the back of a pickle shop. This is the key to your new workshop. If you want it."

Cassandra glanced over to Molly, who nodded so hard she was afraid her head might fly off. Cassandra took the key.

"Congratulations, Mrs. Pepper!" Emmett said. "You're finally going to have the kind of space and tools you need. I can't wait to see what you come up with now. You deserve this."

"Oh, I have more keys here, young man," Hertha said. She pulled another from the ring and placed it in Emmett's hand. "I did say we wanted the most promising inventors . . ."

Emmett stared at the key as if it were the Star of Ceylon. But then he looked up at his father. "Papa, do you think—"

"Of course you're taking it!" Captain Lee beamed. "There's an apartment attached to that workshop. To both of them!" He nodded to Cassandra and Molly.

"You mean we get to *live* in the Guild Hall?" Molly asked. She grabbed Emmett's hands. "And be neighbors?" She was practically levitating with joy.

The captain nodded. "*And* these incredible women are going to build me a new ship," he said. "A speedy, futuristic one even faster and grander than Bell's *AquaZephyr*. I'm finally going to be a real captain again!"

"That's ... that's wonderful," Emmett said. He seemed torn. "You've really missed being at sea, haven't you?"

"Put your worries back in your pocket," his father said. "I'm not going to ask you to come with me. And I won't be gone for long. Just short voyages here and there. I could, however, use some new navigation equipment. Or a communication device for talking to family back on shore. Maybe some kind of machine that makes sea rations taste better. You wouldn't happen to know any inventors who might be interested in working on these projects for me, would you?"

Emmett embraced his father.

Molly couldn't stop smiling. After everything they'd been through, all the mistakes she'd made, all the times she'd thought she'd lost everything, now she was suddenly looking at so many new beginnings, so many second chances. Maybe some of her bad decisions hadn't been so bad after all.

"Well, Molls," her mother said. Cassandra put an arm

around her daughter and together they surveyed their ecstatically happy friends. "Looks like Emmett's going to have his hands full for a while, so I'm going to be in the market for a new lab assistant . . . or perhaps an *old* one?"

Molly smiled at her. "Thanks, Mother," she said. "But you should have the MOI find you someone who really wants—and deserves—the job."

"But what will you do, Molls? I can't imagine you'll be happy assisting Jasper at the pickle counter."

"No, I think that job belongs to Robot," Molly said. "But don't worry about me. I've got plenty to do." She picked up her pencil and notepad. "After all, this world's not going to change itself."

EPILOGUE

Found
Washington, DC, March 4, 1933

THE ATMOSPHERE OUTSIDE the US Capitol building was jubilant as a record-breaking crowd gathered to witness the inauguration of President Roosevelt. Molly flipped up her coat collar to protect herself from the brisk wind as she stood in the bleachers, looking for her old friend. It had been a while since they'd seen each other, but the moment she laid eyes on Emmett, inching down the row of seats toward her, she felt at home. When he reached her, Emmett tucked in his scarf and leaned back to take a good look at her.

"You've got more gray hair than last time," he said with a grin.

"And you've got less hair in general!"

The two hugged each other, laughing.

"How's Orla?" Molly asked.

"Oh, she's great. Asks about you all the time. Luddie?"

"Good, good. We should all get together soon."

"Yeah, maybe at Jasper's. His place is certainly big enough. Yeah, that would be really nice." He let out a misty puff of breath as he took in his surroundings— the capitol dome rising majestically in one direction, the antenna-less Washington Monument looming in the other. "This is the first time I've been back, you know."

"Since when? Wait, you mean the day of you-know-who's final gambit?" Molly asked, squinting at him. "Not since then? Really?"

"We non-muckrakers don't have need to spend as much time in the nation's capital as you," Emmett said. "Though I've read enough of your stories to feel like I've been here."

She grinned. "Yeah, I suppose I've gotten a few good ones in over the years. Though honestly, none as surprising as when we found out Balthazar Birdhouse was a real person."

Emmett laughed. "Well, thanks for suggesting we meet up for the inauguration," he said. "If there was ever a good reason to come back to DC . . ."

He caught Molly staring up at the peak of the Washington Monument. "Hard to believe it's been almost fifty years," he said.

"Is it weird to think of those as good times?" Molly said. A tear welled up in the corner of her eye. She dabbed it with a glove, telling herself it was just the cold. "Ah, I know it shouldn't still bother me after all this time, but it does. You think anyone will ever get to learn what really happened that day? Or at the World's Fair? Or in Antarctica?"

Emmett raised an eyebrow. "You know, your name *has* been in the papers since then."

"But that's me writing about stuff *other* people have done."

"Exactly," said Emmett. "Things those other people shouldn't have been doing, which you uncovered and told the rest of the world about."

"I know, I know," Molly replied in a self-mocking sing-song. She raised her chin to let the bright sun warm her face. The history books may have skipped over her, but she would never have traded the life she'd lived. And was still living. She was only sixty-two, after all. Her story was far from over. "Sometimes I just wonder how much of a difference we really made."

Emmett smiled at her. "You're never going to be satisfied, are you, Molly Pepper?"

She chuckled. "Heh. When you're satisfied, you stop trying."

"Well, who knows," said Emmett. "Maybe Roosevelt will finally free us from those confidentiality contracts. I've heard that—"

The band on the flag-draped stage began playing "Hail to the Chief."

"Ooh, they're starting!" Molly said. "This is it."

The crowd hushed as the president-elect walked onto the stage, to join the chief justice of the Supreme Court, who was waiting to administer the oath of office. Everyone in the bleachers was standing, so Molly lifted herself onto her tiptoes (aging hadn't made her any taller) and Emmett let her lean on him for a better view. Molly mouthed a quick thank-you to her oldest, dearest friend, then immediately turned back to the action and pushed her glasses up the bridge of her nose. She didn't want to miss a moment of the swearing in of President Eleanor Roosevelt.

Afterword: What's Real and What's Not in 'The Final Gambit'

This book is a work of fiction, but many of the people, places, and things that appear in these pages actually existed in world history. So what's real and what's not?

Cowmen of Florida: Many people don't realize this, but in 1800s America, cowboys were not limited to the Wild West. They could exist pretty much anyplace that had cows. That includes Florida, where there were quite a few. Though, yes, they preferred to be called cow*men*. And Punta Rassa—a real city—was one of the centers of cattle culture back in the day. Punta Rassa looks very different today. Far more luxury hotels than coffin makers.

Washington Monument: In the real world, President Chester A. Arthur didn't rush the construction of the Washington Monument, and it was finished, as planned, in December of 1884, at which point a lightning rod was installed at the top. But it worked a little too well and within six months, it had attracted so many lightning strikes that it melted. It was replaced by a rather silly-looking crown of *eight* spiky lightning rods that remained in place until 2011.

The Smithsonian Institution: When the Smithsonian was founded in 1846, its museum holdings were housed entirely in the red stone "castle." But as the institution grew, they added more and more buildings and galleries, the first of which was the Arts and Industries Building. The Smithsonian now consists of nineteen museums (seventeen of which are located in Washington, DC) and the National Zoo, but the castle is still its headquarters. And yes, the Smithsonian does have George Washington's salt and pepper shakers displayed as part of his battlefield mess kit.

The Star of Ceylon: The Star of Ceylon is a fictional gem, but it is based on the real-life Star of India, which was for decades the largest sapphire in the world. Despite being called the Star of India, it was discovered in Sri Lanka, which at the time Perilous Journey takes place was known as Ceylon. Rector might have particularly sought a sapphire to disperse his beams because sapphires are known for their high conductivity, which is why they are frequently used in the production of lasers today.

The Mind-Melter and Magneta-Ray: The real Thomas Edison actually attempted to build some frighteningly similar instruments of warfare—an "electronically charged atomizer" that would cause soldiers on a battlefield to drop into sudden comas, and giant electromagnets that could catch bullets in mid-air and hurl them back at the enemy who fired them. Luckily for everyone, these projects were never completed. Was Edison was really a criminal mastermind in disguise? Probably not. But the similarities to Rector's fictional weaponry are kind of eerie.

The Election of 1884: Thomas Edison never ran for president. Though, if he had, who knows? He might have won. The actual presidential election of 1884 featured only New York governor Grover Cleveland and James G. Blaine, who had been secretary of state to Chester A. Arthur. Cleveland won. Some people must not have liked the job he did, because he was defeated by Benjamin Harrison when he ran for reelection in 1888. But people must have liked Harrison even less, because they reelected Grover Cleveland in 1892, making him the only person to serve two non-consecutive terms as president of the United States. Politics are weird.

The *New York World*: The *New York World* was a real newspaper that really was taken over by Joseph Pulitzer (after whom the Pulitzer Prize is named) in 1883. It was the *World*, under Pulitzer's reign as editor, that published some of the real Nellie Bly's most famous and most important reporting, such as her exposé on the horrible conditions at Blackwell's Island insane asylum and her real-life race around the world, which she completed in seventy-two days, beating the fictional journey in Jules Verne's *Around the World in Eighty Days*. Nellie Bly was very cool.

Eleanor Roosevelt: In real-world 1933, it was Eleanor Roosevelt's husband, Franklin D. Roosevelt, who was sworn in as president. At that point in American history, women had only had the right to vote for thirteen years and very few had risen to elected positions. But based on all the amazing things Eleanor Roosevelt did *without* being president—advocating for civil rights, working to expand the roles of women in the workplace, aiding World War II refugees, writing a regular newspaper column, and becoming the first chair of the United Nations' Commission on Human Rights—I think she probably would have done a pretty awesome job in the Oval Office. At the time of this writing, the United States still has not elected a woman president. If that last fact makes you as unhappy as it does me, what are you waiting for? Get out there and let people know how you feel. Advocate for change, even if you're a kid. And when you're old enough, vote. After all, the world's not going to change itself.

—Christopher Healy, 2020

Acknowledgments

As this adventure comes to a close, I would like to give one more round of thanks to the people who aided me across this entire three-book journey—I would undoubtedly have stalled along the way without the input and assistance I received from you all: my excellent editor, Jordan Brown; my awesome agent, Jill Grinberg and the whole crew at Jill Grinberg Literary; my always-up-for-brainstorming wife, Noelle Howey; my never-misses-a-typo son, Dashiell Healy; my ever-inspirational daughter, Bryn Healy (the closest thing to a real-life Molly Pepper I'll ever see); Debbie Kovacs at Walden Media; Kevin Chu at the Museum of Chinese in America; Cheryl Pientka; Shenwei Chang; Barry Wolverton; Jennifer Chu; Martha Brockenbrough; Christine Howey; Tiffany Dayemo; Geoff Rodkey; and my lovable pooch, Duncan, who told me in no uncertain terms how upset he would be if I didn't finally put a dog in one of my books.